The True Tales of Bad Benny Taggart

#MADEINDADE

#MIAMISOMETIMES!?

The True Tales of
Bad Benny Taggart

Timothy Schmand

Jitney Books

For M, B & J

I

The Spirit Club had decorated one of the over-sized bulletin boards in purple and gold, Halpert's colors. Purple construction paper trimmed into the shapes of footballs and oak leaves sailed across a yellow background. "Beat Meadow Park," written in fat purple letters, arced atop the display. Benny Taggart leaned against the lockers opposite the sign and tried to figure out which letters he could move to make other kids laugh. "Beat Me," was the only phrase he saw. He decided no one would get the word "prick" from "prek." If he had other letters, he'd put up something really funny -- "Beat Meat." "Fuck You." "Eat Shit." He imagined kids laughing when they saw it, thinking whoever did it must be a really cool guy. Maybe he'd spend the rest of the school year sneaking around, changing bulletin boards. He could cut out his own letters, draw funny pictures of the real asshole teachers, though he knew all teachers were assholes, mostly. He'd sign each one, BBT -- Bad Benny Taggart. No one would know who he was, like a ghost or a spirit, but he'd be famous.

Benny smiled at the idea. He'd be careful; not get caught. But he couldn't figure out when he'd be able to do it. Forty-five minutes after final dismissal and the school still echoed with laughs, shouts and the metallic banging of lockers. It surprised Benny that kids hung around school. He wondered what they were doing. Sucking up to asshole teachers? Finishing their detention?

He heard girls approaching -- voices quick and snappy, their words chirpy and jumbled together -- a foreign language to his ears. They appeared from around a corner. There were three. Two wore blue jeans, black leather boots and Halpert Middle School jackets. Their heels hit the floor and their chewing gum cracked in a rhythmic staccato. The girl passing closest to Benny had long black hair, wore a short red skirt and brown leather work boots. Benny thought if he squatted down, as she passed, he could see up her skirt. The girls glanced at Benny, made eye rolling contact, laughed, and pulled their books tighter to their chests. Benny's face reddened. He tried to look tough, while wondering about their tits. He wondered about tits in the same way that he wondered about fucking. Tits and fucking -- words he'd used for years suddenly made sense in a way they never did before. He wondered when he would touch a girl's tits or maybe fuck one. Maybe if he stayed after school more often? No, he'd had enough of that. The principal at his last school, Ottem Elementary, told Benny he had detention more often than anyone before him and if he didn't change his ways, middle school and perhaps his entire life would be very difficult. Asshole.

Benny watched the girls disappear around a corner, then looked back at the bulletin board. "Eat Krap." He saw it plain as day. He laughed. Everyone could read that. "Eat Krap."

He started across the hall to see what he'd have to do to change the sign but stopped half-way. Benny had another purpose for staying after school, and he didn't want to screw that up. He'd stayed late to give his *Environmental Studies* teacher, Mr. Singerman, a wallet-size copy of his school picture. He leaned backed onto the lockers, unrolled the glossy sheet of repeating pictures of himself and scrutinized his image. He liked the way his hair looked -- moussed by his mom so it stood straight up -- but the photographer had said something that made him smile, so he couldn't use the scowl he had practiced all that week. Instead, he wore a goofy smile that made his chipped front tooth the focus of the picture. He winced. The photographer was a real asshole.

Benny glanced through the classroom door, beside the bulletin board, and watched Mr. Singerman's shadow drift across the green chalkboard. Singerman was a good guy. If it wasn't for him, Benny thought, I wouldn't even hang around here. Singerman didn't mess with you. He was funny.

From his very first day at Halpert, Benny knew Singerman was all right. Dressed in a white lab coat, he stood in front of Benny's Environmental Studies class and said, "The environment is like your bedroom. If you leave smelly socks, dirty cups and plates lying around, your TV running all the time, the place is going to get," he paused and held his nose, "pretty darn stanky."

Benny laughed and clapped his hands with the rest of the class. Singerman was okay. Not like those teachers at Ottem. They didn't really teach anything, they just talked about stupid stuff. And

Benny didn't do half the things they claimed he did. At least they couldn't prove it. If Benny had known that a jaw breaker fired from a sling shot could shatter someone's glasses, he wouldn't have done it. And, he wasn't really aiming. The kid stepped into it. It's not like he lost an eye, too much. And the time the art room got trashed. He smiled at the memory -- the plastic bottles of tempera paints hurled against the wall – green dripping through red dripping through blue; after the first – he couldn't stop. Splat. Splat. Splat. Splat. Splat. Construction paper by the reams launched into the air fluttered down like giant snowflakes. The room smelled of paint -- chalky and sweet and the drying cut wood aroma of freshly unbound paper. The art room resembled settled chaos when he snuck out. But did anybody see him do it? No. They chose him because it was easy. He was glad to be out of that place. Now that he was in middle school, those jerks at Ottem couldn't touch him.

Benny leaned his head against the locker at his back. It had been a long day: his backpack, bulging with textbooks, made his shoulder ache; his baggy jeans kept sliding lower and lower on his hips -- he tugged at them repeatedly so as not to stumble when he walked.

As fewer students and teachers passed and the corridors grew quiet, Benny wondered if the guy was ever going home. He could have given Singerman the picture after class, but Benny wanted to talk to him alone. Like a friend. Benny thought it would be nice to have a friend. The lights in the classroom blinked out. Singerman appeared at the door. He wore his black hair combed over a shining bald spot and rimless glasses magnifying his eyes with fish tank clarity. He turned and locked the classroom door, turned back and smiled at Benny.

Benny grinned.

"Waiting for a bus?" Singerman asked.

"No," Benny said, laughing.

"Spending the night?"

Benny shook his head.

"Well, I'm going home," Singerman said.

He started down the corridor.

Benny jogged to catch up and fell in step with him. "I want to give you my picture," he said.

Singerman stopped and pushed his hands into the lab coat's pockets. "I'd rather be receiving your first paper. It's two weeks late."

Oh, shit, Benny thought, not that again. "Well, here, I just want to give you my picture," he said, hiking the backpack higher onto his left shoulder and, using both hands, began to tear free an image of himself.

Singerman put a hand on Benny's shoulder. "Give it to me when you hand in your paper."

"The paper doesn't matter," Benny said. "I'm leaving soon. I'm going to Florida, to live with my dad." Benny never met his father, but that didn't matter. He knew his dad was the guy clowning with his mother in the picture she kept in the drawer, hidden beneath her underwear. He lived in Miami. Benny knew that. Someday, soon, sooner all the time, his dad would show up and ask Benny to come and live with him.

"I'll take the picture when I get your paper," Singerman said. He left Benny standing in the hall.

Screw you, asshole, Benny thought, as Singerman disappeared through the door into the teachers' lounge. He folded the sheet of pictures in half, then half again, and stuffed them in his back pocket.

***

"Benjamin. Benjamin Taggart."

His mother's voice woke him from a deep sleep. Her car keys made a grating jangling noise when she dropped them on the glass topped vestibule table. Benny hated that sound; the noise of an accident about to happen.

"What?" he croaked, rubbing his eyes. Benny had eaten half a package of Oreo cookies when he'd come in from school and fallen asleep on the couch watching Captain Bob's Cartoon Playhouse. His school pictures lay creased beneath crumpled cellophane and cookie crumbs on the coffee table. He opened his eyes -- the local news was on. "What?" he yelled again.

His mother bore a strong resemblance to the photo in her weekly 'Julie Taggart Real Estate' ad in the Buffalo News Sunday

"Your New Home" Section -- *From downtown to the southtowns your residential (and commercial) real estate specialist.* The five-year-old photo showed the difference between 29 and 34. Julie still permed and colored her hair from dark chocolate to mocha to blonde highlighted tips, but her brow wasn't as smooth and the chin-line no longer sleek. Her eyes at 29, even in the blurred newsprint, looked bright and optimistic. By 34, they'd grown wary and watchful, with tiny bags pouching beneath her lower lashes. Her smile, still her best feature, shone brightly, not from inner joy but as a practiced response to all news, good, bad and devastating.

"One of your teachers, a Mr. Singerman, called my office today," she said, walking out of her high heels as she crossed the family room's beige shag carpet. She stopped halfway and standing on one foot reached with her right hand to poke a finger into a run in the left calf of her panty hose. She whispered, "Damn," to herself, stepped behind the bar pulled up her skirt and shimmied out of the panty hose, balling them into a trash can filled with earlier pairs, before pushing her skirt back down over her thighs.

Benny sat up and rubbed his face with both hands, listening to the ice cubes crack as the scotch spilled over them. Fuck, Singerman. He looked up. His mother wore a blue silk blouse with tiny gold buttons.

He couldn't see his mother's eyes and except for the tone in her voice, had no way to judge her mood.

She sipped the scotch. "Jesus," she sighed, "I've been looking forward to that since about eleven." She took another. "A Mr. Singerman called my office this afternoon," she said. "Imagine that? I had a client sitting right across from me. But then again, Benjamin, what do I have to do all day but sit at my desk and wait to hear from your teachers?" She came out from behind the bar and dropped down next to him on the couch. The sweet aroma of her perfume with a hard bite of sweat and the medicinal smell of scotch drifted down with her. "He said you've missed an important assignment. He asked if there were any problems at home." She laughed.

He hated her when she did that.

"No problems here, right, Benjamin? What problems could we be having?" His mother shook her head and stared for a moment at the television. "I know," she said smiling, while pretending to look at a watch that wasn't on her wrist, "it's what, October Eighteenth, in the year of our Lord, Nineteen Ninety-three and you haven't killed anyone yet. Or they haven't found the body. I guess that is a little strange." She cocked her head and took another sip.

"You're not funny," Benny said. "I've been good. That stab-in the-back Singerman didn't need to call you."

"That's true, Benjamin. I specifically told them not to bother me unless you violated a Federal or State law. I don't know where they get off calling me just because you're not doing your school-work."

"Quit fooling around," Benny cried.

"You're right," she said, patting his knee. "You're right. Let's get serious." His mother took another sip of scotch and ran a finger around the rim of her glass. "What's this dad stuff all about?"

Oh, shit.

His mother repeated the question.

Benny blinked his eyes and looked up at her. "Tell me about my father," he said.

She stared at him for a moment. She smiled. "He was a pirate or an outlaw," she said. "I forget now. He came by boat or horse."

Benny whined, "Can't you be serious?"

"Okay, serious. He didn't want anything to do with us. Plain and simple."

Benny said something he had been thinking about for a long time. "Us," he said. "Maybe he didn't want anything to do with you."

His mother laughed. "Come on, Benny. Forget about him."

"Then why don't you?" he snapped.

"I have." Her eyes closed for a moment and opened slowly. "Believe me."

"Then why do you keep his picture?"

"What?"

"In with your underwear. I've seen it." In a faded colored photo, seeming to Benny as if it was taken before time began -- he recognized his mother, barefoot, dressed in cut off jean shorts, wearing oversized round sunglasses, her hair past her shoulders, straight and parted in the middle. A boy her age, long hair pulled back in a ponytail, in jeans -- barefoot and shirtless -- draped an arm over her shoulder and faced the camera with his tongue stuck out. Benny had stuck out his tongue and stared at the boy's face, trying to see himself. His mother smiled at the camera, pointing at the boy with her right hand.

"Why you little sneak..." His mother shook her head, then looked puzzled as she lifted the glass to her lips. She turned to Benny and smiled. "That's Meryl's brother, John. I wish he'd been your father. What a nice guy."

"Meryl's got no brother," Benny said.

"He died just after you were born. Cancer," she said. "The big C." The ice cubes rattled in her glass. "Listen, your father never wanted anything to do with us. Okay? He was bad news. Just bad." She looked at Benny and smiled.

"So, I'm like him," Benny said. "I'm like my dad."

His mother shook her head. "Benny, you're not like anybody."

"You know, you could just tell me about him."

"You know," she said mimicking him. "You could just do your homework."

"Do you always have to make everything a joke?"

"Benjamin Taggart," she said. "If I took all of this seriously, one of us would be dead by now."

Benny looked into her eyes, then turned away.

The national news came on the television. His mother coughed twice, clearing her throat. "Now, Benjamin," she said. "What did we decide Halpert Middle School was going to be?"

"A new start," Benny mumbled. He thought, screw you Singerman. Stab-in-the-back.

"Right," his mother said, nodding. "A new start with a...?"

"Clean slate," Benny said. Asshole.

***

The following day, Benny ducked into a boys' bathroom for a smoke just before Singerman's class. When the bell sounded, the bathroom emptied. Alone in a stall, he took a long drag on his cigarette and thought, bullshit. Singerman could go fuck himself. He dropped the butt into the toilet and wondered what bullshit

Singerman was telling the class. Benny wished he could go right into Singerman's room and tell him what he thought about him -- what he thought about the whole fucking-school. "Bullshit," Benny said. The sound of his voice startled him as it bounced around the bathroom's tiled floor and walls -- thick, full, nearly an echo. "Bullshit," he said again, and hooted. "Bullshit, bullshit, bullshit."

He worked his white plastic lighter from a hip pocket and said, "bullshitbullshitbullshit," over the flame. He jerked a small rectangle of toilet paper out of the dispenser and held it just above the lighter. The paper flamed bright and fast, singeing his fingers. Glowing black ash drifted to the floor. Benny snapped out another sheet, lit it and dropped it. He added more and more tissue until flames wavered and shimmered at his feet. He jerked all the paper out of the dispenser and sprinkled it over the fire. Then he rushed from stall to stall snatching paper and tossing it into the flames. Pieces of ash, stirred up by his feet, drifted through the air with the ghostly white smoke.

Watch it, watch it, he told himself. Fire was so wild. He didn't want to leave the flames to get the tissue. He never wanted to leave.

When the tissue was gone and the air filled with haze, he lifted his Environmental Studies textbook from his backpack and began tearing it apart. Color pictures of smokestacks belching smoke became smoke themselves. Rain forests were torched, pristine valleys devoured by Benny's conflagration. He heard and saw nothing except the fire. The gong gong gong of the school's fire alarm was just a whisper in his ears.

As he crumpled a page with practical suggestions for students, the bathroom door burst open and an assistant principal named McIntyre aimed a fire extinguisher at Benny and the flames. He coated Benny and the fire with a white foam. Benny thought he was on fire. He batted at the foam and rolled on the floor. The assistant principal grabbed him and pushed him, face first, against a tile wall.

"All right, asshole," McIntyre said, "calm down."

McIntyre twisted Benny's left arm behind his back, then guided him out into the hallway. He pushed him, not roughly, toward the principal's office. Three firemen, wearing oxygen masks and carrying axes, passed them in the hallway.

"Boy's bathroom," McIntyre said. "Just paper. Here's the bug. I think it's out."

Two cops stood just inside the principal's outer office. McIntyre launched Benny into their grasp with a light push. Benny looked back at the man. A tall thin guy in a white shirt and blue tie. He had gray hair gathered in a ponytail.

"He started it," McIntyre said. "It's out now."

"What's his name?" The cops had turned him around so he faced McIntyre. He felt something cold and hard on his wrists.

McIntyre looked at Benny. "Yeah, what's your name?"

"Benjamin," he said, his mouth dry, tongue heavy. "Benjamin Taggart."

Hands cuffed behind his back, a cop on either elbow, Benny's feet barely touched the floor as they hustled him through Halpert's corridors. They moved fast. He wanted them to slow down. They pushed through the school's doors. Benny squinted at the sun poking through an overcast sky and thought, these guys are not playing around.

The entire school watched as the cops hustled him to the patrol car. Kids laughed and pointed. A few cheered. Some looked scared.

Benny caught a glimpse of his reflection in the patrol car's window, warped and elongated in the curved glass. Except for the two patches he had pawed clean around his eyes, his entire body was still dusted white from the fire extinguisher's blast. What the fuck? Am I a ghost? He looked over the car's roof at the students. One of the cops put a hand on the back of his head and pushed. Benny resisted for a moment, staring at the other kids. They seemed so strange. Benny wondered if he could be one of them. If he was like them. The cop pushed harder and Benny rolled into the back of the police car. The door slammed. Halpert's principal, speaking through a bull horn, called the students back. Benny almost said to the cops, "Hey, I got to go back to school." But they had already turned a corner, and Benny didn't think they would let him.

***

They took his picture, rolled his fingers through ink, then left him alone in a tiny holding room. Benny didn't know what he would say if anyone asked him why he'd lit the fire. No one did. He sat on a wooden chair beside a small table. A handcuff wrapped his left wrist. The right cuff was looped through a metal ring attached to the table. The room smelled of stale cigarette smoke and sweat. Dark stains spotted the room's yellow walls. Benny tried not to think about what the stains might have been. Fluorescent lights buzzing overhead were recessed into the ceiling and protected by a metal grate. Eyes peered at him through a small rectangular window in the door. They spooked Benny. He stopped looking in that direction. He knew he was fucked this time. They had caught him. He could say he was trying to put out the fire, but McIntyre -- McIntyre knew better. Fuck, Benny thought.

A key jingled in a lock and the door opened. Benny didn't take his eyes off the floor. He saw cop shoes, followed by a pair of high heels. Benny looked up just as his mom pushed past a woman cop. "Oh, Benny," she cried, "not again." She shook her head and turned to the cop. "I just don't know what to do with him," she said. "You probably think I've been a horrible mother, but it's not so." His mother glanced at him over her shoulder; she was crying. "What the hell do you do with kids, anyway? Do you beat them? Not beat them? Tie them up in the basement, for Christ's sakes? Do you raise them the way you were raised? Do you buy a book and raise them that way?" She was shouting. "I just want you to know that I'm trying."

The cop looked concerned.

"I'm sure you are, Mrs. Taggart. I'm sure you are."

His mother turned to him; her mouth hung open like she was going to say something. Then she shook her head. "No," she said quietly, "you're not doing this to me again."

Benny wanted to say, it wasn't his fault. He wanted to say it was somebody else. He had been caught. There was nothing he could say that would get him off.

A man in a white shirt and tie stuck his head in the door and said, "Fergie's here."

Benny and his mom followed the woman cop up a flight of stairs and down a corridor to another office. A white-haired old woman, glasses hanging around her neck on a jeweled chain, sat typing behind a gray metal desk. She looked to Benny like a television grandmother. Someone who would call you honey, give you cookies and tell you stupid things that didn't mean shit. He wanted to sit on her lap.

Someone had been painting the office. The wall on Benny's left was about three quarters done, a fresh shadow-free white, elsewhere the color of old newspaper. The room smelled of paint and thinner. Brushes, rollers and an open five-gallon bucket sat on a drop cloth. The entire right side of the room looked finished. A row of gray metal file cabinets lined the painted wall.

"Fergie," the cop said.

The woman waved Benny and his mother into the room with one hand, continuing to type with the other. Benny couldn't believe how fast her fingers moved. The roller zyyzzzed as she jerked the paper out.

She put her glasses on and looked up at Benny and his mother. "Doris Ferguson," she said. "Hearing Officer, Juvenile Court. Benjamin. Mrs. Taggart. This," she gestured at the papers lying on the desk, "is the police report and an incident report from Halpert Middle School. "This," she pointed at the paper in her hand, "is a performance contract that you will both have to sign." She pushed her glasses down on her nose and read over the top of them.

"I, Benjamin Taggart, acknowledge complete guilt and culpability with regards to my actions as described in the attached police and incident reports. I understand that adjudication of charges resulting from my actions has been waived on the condition that I attend Halpert Middle School's Opportunity Class. I understand and acknowledge that I will attend class every day. I will complete all homework assignments. I will work to improve my attitude and will not carry any matches or lighters of any kind. Furthermore, I understand that violation of any of the terms of this contract will result in my immediate arrest and confinement to Juvenile Hall." She stopped reading and looked up.

"Any questions?"

Benny wondered what adjudication meant.

"Couldn't we just get that cop to come in here and shoot him?" his mother asked.

Mrs. Ferguson's eyebrows went up.

"Come on," Benny pleaded. "This is serious." He couldn't believe she'd said that.

"I'm sorry," his mom said. "I don't have any questions."

Mrs. Ferguson smiled at Benny's mother. "We won't shoot him this time. But let me tell you this." She pointed a withered old lady finger at Benny. "The next time you fuck up, kid, you may wish we did."

Benny's head snapped up when the woman said 'fuck.'

"That's right..." She gestured around the room with her chin. "You probably think this is pretty bad, huh, Benjamin?"

Benny nodded. He thought he was about to cry.

The woman shook her head. "This is nothing. We finish here. You sign this contract and you can walk out that door. But."

Benny blinked.

"Fuck up and next time, your mom will go, and you'll stay." She leaned forward on the table. Benny could see veins, purple and blue, beneath the skin on her forearms.

Benny stared at her.

Mrs. Ferguson smiled.

"Couldn't I leave him for awhile, like on a layaway plan?" his mom asked.

***

The day after the fire, Benny squinted against the bright sun as he and his mother walked from the visitors' parking lot toward the school. Wind-blown leaves skittered across their path. Benny had shoved his hands deep into his pockets, walking with his head down. His mother strode beside him, one hand holding the shoulder strapped briefcase against her hip. McIntyre waited for them on Halpert's front steps. He had removed the rubber band from his ponytail and was in the process of retying it.

Asshole, Benny thought, get a haircut.

"Mrs. Taggart," McIntyre said, coming down the steps to meet them. "Paul McIntyre. I'm the assistant principal in charge of many things here, including the Opportunity Class." He looked at Benny and smiled.

"Call me Julie," his mother said, smiling, holding out her hand.

Benny shot a glance at his mother.

Was she flirting with this asshole?

McIntyre took her hand, "I'm pleased to meet you. Though, maybe, we wish under different circumstances."

"Circumstances?" his mother asked. "Oh right." She nodded toward Benny, "The circumstances."

They both laughed.

Jesus, Benny thought, she did that with everyone. He knew it was no way for a mother to act. Everything wasn't a joke. She probably knew it too and did it just to get back at him.

McIntyre turned to Benny. "I believe you have something for me," he said.

Benny didn't know what he wanted. "No," he answered. "I don't have anything."

"The contract?" McIntyre said, nodding. "You do have the contract? That's the most important thing -- THE CONTRACT."

"Oh," his mother said. "I have it." She opened her briefcase and moved her fingers over a sheaf of papers.

"The contract is the most important aspect of our work with Benjamin," McIntyre said. "Often children don't know what's expected of them. The contract lets them know in writing."

"Here it is," she said, handing it to McIntyre.

He waved her away.

"Give it to Benjamin. He should give it to me."

Benny looked from his mother to McIntyre to see if they were joking. It didn't seem so. He took the envelope from his mother and handed it to McIntyre.

"Now, Benjamin," he said. "We have an agreement." Benny nodded. "I didn't hear you," McIntyre said.

I didn't say anything, he thought.

"Tell Mr. McIntyre you have an agreement," his mother said.

"We have an agreement," Benny said.

***

"We call it Opportunity Class because it gives the kids another chance, an opportunity, to come back and rejoin the Halpert community," Mr. McIntyre told Benny's mom as they walked through the corridors toward the classroom.

Benny noticed they had crossed from the new school into the old building, but neither his mother nor McIntyre seemed to care.

McIntyre said the Opportunity Class met in a double study hall, redesigned to satisfy the students' special needs. The door, he explained, was changed from wood to reinforced metal for obvious reasons.

Benny tried to figure out what those reasons might be. Did they lock the kids in? Did they lock others out? Did the kids in Opportunity Class try and throw each other through doors?

He didn't get it.

But McIntyre had moved on, pointing out that, since an incident with a Mr. Crowley, both students and teachers passed through a metal detector each time they entered the classroom. McIntyre assured Benny's mom that Mr. Crowley was no longer on staff, but as a precaution, the rule about the metal detector was still in place. The students' desks and chairs were all fastened to the floor, he said, and the maintenance staff was called the moment one came loose. The goal, McIntyre declared, was to create a safe space for the children.

"Welcome to the Opportunity Class," McIntyre said, stopping before a gray metal door.

Benny realized he was in a part of the school he'd never seen before -- the old building that smelled of mold, cigarette smoke and generations of middle schoolers. The corridor's bare brick walls were broken by radiators spaced every ten yards or so. A rumbling noise came from the other side of the door. He looked at his mother. She smiled at him. She fucking smiled. Jesus, Benny thought, she really wants to get back at me. She's going to put me in there. Jesus.

McIntyre slapped the door with the flat of his hand and the

rumbling stopped. He pulled it open and stepped aside.

"After you," he said.

Benny followed his mother into the room and glanced around. He was ready to be afraid, but it didn't seem too bad. It looked like every other class at Halpert: there were a couple of black kids -- a girl and a boy; the rest were white. Benny counted about twenty. There were more boys than girls. Most of the kids looked older than Benny. Their desks fanned out from a lectern, centered in the front of the room. A bald thin man, dressed in black from sneakers to turtleneck, stood behind the lectern. He gave Benny and his mom a surprised look, then turned back to the class. The guy's head was shiny, as if coated by a fine layer of oil. Benny thought that was funny. In the back of the room, on opposite sides of the class, a man and a woman sat on stools and leaned against the wire grates covering the windows. Their light blue t-shirts read SECURITY. They were huge. Both had their arms folded across their chests. Neither looked happy.

"Benjamin. Mrs. Taggart," McIntyre said, gesturing toward the lectern. "This is Mr. Roberge, the Opportunity Class monitor."

As Roberge crossed the room, Benny noticed he never took his eyes off the students. His clothes billowed out from his legs and arms as he walked, and he looked to Benny like a dancing scarecrow. He seemed to be shaking. It made Benny smile.

Roberge positioned himself with his back to the wall and said those things Benny had heard grownups say every time they met -- "Hello, nice to meet you." "I'm sure he'll do fine." "Yes, yes, I won't hesitate to call." There was something very tight in his voice, like he was about to cry. Roberge escorted Benny's mom and McIntyre to the door in a graceful sliding side-step. The moment he closed the door, a low rumbling sound erupted from the class. Roberge dashed past Benny back to the lectern. He gripped the sides of it, took a deep breath in, leaned out toward the class and screamed, "I'll have quiet," in a long- drawn-out exhalation -- as full and deep as lower register keys banged from a piano. Not a sound came from the students.

Benny backed himself against the chalkboard when Roberge started to scream. He wondered if there was a contract between McIntyre and Roberge. Was Roberge a bad teacher? Was he sent to Opportunity too?

The teacher's face and head turned the color of cherry licorice.

He sucked in a deep breath and let it out. "Okay, Taggart," he said, gesturing toward the desks with his chin, "find a seat."

Benny stood for a moment looking from Roberge to the students. This is pretty fucking weird.

"Taggart." Roberge repeated his name. The teacher's head shook, his lips quivered. "Do you need help?"

The security aide leaning against the window sighed loudly and straightened up.

"No," Benny said, looking at the teacher and the aide. "I got it."

None of the kids looked at him as he walked up the aisle. Halfway up, he slid into a seat. The chair was too far from the desk. He tried to scoot it forward. It was bolted to the floor. Benny shook his head. A safe space for the children.

Roberge took roll call every half hour. That and the clicking sound the clock's minute hand made as it moved around the dial were the only ways to mark the passage of time. No one spoke. No one looked at books. There weren't any books in the room. Just the kids, the teacher, the aides and the rumbling noise. After a while Benny figured out that the sound was a hum the kids made deep in their throats. By the second roll call he was doing it too.

Just after eleven o'clock, Roberge lined them up to go the restroom, dividing boys from girls. The two aides left the room first and moved to either end of the hallway, just past the bathrooms. The kids stamped their feet in unison as they walked. Benny smiled as he picked up the rhythm.

Howls and screams came from behind the bathroom door as Benny waited for the kids in front of him to file in. The aide, just up the hall, didn't seem to notice the sounds. Mr. Roberge stood outside the classroom door, smoking a cigarette. He flicked his ashes into a Coke can. Benny knew some teachers smoked. He'd seen them sneak out to the parking lot at lunch time. But Roberge did it in the hallway, under a no smoking sign. Benny decided they had different rules for the Opportunity Class. They didn't care if the teacher smoked or the kids made noise.

Benny followed the kid in front of him through the bathroom door and into a wildness he'd never seen before. Small rectangles of toilet paper were being thrown by the handful into the air. A kid swung like a gymnast from the metal frames that divided the toilet stalls. Two kids wrestled, rolling around the bathroom like tops. The chaos grabbed Benny as madness and freedom. He shouted "Fuck, fuck, fuck," jumping and turning in a circle as he yelled. As he spun, he caught sight of a tall, thin boy with brown hair dropping to his knees in front of another. The tall boy took the other's dick in his mouth. Benny stopped jumping and watched, fascinated. He's got that boy's dick in his mouth, he thought. Benny wondered how it felt, to have your dick in somebody's mouth. To have somebody's dick in your own. Jesus, you piss with your dick. Still, he thought, as he stared at the tall boy's mouth working back and forth on the other, it probably feels real good.

Benny swallowed a mouthful of drool and looked around. Except for water hissing through the pipes, there was no other sound in the bathroom. All the other boys stood, eyes fastened on the two in the corner. Jesus, Benny thought. His cock was hard.

The standing boy started making peeping noises. The boy on his knees worked his mouth faster. One moaned. One gagged. All the other kids sighed. Benny did too.

Benny had heard about getting your dick sucked. Girls did it sometimes. Now he knew boys did it too. He looked around at the kids next to him and wondered if any of them would do it. He wondered if he would. He shook his head, not because he wouldn't, he knew he would.

He turned to go to a urinal, and somebody grabbed him and spun him up against the wall. Two boys pinned back his arms. Benny couldn't move. A third boy, with a sharp nose and angry eyes, leaned close to Benny's face. "What's your name?" the kid asked.

"Benny Taggart," he answered.

"Wrong." The kid spat a gob of mucus. "You're new meat."

The spit landed on Benny's right eye. He gagged.

"What's your name?" the kid repeated. Benny heard him work up more phlegm.

"New meat," Benny said.

"Wrong." The kid spat again. "Sweet cheeks. That's your name. Sweet cheeks."

Benny closed his eyes to try and keep from crying. The spit slid down his face. He shook his head to get the stuff off. His feet were wet. He looked down. The kids holding his arms were peeing on his sneakers. He screamed and tried to jerk free. The kid that spit on him pressed Benny's throat against the wall with one hand. "Stop moving," he said. The kid leaned close and asked quietly, "What's your name?"

Benny didn't know what to answer. He shook his head, crying. Whatever he said would be wrong.

"Dick face," the kid said. "That's your name. Dick face." He brought his knee up into Benny's crotch. The kids holding his arms let go and he dropped to the floor.

Benny lay on the floor waiting for the pain to end. The other boys left the bathroom. He heard someone counting outside. A man cursed and the bathroom door opened.

"If I got to come in there and get you, you're going to wish I didn't," the aide shouted.

Benny stood up and wiped spit from his face as he walked to the door.

Roberge took roll call again when they returned from the bathrooms. The kid who spit in his face was named O'Ryan. He sat in the very back of the class. On either side of him sat the guys who had held Benny's arms. One was named Blume. The other Lewis. They smiled at Benny. O'Ryan flicked a gob of spit into the air with his tongue and caught it in his mouth.

This really sucks, Benny thought. This really sucks. He had wiped the spit off with his hands, but he could still feel it on his face. His pants' legs and sneakers smelled of piss. He had to get out of this fucking Opportunity Class. He would just tell his mother. She couldn't make him do this. This was fucking crazy.

Lunch was wheeled into the room by one of the old ladies from the cafeteria. Her white shoes and the cart's rubber wheels made no sound as she moved across the floor.

At the two o'clock bathroom break Benny stood outside the rest room. The sounds from the other side of the door let him know that the morning's events were being repeated.

The aide said, "Go now, kid. There's no special trips, here."

Benny thought, I'd rather piss my pants than go back in there. But he didn't say anything. He just shook his head.

The dismissal bell sounded at 3:30, the aides led the kids through the old school and out an exit into the bus parking lot. It took Benny a moment to figure out where he was. He glanced around.

O'Ryan waved. Lewis and Blume smiled. Benny ran across the parking lot and around to the front of Halpert Middle School. He slowed to a quick walk when he was sure O'Ryan and his friends weren't following him.

***

Benny crouched on the floor in the vestibule and waited for his mother to get home. He would show her what they had done. They peed on him. They spit on him. She wouldn't make him go back. She couldn't.

He jumped up when he heard her key in the door. She glanced at him as she stepped into the house and dropped her purse on the glass topped table. She sniffed the air. "Benny, go take a shower. You smell."

"I know," he whined. "I know. Some kids peed on me today."

"They did what?" His mother's eyebrows went up.

"They peed on me. They spit on me." Benny started crying. "They hit me and called me names. A guy named O'Ryan spit on my face. You can't make me go back."

His mother held him while he cried. She ran her hand over the top of his head and Benny thought his mom was crying too. She pushed him back a little. "Where was the teacher? The aides?" Her face was red.

"They weren't there," Benny said. "It happened in the bathroom. They don't come into the bathroom."

"In a bathroom?" Her voice stiffened. "Were you in there fooling around?"

"No," Benny said, shaking his head. "No. I just went into pee and these guys--"

"You're lying to me."

"No," he said, "I'm not." He could tell she didn't believe him.

She shook her head. "I don't want to hear anymore," she said. "I'm sorry, but you're going to have to go back there tomorrow."

Benny didn't say anything. He hated her as much as he hated O'Ryan and Blume and Lewis.

"After I drop you off tomorrow, I've got a closing at eight thirty. As soon as I'm done there, I'll call Paul McIntyre and ask him to look into the problem."

"No," Benny shouted. "No way. I'm not going back there."

"Benny, we have a contract. You have to go to Opportunity Class. I have to take you there. Tomorrow, after the closing, I'll call Paul McIntyre and see if there's anything we can do."

"No," he said. "You don't understand. They peed on me. They spit, right here." He pointed at his face. "I can't go back."

"You have to. We don't have a choice. But first thing, after the closing, I'll call Paul McIntyre. I promise."

Benny shouted. "You don't know what it's like in there."

"Don't yell at me, Benjamin Taggart," she said. "I wasn't the one who got us into this mess."

***

On his second morning in the Opportunity Class, Benny slid out of bed and dressed in the clothes he'd worn the day before. His socks and sneakers were still damp and smelled like piss. If his mother didn't give a shit, then neither did he. Those kids were going to beat him up and spit on him again, but she didn't care. She never cared.

Okay, he thought. Ofuckingkay.

Benny didn't speak during the ride to Halpert. He stole glances at his mother, thinking, bitch -- bitch -- bitch. When his father did show up, he would tell him what a fucking jerk she was. Benny knew why his father left. Bitch. He slammed the car door when he got out. Bitch.

Benny walked fast through the hallways. He had a plan -- he would get to the Opportunity Class before anyone else and not leave the room for any reason. If he didn't leave the room they couldn't get him. He cut left and right around groups of students. He turned a corner and nearly ran into O'Ryan. He groaned, felt a chill.

"Hey, Taggart," O'Ryan said, smiling. "How's it going?"

Benny didn't say anything. He cut around him and walked faster, trying not to look at the kid.

"Hey, Taggart, wait up," O'Ryan said. "If it's about yesterday? That's like an initiation," he said. "Everybody gets it. Don't worry. You're in." He jogged by Benny, turned and stood smiling. "Don't worry. You're in."

Benny stopped and stared at him. He thought of the kids pissing on his shoes and O'Ryan spitting in his face. He nearly cried.

O'Ryan put a hand on Benny's shoulder. "Come on, kid. It's all right. You're in." He reached into his jacket and pulled out a hand-rolled cigarette. "Come on. We'll catch a buzz before class today. Opportunity is so much nicer when you're stoned."

Benny had never smoked anything other than cigarettes. He'd tried to get drunk on his mother's Scotch, but that made him sick. "No," he said, stepping around O'Ryan. "I don't think so."

"Come on, Taggart," O'Ryan said. He walked backwards in front of Benny.

Benny saw the other kids move to the sides of the hallway as O'Ryan backed toward them. They quieted, watching from the corners of their eyes. Benny could see they were scared of him and O'Ryan.

"I told them you're okay," O'Ryan said. "Don't let me down."

"What?" Benny asked, looking from the kids to O'Ryan. He stopped. O'Ryan's momentum carried him two steps further.

"I told them you're okay. You're one of us. Come on," O'Ryan said. "Come catch a buzz."

One of us, Benny thought. One of us. In every other school there had been just one Bad Benny Taggart. In every other school there was just me, and now there is us. I am one of us, he thought.

"Okay," Benny said.

Benny followed O'Ryan deeper into the hallways. They crossed into the old building. "Jesus, where we going?" Benny asked.

"You can't smoke a joint just anywhere, Taggart," O'Ryan said.

Benny believed him and kept going. They walked through an empty, unlit corridor and ducked into a room that Benny figured was under the old gymnasium.

The darkened space smelled like medicine and sweat. O'Ryan flipped on the lights. The row of lamps overhead were housed in metal cages. Army green lockers were built into the walls. A plank bench ran around the entire room. Two doorways, one marked SHOWERS, one TOILET, broke the monotony of the lockers.

O'Ryan crossed the room, stuck the joint in his mouth and began patting his pockets. "Shit," he said. "You got a light, Taggart?"

Benny reached for his lighter. Then he remembered. "No," he said. "If they catch me with matches, I go to juvey."

"Right, right," O'Ryan said. "Hold tight. I'll be right back."

O'Ryan was out of the room before Benny could say a word. As the door slapped shut, he nearly shouted, "Hey, I'll go with you." But the boy was gone. Benny sighed and shook his head. What a strange place, he thought. He walked over and rapped one of the lockers with his fist. It sounded rusty, old, not like the lockers in the new part of the school. Benny sat down on the bench and looked left and right. It was funny being alone in that room. He got nervous. He couldn't be late for Opportunity. He couldn't leave O'Ryan. O'Ryan would show him the ropes. He would be a friend.

The locker room door flew open, smacking against the brick wall. Benny turned to it, smiling.

Blume and Lewis stood on either side of O'Ryan. A weight dropped in Benny's stomach.

O'Ryan grinned. "Hey, Taggart, I got something for you." Blume and Lewis giggled.

"Hey, Taggart, I got something for you, too," Lewis said. "Something long and hard."

O'Ryan smiled at Benny. He looked like a dog about to bite. "Are you ready for our little party?"

Benny groaned, then screamed, loud, in a high-pitched voice.

"I love a loud fuck," Lewis said.

They rushed across the room and grabbed Benny by his arms and legs. Benny took a breath and screamed.

"Nobody can hear you," O'Ryan shouted, laughing. "No one."

Benny squeezed his hands into fists and tried to pull his arms free from Blume and Lewis. He tried to throw punches but couldn't move his arms. He held his body rigid like a board, then squirmed and bucked. It did no good. O'Ryan wrapped an arm around his neck, and repeated, "Come on, Taggart, don't fight it," punching him in the face each time he spoke. Lewis and Blume tore at Benny's pants. Benny kicked and fought. His pants and underwear were jerked away. They pushed him down onto all fours; the floor tiles were cold and hard on his knees. The two boys behind him took turns slapping

Benny's ass, chanting, "We like our sweet cheeks red." O'Ryan stood with his crotch in Benny's face, and said, while lowering his zipper, "You do any fucking thing to hurt me, Taggart, any fucking thing and I will..." O'Ryan slapped Benny in the face. "Understand?"

Benny didn't answer. O'Ryan slapped him again. "Understand?" he shouted.

Benny nodded.

"Say it," O'Ryan shouted.

"Yes, yes, yes," Benny rasped out.

***

Splayed out on the tile floor, Benny spat again and again trying to rid his mouth of O'Ryan's taste. His asshole burned. There was nothing left inside him except what O'Ryan and his friends had put there. And they had stolen something, something Benny didn't even know he had. For a moment, he thought maybe it was all a bad dream. But the tiles were cold, the taste in his mouth real. He pushed himself to his feet. The boys' sperm dripped and ran down his inner thighs. He wiped away the sperm and blood with his underwear.

Benny stumbled through the doorway marked TOILET and cried at his reflection in a mirror above the sinks: his lips were swollen and puffy, the right side of his upper lip gashed open. His left eye was turning black, and his cheeks and jaw were scored with welts from O'Ryan's fists. Benny wanted to hurt something. He had to hurt something. He had to hurt O'Ryan and his friends. Maybe kill them. If he killed them, maybe he'd get back whatever they had taken.

Benny pulled on his pants and shoes and crept through the hallways until he found one of Halpert's side entrances. He made his way home by cutting through yards and hopping fences. Once in his house, he scrubbed his mouth with a toothbrush, stripped off his clothes and stood under the shower until the hot water ran cold. As he dried himself, someone knocked at the front door and rang the bell. He peeked between the shades in the spare room. A police cruiser backed down his driveway. He dropped to the floor, not moving, until he heard the car motor down the street.

Benny, dressed in clean clothes, took his mother's Scotch from behind the bar. He tipped the bottle to his mouth. The alcohol burned the cuts on his lips, and he spat the booze across the room. He poured the rest of the bottle down the kitchen drain, then went out into the garage and refilled it with gasoline from the five-gallon can his mother kept for the lawn mower. He was leaving home for good. He knew that he would never be able to talk to his mom again. If only she'd listened to him. He had to go to school. Well, okay. He had to do this. He had to. He capped the Scotch bottle and returned to his room for his backpack and sleeping bag. The backpack was dusted white from the fire extinguisher's blast. He never used the sleeping bag. They had kicked him out of the Boy Scouts before he could go camping.

Benny spent the night bundled in his sleeping bag beneath the shrubs that grew alongside the garage. The police came to the house two more times before his mother got there and then again for a long time once she was home. Benny crawled down deeper into his sleeping bag and dreamed of his revenge. He knew what he was going to say -- just as he lit the bottle and heaved it at O'Ryan, he would ask, "Scotch?" And O'Ryan and everyone around him would try to get away, but they couldn't. They couldn't.

Benny woke up once in the middle of the night and didn't remember where he was. A neighborhood dog barked. A breeze rattled the branches overhead. Scared and cold, he felt like going into the house. He'd tell his mom he was sorry and beg her not to call the police. Let him hide in the house. He didn't need to go to school anymore. He would study at home. She would see. He could get smart. Real smart. Just like her. But he knew even before he rolled out of the sleeping bag that she wouldn't let him. She'd make him get up, go back there. She didn't care. Nobody cared. Benny rolled over and touched his backpack to make sure the Scotch bottle was still there.

Benny Taggart scrambled out of his sleeping bag just as the sun climbed above the horizon. His lips had thickened and cracked overnight, and his left eye was swollen completely shut. He peed against the garage wall, then lifted his backpack onto his shoulder and cut across his yard and through a shrub.

At the far end of Halpert's sports field, Benny ducked through a hole in the fence and walked beneath the bleachers toward the back of the school. The bottle of gasoline in his backpack didn't weigh much, and he stopped twice to make sure it hadn't fallen out. The second time, as he twisted off the cap, gas spilled onto his hands and his backpack.

The teachers' parking lot, mostly empty, lay between Benny and the school. As he stepped from the grass onto the yellow-lined asphalt, a car wheeled around the corner and beeped twice as it came to a stop. He tried to look normal -- kept walking -- head down, shoulders forward. The car beeped again. Benny glanced to his right. Mr. Singerman pushed open his car door and stepped out onto the pavement.

"Taggart," he yelled. "Benjamin Taggart, how about a hand?"

Benny stopped in the middle of the lot. He thought for a moment about running.

"Taggart," Singerman hollered again. "Come on. I need help with these barrels. They're full of frogs, not monkeys."

Benny turned back. Singerman was hidden behind the open trunk of his car. He held out a barrel marked in bold black letters: FROGS IN FORMALIN.

"Come on, Benjamin, I can't wait all day."

Benny's sneakers made a scuffing sound on the asphalt as he walked up to Singerman's car.

The teacher gestured toward the trunk. "We can get it all in one trip, if we do it right." He glanced up at Benny. The smile on his face collapsed. "What happened to you?" he asked.

"Nothing," Benny said.

Singerman rocked back on his heels and made a face. "If that's nothing, you should be careful. Imagine what you'd look like if something happens?"

Benny didn't mean to smile, but the left side of his mouth moved up, drawing the right side hard across his teeth. "Oooh."

"Ah, only hurts when you laugh, huh, kid?"

Benny nodded, as tears formed in his eyes.

"Well, come on," Singerman said, handing Benny a closed white plastic barrel. "We'll see if we can't clean you up a little."

Benny followed Singerman through the school to the science lab. He placed his barrel on the floor next to Singerman's. The teacher slipped into his lab coat.

"The doctor will see you now," Singerman said.

Benny smiled and winced.

"Right, right," the teacher said. "Don't be funny."

"Yeah," Benny said.

Singerman took hold of one of the straps on Benny's backpack and tried to lift it from his shoulder. Benny jerked away. "Come on, Benjamin," he said. "We'll leave the pack on my..." Singerman sniffed the air, then his hand. "Listen to me," he began, but Benny had already turned and run out of the room.

Benny ran from the sound of Singerman's voice and didn't stop until the teacher's shouts were swallowed in the maze of Halpert Middle School's hallways. He slowed to a walk. He needed to hide if he was going to do what he set out to. He looked from side to side and realized he was in the hallway, just under the gymnasium, where O'Ryan had taken him the day before. He would hide there and wait.

The fire alarm began its wild gong gong gong gong and Benny felt a movement of people like a rush of breath through the building. Singerman was smart. They would empty the school; he'd never be able to get O'Ryan. "Shit," he said.

Benny paused with his hand on the locker room door and looked in either direction before he pushed it open. He stepped in and leaned back against the door. A line of his blood still scarred the tile floor, and his underwear lay in a wad beneath the bench. A gorge rose in his throat; he vomited mucous and anger between his feet. The fire alarm gonged gonged gonged. People ran and shouted instructions on the other side of the door. Fuck, I'll never get O'Ryan.

He knew he had to act. Benny took the bottle from the backpack and held it in his hands. The gasoline was the color of gold. He looked from his blood marking the floor to his underwear and did not hear himself weeping. No other part of his life mattered, except what had taken place in that room. If he couldn't hurt the people, he'd hurt the room. Get the place. Benny lifted the bottle above his head and heaved it at the spot where they'd had him pinned. The bottle shattered. The smell of gas stung his eyes. He used one match to light the book and tossed it toward the gasoline. The lit matches, a golden flame arcing through the air, ignited the fumes. Heat, solid as a punch, knocked him against the door. Benny crouched low, trying to beat out the flames in his hair. I could die here. Or, maybe I'm dead already.

II

Sitting between his mother and his lawyer, Charlie Fallon, Benny tried to relax in a creaky rail back chair in Judge L. V. Williams' chambers. A tall thin black man, wearing a white shirt and a dark tie, sat beside the judge's desk and pushed keys on a small, silent machine every time someone spoke. He smiled when Benny entered the office but gazed up at the ceiling as he typed. The office looked like something Benny had seen on television: bright windows, dark wood panels and full bookcases. A black robe hung on a coat tree behind the judge's chair. After introducing himself and having everyone "state their names," the judge leaned his elbows on his desk and flipped through a blue folder marked *Taggart, Benjamin E. CN#7-203-457*. Black hair curled from his nose and ears. His nostrils made a high-pitched whistle each time he inhaled. It sounded to Benny the way peach skin felt and raised goose bumps on his arms. He wanted to rub the bumps away but was too scared to move.

Benny recognized the blue folder as the one Lynda (he forgot her last name) carried with her each time she came to see him, during his three days in the lock-down-ward at the hospital. She said she was a psychologist. Benny remembered she smelled good, like she had just come in from outside. Lynda had blonde hair and was younger than his mother. She spoke slowly and quietly, nodding when Benny answered. Lynda took notes. Benny thought they might become friends. After their third meeting, he decided to tell her everything: about O'Ryan, the fire, everything. She never came back.

Benny was glad he didn't tell her, or anyone else, that he burned the locker room because he couldn't get the three boys. He realized how much worse that would have made things. Not that things weren't bad enough. His face was scarred and sore from the three boys' fists. His eyebrows and hair were gone, scorched to ash when the gasoline flashed through the locker room. After three days on the lock-down-ward they transferred him to the county holding center. On his way in a guard told Benny he looked like a cancer patient. And, Jesus, the holding center.

Those two days seemed an endless hell.

Thoughts of drunks puking, shitting their pants, rolling in piss or crazies crying out -- night and day -- glaring wild-eyed at him, made Benny's heart race. The wooden chair beneath him creaked in time with its beat. When the creaking began Judge Williams glared at Benny.

Benny knew what the judge wanted: he wanted the noise to stop. And so did Benny, only he wanted it all to stop. His heart beat faster. The chirp grew louder.

Judge Williams inhaled.

Benny winced at the sound.

The judge sighed, and a hard-looking smile formed on his lips. "I see how it is, Mr. Taggart." He closed the file folder and looked to Benny's mother and lawyer. "I'd like to speak to Benjamin alone," he said. "Would you excuse us?"

"Yes, of course, your honor," Charlie Fallon said. And he and Benny's mother stood up.

Benny knew he was in big trouble. As the door clicked shut behind him, he massaged his wrists where the handcuffs had rubbed them raw.

The judge stared down at the folder on top of his desk. He looked up. The smile was gone, his lips were pressed into a thin tight line. "So. You think you can fuck with me, Taggart?"

Benny's chair creaked louder and faster.

The stenographer gazed at the ceiling. His fingers moved over the keys and Benny wondered if every sound was being recorded, his heart, the chair, the judge's breathing.

"That's funny, Taggart. Very funny." The judge's eyes narrowed. "You know, you're not too smart. A smart guy comes in here, cries in front of me, promises he'll never do it again and begs me to let him go." Judge Williams nodded his head. "And you know what I do? I cut him some slack. Not because he's begging L. V. Williams for mercy, but because he respects the court. But you, Taggart. You've been fucking with this court since you walked through that door."

Benny leaned forward. He wanted to tell the judge that he wasn't fucking with the court or anybody. He was just scared – too scared to cry, too scared to beg. Did the judge know what kind of noises they made at night in that holding center? Had he ever tasted that food? Tried to sleep in those beds?

Benny moved his lips, trying to form the words that would save him, but nothing came out.

Judge Williams held up his hands. "It's a little late, Taggart. Just a little late. Most of the time I don't enjoy this." He pushed a button on his phone. "Send Fallon and Mrs. Taggart in," he said.

Benny's mother winked at him as she sat down. Benny felt bad for her. He knew what was coming.

Judge Williams coughed into his fist, said, "Excuse me," and flipped open the file folder. "Benjamin Taggart," he said. "I feel it is incumbent upon this court to communicate to you the seriousness of the crimes you have committed. Within a period of five days you started two fires that endangered the lives of hundreds of people. The psychologists tell me that you're not insane -- that you know what you've done – and on both occasions showed little remorse. Benjamin Taggart, you have left yourself and the court few alternatives."

Benny's chair chirped faster. He feared his heart was about to explode.

"The court sentences you to sixty days in the county penitentiary, five months in the Juvenile Detention Center and six months in transitional housing."

His lawyer jumped up. "Jesus, L.V., the penitentiary? It's a first offense. He's a fucking kid."

"Come on, Charlie," the judge said. "Aren't you sick to death of the molly coddling? Sick kids and troubled kids? Screwed up kids? How about just plain bad kids, Charlie?" The judge pointed at Benny. "You and I both know what kind he is and he needs a lesson. Our whole society needs a lesson and it starts right here."

Benny looked from the judge to Charlie Fallon. Charlie raised one eyebrow and didn't speak. Benny turned to his mom. She stood, motionless, a tear dripped off her nose. Yeah, fuck you guys, he thought. His mother turned toward him, her face red. Benny looked away. Fuck you, too. His nose stung. He blinked and felt a tear roll down his cheek. Benny thought about running out of the room. Make them run. He wouldn't go so easy. This fucking judge, Benny thought, what does he know about kids? What does he know about me? Benny jumped out of his chair and cried, "I'm not going. You can't make me."

The judge and his lawyer looked bored. The stenographer tapped the keys on his little machine.

Only his mother seemed to listen. "Don't let them take me," he pleaded. She stood up and hugged him. He felt her sobbing. She pulled him closer. Benny felt his mother's hands on his back, smelled her perfume and clothes. For a moment, he felt like he'd won something. They could see he didn't have to go to prison. He was okay. He could be a good kid. His mother patted the top of his head. Other hands clutched his elbows. They pulled Benny away from his mother. He didn't look back to see who held his arms. Instead, as he backed out of the office, he watched his mother, lawyer and the judge. They seemed to be waiting to get this nasty problem out of the way before going on with their lives. Benny wrestled one arm free.

"Fuck you," he shouted.

The stenographer's hands moved across the keys.

"Fuck you all."

***

A dozen others rode with him on the bus to the penitentiary. They were all older, but seemed tired and scared, too. The bus was cold. Benny's teeth chattered. He could see his breath. Wearing only thin coveralls, he rubbed his arms to get warm. Body tense and teeth clicking, he tried not to think about prison.

Two guards had taken him from the judge's office and made him change into prison issue blue, one size fits all coveralls. A guard helped him cuff the suit's arms and legs, but he still tripped over the extra cloth as he walked. They chained him to a bench while waiting for the bus. He cried, mute draining sobs, until he slept. A guard jostled him awake.

Benny spent the ride peering through metal grates that covered the bus's windows. In a small town named Enid, he saw a corn stalk and pumpkin display, carved jack-o-lanterns. A banner, stretched between lamp posts, announced a Safe Night Halloween Party. He remembered that year he dressed as a convict. He wore a black and white striped outfit. His mother blackened a beard on his chin with waxy smelling make-up. Benny stared at the fall colors, smelled burning leaves and smiled at the memory of himself, forgetting for a second his destination.

They passed through the town and traveled for what seemed like hours. Just when Benny thought they'd never arrive, the prison loomed up ahead. Set in the middle of a huge green field, its gray walls and guard towers made Benny think of a castle. The bus rolled slowly up the entrance road and passed through a heavy wooden gate into a chain-link cage. Benny fell in line and followed the others out of the bus. Guards, dressed in black baseball caps and shiny black nylon coats, stood on either side of the door, directing the men to stand in line. Benny followed the man in front of him, not taking his eyes off the cold damp asphalt. "Toes on the line please, gentlemen," a voice said.

Benny spotted the thick yellow line painted on the asphalt and scuffed his feet forward. The guard said, "Thank you, gentlemen. Please respond, 'here,' when your name is called."

The guard called their names in alphabetical order. Benny listened to the men around him. Some shouted their answers, others whispered. Benny wondered what his voice would sound like. Finally, the guard hollered "Taggart, Benjamin." As Benny squawked out a trembling "here," someone behind him shouted, "Flagged."

The guard with the clip board said, "Mr. Taggart, two steps forward, please."

Benny never counted anything as carefully as he did those steps. One step. Two. He stared straight ahead. A tear trickled down his cheek.

"Jesus Christ," the guard said. "How old are you?"

"Twelve," Benny replied, standing straight as he could, believing good posture helped somehow.

"Twelve!" the guard shouted. "File," he yelled. "Mr. Taggart's file now."

Another guard handed him a file folder. He flipped it open and said, "Jesus, Mary and Joseph, this ain't a nursery." He slapped the folder closed. "Mr. Taggart, what happened to your face?"

"I got beat up," Benny said. "And I got burned."

"I see," The guard said. "Mr. Kerns," he shouted, "take over. Mr. Taggart, come with me."

The guard locked his hand around Benny's elbow and dragged him to a black metal door recessed in the stone wall. Benny looked up for the first time and saw the guard was the biggest man he'd ever seen. He had to be seven feet tall. Benny stood eye level with the guard's belt and his arm disappeared in the man's grip like a baseball in a fielder's glove. The guard pushed a button; a buzzer sounded.

"Yes," squawked a speaker.

"Mr. Grant plus one," the guard said. The door swung open. They stepped through. The door closed behind them.

A guard on the far side of a woven metal grate, said, "Mr. Grant plus one."

"Correct, sir," Grant said. A door, like a fence gate, buzzed as it swung open.

Once through the grate, the guard released Benny's arm. He placed his hand on the top of Benny's head and tilted it back, until their eyes met. Grant's head and face reminded Benny of the jack-o-lanterns he'd seen from the bus. The man's eyes were big as fists, his mouth crooked. Grant said, "Mr. Taggart, it would be best for you to follow me. I will not look back. But should I do and discover you're not there, you will regret it. This is a penitentiary, Mr. Taggart. I don't know where else you've been during your brief time on this planet. But I can assure you, you've been no place like this. Do you understand?"

Benny tried to nod but couldn't.

"Do you understand, Mr. Taggart?"

Grant's fingers tightened on Benny's head. "Yes," he said.

The man squeezed harder. Benny winced.

"We're all gentlemen here, Mr. Taggart. You should show me the same respect I've shown you."

Benny tried to nod again. "Yes sir," he said.

"Yes sir, Mr. Grant, is considered the gentlemanly response."

"Yes sir, Mr. Grant," Benny said.

"Thank you, Mr. Taggart." Grant released his grip, turned and started away. Benny rushed to keep up.

The prison, though warm and dry, had a damp bitter smell that Benny decided was fear. He could smell it on himself. Creamy yellow paint, gleaming as if still wet, covered every surface -- walls, stairways, grates, and railings. As he followed Grant upstairs and along corridors, Benny ran his right hand along the wall. It trembled as if struggling with a great weight. They met no other prisoners, but Benny heard them. Howling and shrieking like angry fans at a football game. The cries came from the other side of the wall.

Grant stopped before a gated passageway. He pushed a buzzer, said, "Mr. Grant plus one." The gate opened. They traveled a short corridor into an office lined with gray metal file cabinets. A man with a droopy black mustache, wearing a starched gray uniform sat behind a wooden desk. "Mr. Barclay," Grant asked," Is he in?"

Barclay nodded. "He is, Mr. Grant. I believe he's working on next year's budget."

"I must see him immediately."

Barclay nodded, picked up a phone, punched two numbers and grinned at Benny. "They're getting younger, aren't they Mr. Grant?"

The grin disappeared, and the man stared at the phone. "Sorry to disturb you, sir. Mr. Grant has asked to see you, immediately." He grimaced at the receiver.

"Yes sir," he said. "Yes sir."

Barclay put the phone in its cradle and gestured toward a wooden door.

"He's all yours, Mr. Grant."

Grant crossed the room. He looked back at Benny. "Come along, Mr. Taggart," he said. "The warden's a busy man."

Benny rushed after Grant. The guard rapped once on the door, pushed it open and prodded Benny ahead of him into the office.

Four leaded glass windows on the far wall captured the sunset and splashed a thin pink light around the room. A substantial wooden desk stood before the windows. The backs of framed pictures, a glowing lamp and a phone stood atop the desk. Benny saw no one else in the office. Grant stepped into the room and closed the door. Something shifted off to Benny's left.

"Mr. Grant," a voice asked, "Do you have any idea how much money we spend on toilet paper each year?"

"No, warden, I don't," Grant said.

"You wouldn't want to."

Benny turned to the voice. A computer screen glowed green

on a small corner desk. A black man in a blue shirt and pink tie spun away from the keyboard. He rocked back slowly and grinned. He lifted his glasses from the bridge of his and propped them against his forehead. He squinted. "Well, Mr. Grant, I see Judge Williams has made good on his campaign promise."

"It would appear so, sir." Grant replied.

"Thoughts, Mr. Grant?"

"We've got him for sixty days, sir."

The warden chuckled. "Enough to make our lives difficult, but not long enough to require a permanent solution."

"The general population is out, sir."

"Agreed."

"Solitary for a twelve-year-old wouldn't look..."

"Agreed. Options?"

"Only one, sir."

"Make it so, Mr. Grant." The warden turned his eyes to Benny. "What's your name, son?"

"Taggart," Benny said. "Benny Taggart."

"What happened to your face, Mr. Taggart?"

"I got beat up."

The warden nodded. "Mr. Grant, do you think Mr. Taggart will be visiting us again?"

"I couldn't say, sir."

The warden pursed his lips. "Make sure he doesn't want to."

"I'll try," Grant said. "Thank you for your time, warden."

The man nodded and turned back to his computer.

Grant pressed a hand against Benny's back and swept him out of the office. Barclay nodded as they passed, then looked down at a sheaf of papers on his desk. Benny followed Grant through a warren of hallways and corridors. They passed through a grate. The guard manning it asked Grant a question.

"Not now," he replied, and kept walking toward a rolling door built into the wall ahead of them. "Grant plus one," he shouted.

"Plus one," barked a speaker.

As the door rolled open, the prison's smell and sound washed over Benny with such ferocity that he gagged, swallowed and gagged again. He tried breathing through his mouth, but the air tasted as bad as it smelled. Grant led him down a corridor and through another grate into a huge open room. Tiered floors rose seven stories on all sides. Men leaned against railings overhead and gathered at picnic benches on the floor in front of them. Their voices, men wise and hard, thickened the air. Benny eyed the cell block. If he had to spend sixty-days there he'd go crazy. The sound. The smell. Benny concentrated on Grant's back and trailed him through rows of picnic benches. Some of the men smiled, others frowned and bared their teeth. One barked and licked his chops like a dog.

"Hey, Grant," someone shouted. "That one's too small to keep. Don't you have to throw him back?"

The guard stopped. Benny walked into the back of his legs. Grant snatched Benny by the arm, held him in the air like a prized fish.

Benny squirmed and looked out at the men, all dressed in the same blue coveralls.

The prisoners clapped their hands and whistled.

"Gentlemen. Gentlemen," Grant shouted, waving them quiet with his free hand. "This child should look familiar to you all. He is you at twelve, when you were taking your first steps down the road that brought you here. Mr. Taggart is new to this world. Who would like to teach him the rules?"

The room erupted. Men jumped up, pointing thumbs at their chests, each demanding the chance to teach Benny something.

The men terrified Benny.

They looked like they wanted to eat him.

Grant shook him like a doll and lowered him to the ground. He bent over and whispered in his ear. "See your future, Mr. Taggart?" He grinned at Benny, and said, "This way."

Grant walked quickly, though not fast enough for Benny. The men touched him and spoke to him. They talked about his mother, they talked about his ass and his mouth, about what a good little boy they would make him. When they reached the other side of the room, Grant spoke to the guards, a grate swung open and they moved on.

They passed through two more doors; the last one read Authorized Personnel Only. Benny followed Grant into a room holding about twenty men. Cells, doors open, lined three of the room's four walls. It looked like a small zoo, where they let the animals out during the day. A radio played quietly. Benny heard muffled conversation and the scuffing of slippers against the floor. Two men, one fat the other thin, leaned on their elbows over a chess board. Others paced around. A few sat at a picnic bench and talked.

An older man, with wavy white hair and clear blue eyes, looked at Benny from the picnic bench. He blinked and rubbed his eyes. "Hello, little boy," he said. "Do you like puppies?"

All the other men in the room turned toward him. There was silence, then a moan. The fat man leapt from the chess board, upsetting the pieces, and rushed up to Grant. "How old is he? Where's he from?"

Grant swatted the man out of the way, grabbed Benny's arm, crossed the small cell block and jerked Benny through the door of a cell. "Welcome to your new home, Mr. Taggart."

Benny looked back at the men gathering outside the bars.

Grant stepped out of the cell, looked toward the cell block's entrance. "Cell twenty-two," he cried. "Twenty-four-hour lock down, unless manned supervision."

A voice responded, "Twenty-four-hour lock down, unless manned supervision." Something hammered in the wall and the cell door wheeled closed and locked.

"Mr. Taggart," Grant said, "have a nice day."

The moment Grant left, the men crowded the cell's bars. Benny backed up against the far wall. The men snaked their arms through the bars and motioned Benny to them. They pleaded for Benny, smooched at him, waggled their tongues at him. "Come here, little boy." "What's your name son?" "Do you like girls?" "What happened to your face?" "Let's play a game." "Do you like candy?"

***

In the penitentiary Benny's life was defined by his cell. He learned the second day to hang a sheet across the bars during the day. He struggled to remind himself that things existed beyond it. It was easiest to remember when they took him, alone, to a small exercise yard. A guard, usually Mr. Harlan, arrived every day after they picked up his dinner tray. The men on his cell block lined up and ogled him during his arrival and departure. The prisoners in general population hooted and jeered as he passed. Benny tried to rush Mr. Harlan along until they were beyond the other prisoners. Once outside, in the dark, he paced back in forth in the yard. His jacket and coveralls too big. Neither kept him warm. It didn't matter. He could tilt his head back and smell something other than fear. On clear nights he saw stars overhead. When it snowed, the flakes reminded him of a time when he wasn't in prison.

Mr. Harlan, the guard stood in the yard's center smoking. He inhaled the smoke deeply and exhaled with great audible sighs. "You know, Mr. Taggart, we're both prisoners here," he said one night.

Benny lifted his chin from the near warmth of the oversized jacket. "What?"

Mr. Harlan exhaled a cloud of smoke.

"We're both prisoners. I'm inside, just like you."

Benny laughed. "Yeah, but you can go home."

"I come right back tomorrow."

Benny exhaled, his breath visible in the cold air and pointed back toward the door, "But those guys in there aren't trying to get you to suck their cocks. Those guys outside my cell. Fuck." He shook his head. "You go home and come back. I stay here."

"You're right, Mr. Taggart. You're right."

Benny smiled at the comfort of an adult telling him he was right. "Mr. Taggart," the guard said. "Look at me."

Benny stopped and turned to the guard.

The guard dropped the cigarette butt and ground it beneath his boot. "It's your face. You look scared. They see it. They... Well, they ain't in here for being good people."

"I can't wear a mask," Benny cried, thinking Mr. Harlan was a nice guy but pretty dumb.

"No, you can't. But, Jesus, you look scared. Don't look so scared. Hide behind your face." Harlan shook his head. "They look at you. They scare you. They win. Don't let them win."

Benny nodded. "Don't let them win."

Alone in his cell, as the child molesters clucked and whimpered on the other side of the sheet, Benny spent hours working up the nerve to look at his face. Hairless, bruised, and scabbed, Benny had nightmares about the way it looked. He feared the wounds would never heal. People horrified by the sight of him would run when he approached. It frightened him, too. It reminded him of where he was and how he got there.

To look at his own face, Benny approached the stainless-steel mirror riveted to his cell wall with his head tilted to the left. Warped and oblong, it distorted his features as a whole, but individual parts appeared as they were. His right eye was fine, and he could stand to look at it. Once comfortable, he'd slowly let the rest of his face cross the mirror. His lips were no longer swollen, but the cuts still hurt when he drank or ate. The black and blue marks around his left eye had developed a greenish tinge. His eyebrows and lashes had been singed off by the fire. A thick scab formed above his left eye. He touched the top of his head gently with his fingertips. Hair gone, skin peeled and flaked, his scalp cracked when he touched it. He backed away from the mirror and looked hard at his whole face and its warped reflection. Benny knew what O'Ryan had done with his fists and what he had done himself with the bottle of gasoline. The difference between those things didn't matter, because now, it was all just his face.

Benny took Mr. Harlan's advice and tried to see his face as a mask. He worked hard to make it placid, calm, nothing. After three full days before the mirror, Benny understood its ticks -- its muscles, what he could move together, what separately. He developed combinations of eyes, cheeks, lips and brow that said joy, danger, grief and nothing.

Benny wore his nothing face through the prison and while the other prisoners hooted and whistled at him, it didn't matter, because in that face he believed he really wasn't there.

He wore his nothing face to the smudged window that separated him from his mother the first time she came to visit.

"I brought you a cake with a file in it," she whispered. "But the guard took it away."

Benny raised the left side of his mouth, and gave his mother, a 'that's almost funny' smirk.

Her smile dropped a little. Benny knew his face worked.

"So, what do you do in there all day? Make license plates?"

Benny could see she thought that funny. He gave her the full 'nothing' face. "That's not funny," he said. "Don't even think it's funny."

He got her with that one. He got her good. He knew it.

She stopped smiling. "You look different," she said.

"Well, I'm sure being locked up in this fucking place has nothing to do with it."

"Don't talk to me like that," his mother said. "It's your fault. I tried to help." She shook her head. Benny knew she was about to cry.

"Oh, yeah," he said. "Like you helped my father." He sharpened his face like a knife and jabbed. "Now, I know why he left." He waited for her tears to begin. As the first tear drop streaked down her cheek, he stood up and said, "See ya."

"Benjamin Taggart," his mother said. "Come back here. Benny, you little son of a bitch, come back here," she shouted. "Your father didn't leave, Benny. I threw him out. Did you hear me? I threw him out. He was no good."

Benny didn't turn back. As the guard walked him through the prison, some men whistled and made kissing noises. Benny turned his face on then, and they stopped.

III

After sixty days in the penitentiary, Benny arrived at the Juvenile Detention Center like a major leaguer being sent down to the minors. A light snow, like confetti at the end of a parade, fell as the prison transport van stopped outside the Center's gates. Work crews paused, basketball games stopped, and Benny could feel all the boys' eyes on him as he hopped down to the pavement. He knew what they were staring at: the county's rule about transporting penitentiary prisoners, (full shackles required -- no exceptions,) made Benny Bad.

The guard and the van driver stood on either side of him and gripped his elbows. He jerked his arms away. "Jesus, you don't have to touch me," he said, staring straight ahead.

The driver said, "No, Taggart, we don't have to. We like to."

Everybody wants to be funny, he thought. Screw them. They don't have to touch me. I'm not going anywhere. Jerks.

Benny could see his breath and felt the chains on his wrists and ankles growing cold. He turned his head slowly, letting his eyes fall across the boys on the other side of the double chain link fence. A tall black guy, slick with sweat, a steamish vapor rising from his hospital green coveralls, stood on the basketball court, pumping the ball up and down in a cold, slow dribble. The tinny sound of the ball against frozen pavement echoed off the Center's buildings and annoyed Benny. He laid his eyes on the boy and held him in his stare. He pressed harder. The boy stopped bouncing the ball.

"Let's go, Taggart," the guard said, squeezing Benny's elbow.

The chains running from his waist to his wrists and ankles made a jingling sound as he moved in a slow stutter step along the fence. He made walking look more difficult than it was, knowing that to look bad was to be bad. Beyond the fence, gray cement buildings rose like tumors through the snow. Corridors of chain link fence connected the buildings. He smiled as they passed through the first gate. It was like entering a playground. All the buildings had windows. The fence -- shit, he thought, I can see through a fence.

Benny turned his head left and right, looked through the Juvenile Detention Center's fences and off to the surrounding fields. I can do this easy, he thought. Easy.

As they approached the building, Benny saw his reflection in the door's wire run glass. He saw an ugly boy, dressed in oversized blue coveralls. The boy had no eyebrows, his face looked peeled and raw, the remnants of a scab hardened above his left eye, his hair sprouted in clumps. Benny looked away from his face. His head itched. He couldn't scratch it because of the shackles.

The door made a buzzing noise. The guard pulled it open.

The office was warm and smelled of pine scented cleaner. A tiny green plastic Christmas tree stood on a low counter that cut the room in half. Benny smirked when he spotted it. "Christmas is over," he said, quietly. Whether anyone had heard him or not didn't seem to matter. No one replied. Two boys -- one black, one Asian -- stood on the other side of the counter. They both wore green coveralls; the word HONOR had been written in gold over their breast pockets. Beside them stood a guard in a dull brown uniform. Benny looked into his eyes and held up the cuffs. "I'm not going anywhere," he said speaking out of the corner of his mouth to the driver. "How about taking these damn things off?"

"Not till somebody signs for you, Mr. Taggart," the driver said. He slid a clipboard across the counter to the guard from the JDC. "Sign for this monkey and he's all yours."

Benny shook his head. What an asshole.

The guard's pen scratched across the paper. He handed the clipboard back. The driver snapped off a receipt and placed it on the counter. "He's all yours," he said.

The guard unlocked the cuffs and pulled the chain through the restraint on Benny's waist. Benny massaged his wrists and ran his hands over the top of his head. He smirked at the boys in their HONOR uniforms as flecks of dried skin snowed down around him. The boys smiled. Benny was prepared to tell them, or anyone else, what it was like to be the youngest dude ever in the county pen. He would tell them how he could do anything he wanted in his cell: hang pictures of naked girls, swing from the bars and shout, "fuck fuck fuck"; how he could sleep when he wanted, stay awake when he wanted, because they never turned off the lights. He'd tell about the guard who brought him Mars Bars and magazines, and how he did his time the hard way, with murderers and rapists and nobody fucked with him.

But there were things Benny would never tell anyone. How they locked him up with the child molesters because the guards had more control there. How he begged a guard to let him hang a sheet across his cell, so the perverts couldn't watch him. And how, after that, he'd see their shadows and hear them moan as they stroked their cocks. He'd never tell them how one molester, who claimed to be a lawyer, crept up to his cell and pleaded with Benny to let him suck his cock. The lawyer offered food, money, everything he owned just to touch and taste Benny's dick. He wouldn't tell anyone how you couldn't sleep because the noise went on all the time, and how he hated his cell at first and then became afraid to leave it. He'd never tell them about the men who shouted and whistled at him as he walked through the prison and about the guys who argued over who would get to butt fuck him first. How he went nowhere without a guard and even then, he was scared -- so scared. And finally, he knew he would never tell anyone about his face.

On his first night in the JDC, after lights out, Benny had heard some boys in the dorm room crawl from their beds and creep along the floor on their hands and knees. Muffled grunts and groans rose from the beds around him as the boytoys jerked or sucked off others. Benny wondered what he would do if anybody crept over to his bed and put their mouth on him. His cock got hard; he rolled onto his stomach.

On his second day in the JDC one of the boytoys, who called himself Sheila, sat next to Benny at dinner and offered him his dessert: a chocolate brownie with three M&Ms pressed into it. Sheila wore mismatched gold-colored earrings -- a thick hoop in his left ear, a crescent moon in the right. The gold plate stood out like real treasure against Sheila's brown skin. He wore a multicolored scarf twisted into a turban on his head and dusted his lips red with raspberry Jello mix stolen from the kitchen. As he reached for the brownie, he looked into Sheila's eyes. "Are you sure?" he asked.

"Oh, I'm more than sure," the boy replied, raising one eyebrow and pursing his lips.

That night after lights out, Benny felt a hand slide up under his blanket. Cool fingers moved in circles along his thighs and lingered over his balls before grasping his prick. Sheila's mouth and tongue worked his cock. Benny remembered the taste of Sheila's hand, placed over his mouth to muffle Benny's moans.

Four days after his arrival at the JDC, Benny sat in the back of a remedial algebra class watching the boy next to him, Arthur, sketch out a tattoo design. It was supposed to be a snake coiled to strike. Arthur wanted to put it on Benny's shoulder. Arthur, red haired with milk colored skin, doodled on himself the way other kids scratched in their notebooks. The boy had covered himself in an awkward web of blue ink-- from the words LOVE and HATE on his knuckles, to a blurry eye etched into his left calf.

Arthur slept in the bed next to Benny in C dorm. They were the same age. Arthur had stolen purses from old ladies in his neighborhood. He wore a Casper the Friendly Ghost mask and snatched the pocketbooks as the old ladies left evening Mass. The cops staked out the church and beat the shit out of Arthur when they caught him.

Arthur told him the other kids had known Benny was coming to the JDC three weeks before he arrived. He asked if it was true that Benny had torched a house full of bikers for messing with his mother.

Benny shrugged his shoulders and gave Arthur an 'I don't want to talk about it' look. Arthur said, "That's cool," but asked, "Were there really thirteen bikers? Did they hurt your moms bad?" Before Benny could speak, Arthur said, "Yeah, yeah. I guess I wouldn't want to talk about it either." Then Arthur told Benny he was lucky he didn't get the death penalty, that the judge must have been a pretty cool guy to understand nobody messed with your moms.

Benny thought of Judge L. V. Williams and shook his head.

"We're cool," Arthur said. "I get it. Don't talk about it then."

Benny didn't know what he'd tell people about the fire, but if they wanted to believe he torched some bikers, that was fine with him. During his time at the JDC nobody had messed with him. All the boys knew who he was and nodded he passed. Arthur said they called him *Bad* Benny Taggart, which made him smile. Benny figured it was his face and the rumors. He worked to look bad to these guys. Benny never relaxed his face. He held it taut and bad. He made it crazy, and the rumor spread.

Arthur held up his drawing of the snake, and whispered to him, "Taggart, a snake is your power sign. Strike quick and deadly."

Benny nodded his head, but the thought of letting Arthur at his body with needle and ink made his palms sweat. Arthur knew how to spell, but his rendition of a coiled snake looked like a worm eating a twig. He was about to tell Arthur he wasn't sure about the tattoo when the teacher, Miss Jones, shouted his name. "Benjamin Taggart," she said.

Benny snapped his head forward, made himself look stupid. "Huh?" he replied.

An HONOR boy stood alongside Miss Jones. "Counseling," the teacher said.

"Counseling? The fuck is that?"

Arthur looked down at the design and whispered, "Go on, Taggart. We all do it. Ain't nothing."

Benny followed the HONOR boy through the JDC's corridors. Their sneakers squeaked like mice on the floor's over-buffed tiles. The squeaking and his own breathing were the only sounds Benny heard. After two lefts and a right turn, a sign hanging from the ceiling read COUNSELING. Six doors, three on each side of the hall, made up the section. "You got Sharkovsky," the kid said, pointing at a closed door.

Benny knocked.

"Yeah," came a shout. "It's open."

Benny tried the doorknob. It turned in his hand. The last door he had opened was at Halpert Middle School, and through that door he had heaved the Scotch bottle full of gasoline. That door had led him to this one. He hesitated for a moment, grunted and pushed the memory of Halpert Middle School out of his head. Benny put on his nothing face.

In the office, an overweight middle-aged man rose from behind a desk near the back wall. Above his head hung a hand-scrawled sign, "Roy's Place." The guy's hair was greasy and his nose curved at a strange angle to his face. He wore a blue striped short-sleeve shirt that looked like it had been slept in.

"Name's Roy Sharkovsky," he said, and held out his hand.

"Taggart," Benny said, keeping his hands at his side, and concentrating on his 'nothing' face.

The man looked at his hand and shrugged. "Pleasure," he said and pointed to a chair.

Benny sat down and stared at his hands.

"So," the counselor said, shaking a cigarette from a pack of Marlboro 100s and clenching it between his teeth, "you're the Bad Benny Taggart I've heard so much about." He leaned back in his chair and put his feet, one atop the other, on the desk.

"I guess," Benny said, not looking up.

"Well, Taggart, whether you guess or not, you caused quite a stir when you came through those gates."

Benny couldn't help it: he smiled.

"By the way the kids talked you would've thought Al Capone arrived." Sharkovsky shook his head. "Every kid that walked through that door last week began," Sharkovsky's voice became squeaky and nasal, 'Hey, Sharkovsky, ya' hear? Bad Benny Taggart's coming to the JDC.'" His voice returned to normal, "Bad Benny Taggart."

Benny felt his whole body smile. He looked straight at Sharkovsky. "That's me," he said, grinning. "Bad Benny Taggart."

Sharkovsky grinned back at him. "Well, you don't look so 'bad' to me, Taggart." He picked up a blue folder and waved it at Benny. "What? You do sixty days in the county pen surrounded by kid-fucking perverts and you think you're a wise guy? It's all here, Taggart. The sheet. The guards. Your daily stroll." Sharkovsky shook his head grinning. "Get the fuck out of here, Taggart. You think you're something special, but you're not. You're just one of those little weasely guys." The counselor pointed at a stack of folders. "Not like these guys. These guys make sense. They rob. They kill. Run drugs. I know what they're up to. But you, Taggart, you burn bathrooms and locker rooms. What is that? I mean bathrooms. Jesus. What? You hate taking a shit? I don't even know if I think you're a torch. A torch, I mean a real one, lights a building, hangs around in the crowd and watches it burn -- enjoys it. Jesus, Taggart, bathrooms? I mean, come on. What's going on here?" He tapped the side of his head. "Are you a torch, or what?"

"Why don't you tell me," Benny said, struggling to hold the smile on his face. Benny decided Sharkovsky was an asshole. He wanted to put on his 'we both know you're an asshole' face, but he knew if he did, the asshole would have won something.

Sharkovsky laughed, dropped his feet from the desk and

leaned forward, halving the space between him and Benny. "You know what they say in my business, Taggart? They say, you get a kid who wets the bed, hurts animals and lights fires, and you got a nut case. A real crazy that's going to end up snuffing someone. Not for any reason in particular, but just for... ah, who knows?" Sharkovsky nodded, pulled the unlit cigarette from his mouth and flipped it over Benny's shoulder into a trash can in the room's far corner. "Who knows? I don't." He shook another out of his pack. "So Bad Benny Taggart, just between you and me, you hurt animals? Like to tie cats up and cut their ears off? Ever hammer a puppy to death with a baseball bat? What do you say, Bad Benny Taggart? You wet the bed?"

Jesus, who is this guy? Benny dropped the muscles in his face and put on his baddest Bad Benny Taggart.

"Nice face, Taggart. Oooooh, I'm so scared. Well, fuck you." Sharkovsky slapped his hand down on the desk. "Answer the questions. You wet the bed? You hurt animals?"

Fuck this guy, Benny thought. Asshole. "I don't wet the bed." He tried to say it quietly between clenched teeth, but he heard himself shouting. "I don't wet the bed," he repeated, almost crying.

Sharkovsky was on his feet and in Benny's face. "You want to spend the rest of your life inside?" the counselor shouted. "You want to be a lifer? You want to get up and go down, every day, on somebody else's say so?"

"Fuck you," Benny shouted, leaning back in his chair, trying to scoot away from Sharkovsky. The chair was bolted to the floor.

Sharkovsky shouted questions. He moved closer. Benny felt his breath and spit as the counselor shouted in his face, but he no longer heard the questions. This fucking guy was pushing him. He would have to push back. Benny heard himself scream when he leapt out of the chair. He barked and growled like a dog, cried and screamed like a child, and shouted "fuck, fuck, fuck" as he tried to bite and kick Sharkovsky. The counselor turned Benny around and wrapped him in a hug. Benny jerked and squirmed. Sharkovsky repeated in his ear, "Don't be afraid, Taggart. Let it go, let yourself go."

Benny wore himself down in the struggle with Sharkovsky. He wept blindly and selfishly, as he saw himself not as Bad Benny Taggart but as pitiful, a frightened child, as scared of his past as he was of the future. His body shook. He wheezed and gasped for air.

Sharkovsky eased him back into the chair and stood behind Benny rubbing his shoulders, telling him that things could be okay. That crying was okay. "Let it go, kid," Sharkovsky said. "Let it go."

Benny cried for everything that had ever gone wrong in his life. He cried for being alone, for not having friends, for the way he scared people and the way he scared himself. His bones felt like rubber. He slid out of the chair. "Jesus," he said. "I've got to lay down."

Sharkovsky dropped back into the chair behind his desk. "Lay on the floor," he said. "Fuck if I care."

The cool tiles felt good through Benny's sweat-damp coveralls. He closed his eyes and tried to think, but his mind felt empty. He searched for something he was sure of. His name -- Benjamin Taggart, he knew that. But for a moment even that truth wavered. He opened his eyes and stared up at the ceiling. Who is this guy?

**

Benny learned that every boy went to counseling once a week. Some thought it okay, almost fun. Some thought it sucked. Some didn't think. Benny couldn't wait for the next Monday. When the HONOR boy showed up in his remedial algebra class, Benny leapt out of his seat before Ms. Jones could call his name. He walked with long strides through the corridors, knocked once and pushed through the door as Sharkovsky shouted, "it's open."

Benny dropped into the chair, leaned back and gave the counselor his real face. "What do I get if I tell you everything?"

Sharkovsky smirked. "What do you mean, get?"

"I mean. I tell you everything. I mean, everything! Can that get me more time inside? I don't want anymore."

Sharkovsky took a cigarette from a pack in his breast pocket. He clenched the filter between his teeth. "I won't bullshit you, Taggart. There's some stuff you could say that would keep you in here, or maybe some other place, for a long time. But I don't think that's it with you. I know boys more fucked up than you ever thought of being who, right now, are on the other side of the fence."

Benny stared straight faced at Sharkovsky. No mask, no Bad

Benny Taggart. Benny hated the idea that his file might say he was crazy. He wasn't crazy. Or was he? Was he crazy because he wanted to kill those three boys? "Do you think I'm crazy?" Benny asked loud, hard between a cry and a shout.

Sharkovsky startled back in his chair. "I don't know. Do you think you're crazy?"

"Would you tell me if you knew?"

"I might," he said. "What's it worth to you?"

"What?"

"That's a joke."

"I don't like jokes," Benny said. "My mom jokes. Everything's a joke with her."

"Are you a joke with her?"

"I think so," Benny said. "I couldn't ask her. She'd make a joke."

Sharkovsky nodded. "No jokes."

"Thanks," Benny said. "And you'll tell me if I'm crazy."

Sharkovsky flipped the cigarette over Benny's shoulder into the trash can in the room's far corner. "Yeah. I'll tell you."

"Okay," Benny said. "I started two fires. Okay? The first one, I don't know. I was screwing around. A teacher pissed me off, okay. Sometimes. Sometimes, I get going and can't stop myself." Benny stopped and took a deep breath.

Sharkovsky shook another cigarette from the pack and stuck it between his teeth.

"When it happens..." Benny paused. "When it happens, I'm free. I'm happy. I fly. I was flying during that fire. Flying." He smiled at the memory.

Sharkovsky nodded.

"The second." Benny looked to his right, shook his head; tears smarted his eyes. He took a breath. "The second fire was different – I wanted to kill three boys." Benny had replayed the events so many times in his head, his telling flowed out as if a narrative to someone else's life. Benny's voice trembled and cracked. He told Sharkovsky about Opportunity Class, and his first meeting with O'Ryan and Blume and Lewis. His start to the second day. O'Ryan and the joint. Lewis and Blume. The locker-room. His rape. Hiding from the cops. The gas. The Scotch bottle. Singerman, the fire alarm, the locker room.

"You know," Benny said. "When the gasoline flashed, I thought for sure I was dead. I hoped I was dead." He stopped speaking. His body felt weightless, as if he would drift right up out his chair, like a helium-filled balloon. He looked up at Sharkovsky then down at his hands, balled in fists on his lap.

The counselor tossed a cigarette over Benny's head, shook another from the pack and clenched it between his teeth. "It's pretty fucked up, Taggart."

"Yeah, I know."

"Have you talked about this with anyone? Another counselor?"

"No," Benny said, "Who could I tell? Who would've cared?"

Sharkovsky nodded and sighed. "Okay. You know how it felt then. How about now?"

"I'd like to burn those mother-fuckers but know I can't."

"Because you're inside?"

"No, because it won't fix it. Nothing can."

Sharkovsky tilted his head to the left. "Is something broken?"

"Fucking-A, Sharkovsky, weren't you listening. They stuck their dicks in my ass."

"I got that, Taggart. Tell me, what's broken?"

"Me," he said. "I'm broken."

"Okay," Sharkovsky said. "Let's try and fix you."

"Yeah, right, "Benny said. "There's nothing can fix what they did. Nothing."

"Taggart, you can't fix what they did, but how about we work on fixing you."

"Me?" Benny smirked and exhaled through his nose. "You going to fix it so I don't think of them every time I take a shit? You going to make the dreams go away?" Benny stood up, held out his arms and spun in circles. "Fix it? How will you fix this, Sharkovsky? I want you to. Believe me. How?" Benny wobbled left and right, dizzy from spinning.

Sharkovsky gestured with his chin. "Sit down."

Benny looked back and dropped into the chair, his hands resting on its arms.

"Okay, not fix. Wrong word." Sharkovsky sat forward in his chair, placed his left elbow on the desk and supported his chin with his hand. "Taggart," he said. "You're plenty fucked up."

A laugh popped from Benny's mouth. "Good job, Sharkovsky," he said, "Yeah, I'm fucked up."

"Right," Sharkovsky said, "Guys in here. Guys in prison. They're just like you -- plenty fucked up."

"Great. I'm fucked up. So's everybody else in here. And you, Sharkovsky?"

"Listen Taggart, don't cop attitude with me. You're inside. You might not have been crazy when you tried to burn those guys, but in the end it's all the same."

"Aw, man," Benny whined, "You're fucking with me."

"I'm fucking with you?" Sharkovsky shook his head. "I'm not doing shit, Taggart, but giving you the real deal. What do you want to hear from me? You want to hear that you're all fucked up because of what those guys did? You won't. I read your record, Taggart. You were on your way here, with or without those guys. You're fucked up. You need to figure out how not to act on your desire to fuck up."

"You're giving me a headache," Benny said.

"It's a start," Sharkovsky replied. The counselor opened a desk drawer, held up a small notebook and tossed it at Benny.

Benny clapped his hands together. The book dropped at his feet. "Good hands, Taggart," he said. "Now, sometimes this works and sometimes it doesn't. For next Monday, I want you to write down every time you ever fucked up. Number them so you'll have a count."

Benny squinted, that was a lot of work. "Every time?"

Sharkovsky nodded.

Benny opened his mouth to ask what Sharkovsky he meant exactly by "fucked up."

The counselor held up his hand. "Time's up," he said. "Have a good week."

"But."

"Get the fuck out of here, Taggart."

Benny examined the notebook as an HONOR boy walked him to his next class. Small enough to fit in his coverall's breast pocket, the notebook had a shiny red cover and a spiral metal binding. Thin blue lines crossed its white pages. The cover said it had sixty pages. Benny thought he should have told Sharkovsky he needed a bigger book, but he knew the counselor wouldn't have laughed.

In a darkened classroom, while his history teacher showed a film about the Cherokee Trail of Tears, Benny wrote his name on the cover of the notebook. Boys around him made farting noises, shouted, "Eat shit," and threw paper around the room. Benny traced and retraced Bad Benny Taggart into the notebook's cover as different images of Native Americans danced across the screen.

That night while the other boys in his dorm watched TV, Benny sat on his cot and stared at the blank first page. He tried to figure out what Sharkovsky meant by fucked up. Did he fuck up if he did something wrong, or did he fuck up only if he got caught? He decided a fuck up was every time you did something wrong. He tried to remember the first time he fucked up and as he did a flood of fuck ups poured through his mind: the fire in the bathroom; trashing the art room at Ottem Middle School; writing "fuck you" backwards on the Ottem principal's window; throwing snowballs packed with stones at cars; shooting the jaw breaker from a sling shot; in kindergarten, trying to flush the shoes of a boy he didn't like down the toilet. He wrote them all down, numbering each one. At lights outs, he had nineteen fuck ups.

Benny shoved the notebook under his pillow and stared into the dark. The next morning, he sat up in his bunk and added four more, including the fire in the locker room. During breakfast he recollected slapping Henry Mojica, the smallest kid in his first-grade class, and it ruined his appetite. By dinner time he was up to sixty-three fuck-ups. By Sunday afternoon he'd listed eighty-seven. Eighty-seven times that he could remember doing things that everyone would agree were wrong. Benny felt drained by it all. Remembering all that stuff, the good times, not getting caught -- the bad times, getting caught, made him feel old.

On Monday morning during remedial algebra he added eighty- eight, the dissing of his mom when he was in prison. The HONOR boy walked through the door, and Benny followed him to Sharkovsky's office. He rapped once.

Sharkovsky shouted, "It's open."

Benny stepped through the door and dropped down into the chair. Sharkovsky leaned over his desk, writing. His pen made a scratching noise.

"How was your week, Taggart?"

"Good," Benny said. "Real good."

Sharkovsky nodded and looked up. "Did you do the book?"

Benny nodded and lifted the note book out of his breast pocket. "Yeah," he said.

Sharkovsky stuck a cigarette between his teeth.

"Tell me about it."

"I'm not sure what you want me to say."

Sharkovsky shrugged. "Whatever you want."

"I got up to eighty-eight, going all the way back to kindergarten. Sometimes I kind of hurt people and that makes me feel bad and sometimes I didn't and the things I did were funny. At least they seemed funny when I did them. Now, they seem kind of stupid."

Benny opened the notebook and flipped through the pages. "I don't know what else to say about this stuff, except that I did it all." He closed the notebook, read his name scratched in the cover, and looked up at Sharkovsky. "Well?"

"Well, what?"

"What next?

Sharkovsky tossed the cigarette over Benny's shoulder into a waste basket near the door. He shook out a fresh one and stuck it between his teeth. "Yeah, you're right, Taggart. You did it all. And there's probably a few times you fucked up that you don't remember -- so let's just say that you fucked up one hundred times."

"Okay," Benny said.

"I think anything you did once you can do again. Don't care how stupid it is, we're just that way. From now until you leave the JDC, every Monday you come in ready. Ready to do one or two things on your list."

"Do?" Benny said.

"Yes, do. Act." Sharkovsky nodded, "You spend too much time in your head. You need to get out -- see what the world sees."

"That seems too simple," Benny said.

"I know," Sharkovsky said, "If I was a really bright guy and thought up great therapies, you think I'd have ended up working with little pricks like you?"

"I guess not," Benny said.

Each week they acted out a fuck up on Benny's list. Sharkovsky pretended he was Benny; Benny played the victim. Even when Benny didn't think he'd hurt anyone, Sharkovsky showed him he had. Benny cried a lot during the sessions. Sharkovsky told him it was good to cry when you felt bad. Important. A kid needed to cry.

During Benny's final counseling session, he and Sharkovsky acted out the last entry in the notebook: the time he dissed his mom at the penitentiary. They spent two entire sessions preparing for it. During one they talked about Benny's feelings toward his mom. In the next they imagined her feelings toward him.

At the start of the final session, Sharkovsky left his office for a moment and returned scowling, the way Benny had to the visitors' glass in the penitentiary. Benny giggled when he saw Sharkovsky's face, not because it was funny but because he was nervous.

"You look like somebody peed in your cereal," Benny said, grinning.

"That's not funny," Sharkovsky said. "You think it's funny." His face darkened.

Benny's grin froze. "Well, no, I guess it's not funny."

"No," Sharkovsky said. "It is funny to you. You think everything about me is funny. Nothing's serious with you."

"That's not true and you know it. You've brought me nothing but heartache and worry, so I laugh any chance I get."

"You laugh at me," Sharkovsky pointed his thumb at his chest.

Benny shook his head, "I'm not laughing because you're funny. I'm laughing because you scare me. You came through that door looking like you wanted to kill me."

"You think I want to kill you?"

"You do pretty strange things," Benny said. "I never go to sleep at night without wondering what you're doing in your room. I don't think you'd kill me on purpose, but maybe by mistake."

"Is that why you laugh at me all the time?" Sharkovsky asked. "Because you're afraid of me. Afraid I'm going to kill you."

"I don't laugh at you. I love you, but you scare me."

"What did you say?"

"I love you," Benny repeated. "But you scare me."

Sharkovsky's face relaxed. He shook a cigarette from his pack.

Benny waited for him to speak, but he just rolled the cigarette back and forth in his mouth. "Do you think that's true?" Benny asked.

"What I think doesn't matter," Sharkovsky said.

IV

Five months and two days after entering the JDC, Benny Taggart was on his way out. Knowing the kids on the work details watched his every step, Benny, *The Bad Man*, strutted through the caged walkway connecting the JDC's dorm and its main entrance in the punked-up gait of a serious player. His feet danced a 'too bad' pattern across the asphalt, while he rocked from side to side and popped the air with his right fist. Benny had entered prison seven months before -- voice cracking, eyes startled. But as he left lockup -- dressed in green coveralls with the letters 'JDC' stenciled in bold yellow strokes on his back -- his buzz cut hair laying thick as a beaver pelt across his head -- the short sleeves of his coveralls rolled into tight bundles, swelling the appearance of his biceps, he knew the show and put it on full display.

He slowed as he approached the end of the caged corridor that separated the JDC's dorm from the main entrance. Late spring -- the air smelled of wet mud and new grass, and the sun, knifing through threatening clouds, gave the entire complex a raw, threatening look.

Coveralled boys, armed with paint brushes or rakes or shovels, poked listlessly at their tasks. The concertina wire topping the fence flashed like lightning. Through the Administration's wire-run glass window, Benny could see Sharkovsky. An unlit cigarette bobbed in his mouth. Fucking Sharkovsky, Benny thought, and really put on the punk for the last few steps on the inside.

A kid on a work detail shouted, "All right, Mr. Bad."

Benny popped the air one more time with his right fist, hit the button next to the door with his left and said, "Benjamin Taggart" crisply into the tiny speaker above the button. The door made a buzzing sound, and Benny pulled it open.

Roy Sharkovsky, half sitting on the edge of the guard's desk, tossed a chewed cigarette into the trash can at his feet. "*Bad* Benny Taggart," he said. "On his way out of the JDC." He held up a hand.

Benny slapped it. "All right," Sharkovsky said. "All right."

55

***

Dressed in white, government issue sneakers, stiff new jeans and a new white t-shirt, covered by a hooded green sweatshirt, Benny rode the first few miles from the JDC with his head hanging out the passenger window of Sharkovsky's car. A new duffel bag, filled with the rest of his "outside" stuff, lay across the back seat. He whooped and yelled, "All right," as they passed a field of muddy cows. Sharkovsky shouted that he could play the radio if he wanted, but it all seemed too much and too little to Benny. He was out, but it didn't feel any different.

Benny looked over at Sharkovsky as the counselor flipped a chewed cigarette over his shoulder into the back seat. "I want to feel out," Benny said.

Sharkovsky glanced at him. "Well, you're not out. Remember that. Six months, you're out. Even then you're not really out. Guys like you don't get out until you're thirty. If you're still alive at thirty and not inside, you're out. But six months -- it's something to shoot for. Getting in is easy, Taggart. Any asshole can do that. Out? That's the bitch."

"Yeah, I know. I just want to feel out," Benny said. "Do me a favor?" Sharkovsky shrugged. "Pull over," Benny said. "Over there."

"You need to take a leak?"

Benny smiled. "Just pull over and let me walk a little. And you pretend you're not here."

"You pretend," Sharkovsky said. "I ain't pretending shit."

"Pull over?"

Sharkovsky eased the car onto the road's shoulder. Stones popped under the tires. Benny smiled at Sharkovsky then stepped out of the car. Out. He turned his eyes away from the car; he could hear its engine idle. He walked ahead of it, trying to forget it existed, stepping fast, hard. The air felt damp, smelled of cow shit and freedom. Benny turned his head, left to right, scanning the horizon. A stand of leafless trees. Low-bellied power lines slung between pylons. A barn roof like one from a children's book. Out, he thought. This is it. I'm out.

A three-strand barbed wire fence paralleled the road. It looked low enough to vault. The idea of crossing a fence on his own, without asking anyone, made Benny grin. He moved his feet in a quick skipping motion, broke into a run, scampered down a bank, leaped across a drainage ditch, took two steps and was airborne over the fence. He landed feet first in sticking wet mud.

The car squealed to a stop. The door opened. Sharkovsky's head popped up over the roof. "What the fuck are you doing?"

"Just jumping a fence," Benny said.

Sharkovsky stared at him, then nodded. "Make sure you clean that mud off your shoes before you get back in this fucking car."

Benny kicked his feet. Clods of mud flew out into the field. Out, out, out, he thought. He backed three steps from the fence, ran alongside it and leaped into the air. His left foot caught the top strand. He landed in the soft spring grass on the roadside of the fence. He lay still for a moment; nothing hurt. He laughed.

"Jesus, Taggart," Sharkovsky yelled. "Get up off the ground. You're worse than a damn dog. Get in the fucking car."

Benny pushed to his feet and walked to the car. He pulled the door open and dropped in next to Sharkovsky.

"Look at those fucking sneakers," the counselor said. "You got another pair?"

Benny looked at his shoes, mud-splattered and wet.

He shook his head.

Sharkovsky reached into the back seat and handed Benny a brown paper bag. "Here," the counselor said. "A gift for your work."

Benny looked at Sharkovsky, then tore open the bag. A pair of red hi-top Converse-Allstars fell onto his lap. "All right," he said. "Red Cons, man. Thanks."

"Yeah, well," Sharkovsky said. "Save them. Wear them to school." He looked down at Benny's feet. "You can't wear those."

Benny held one of the sneakers at eye level turning it over in his hands. Cherry soda red, he smelled the musky scent of new rubber and canvas. He knew when he wore them he'd feel out; he'd be out. Benny twisted in the seat, opened the duffel bag and stuffed in the sneakers. "You know, Sharkovsky," he said, turning back, "I really thought you were an asshole when we first met."

"And now?"

"I was wrong," Benny said. "You're ofuckingkay, Sharkovsky."

"Well, Taggart, I thought you were an asshole, too."

"And now?"

"You're still an asshole, Taggart." Sharkovsky stared at him for a moment, then smiled. "But you did the work. A lot of guys don't."

Sharkovsky stopped at an intersection. An eighteen-wheeler blew by the front of the car. Benny grinned when he saw it. He'd forgotten big trucks existed. Sharkovsky moved the car forward. "I talked to your mom last night," he said.

"You did?"

"I told her about your placement and gave her your number. She's going to wait a week, till you're settled, then come see you."

"Was she mad?"

Sharkovsky shook his head. "No, she said to say hello, and that she loves you."

Benny looked out the window, smiling. Sharkovsky was right. Do the work. You can turn it around.

***

Sharkovsky piloted the car into an older and more elegant part of the city than where Benny had lived. The houses, each at least three stories tall, sat separated from the street and one another by large front and side lawns. This looks great, Benny thought. I'm going to live in a mansion, like a rich guy.

The counselor turned the car into a long blacktopped circular driveway. Halfway up the drive, a white passenger van squatted on two flat rear tires. Sharkovsky swung the car off the blacktop and followed the sloppy mud tracks across the lawn. The house before them, like its neighbors, was three stories tall and built of sand-colored brick. Four stout brick columns supported the second and third stories above the porch. A rusting lawn mower stood like a memorial to a lost cause in the middle of the patchy front lawn, and screens, from the windows on the second and third floors, littered the porch roof and the shrubs that grew tight against the house. Benny squinted at the jumble of objects covering the porch: a burnt green bicycle frame, an old wing-backed couch standing on end, a bench press -- the weights on one side tipping awkwardly toward the ground -- a brown and bare Christmas tree tipped against the front windows, and what Benny thought was a mannequin, at first, until its right hand moved slowly up to its mouth and cigarette smoke drifted across the yard. The mannequin raised its left hand in a slow half-hearted greeting. The mannequin became a man, wearing a black and white horizontal striped long-sleeved t-shirt. Graying brown hair, pulled back in a ponytail, encircled his smooth, bald head. Tobacco stained his mustache a butterscotch brown and a bright white cowry shell was woven into a wisp of a beard.

Benny turned toward Sharkovsky. He opened his mouth, but he didn't know what to say.

Sharkovsky pulled up in front of the house and slid the gear shift into park. He shook a cigarette from the pack and stuck it between his teeth. "Okay, this is the deal, Taggart. I'm being straight with you because you've been straight with me." He shifted the cigarette across his mouth. "The easiest part of getting it together is the stuff you do inside. Even when you want to fuck off, you can't. Here, Taggart, you're on your own."

Benny glanced up at the house. Suddenly he was as afraid of the group home as he had been of the penitentiary. He nodded his head, tried to smile. "Don't worry about me," he said. "I think I got it."

Sharkovsky tossed the unlit cigarette into the back seat. "Every place has rules, Taggart. Figure out what they are -- try and stick to them -- and you'll do fine. You got that? That's the best I got." He said, "The best."

"I got it," Benny said.

"All right, Bad Benny Taggart, let's show them your stuff."

Benny said, "Yeah," and pushed the car door open, feeling like he knew something about his future. Three raw eggs, bap-bap-bap, splatted against the car's roof. Benny ducked and scrambled behind the car door. He poked his head up and tried to see where the eggs had come from. He heard laughter from behind a blue curtained window just above the front porch. "Jesus Christ," he said.

Sharkovsky shouted from the far side of the car, "No more eggs, Peter. This is a new shirt."

"Fuck you, Sharkovsky. Peter throws eggs at whoever he

wants," came a high shrill voice from behind the curtain. "Peter does whatever he wants." An arm flashed at the window. An egg broke against the windshield.

"What the fuck is this?" Benny shouted.

The smoking mannequin walked slowly down from the porch, turned and faced the house. "Aw, Peter, man," the dummy said. "Don't waste the eggs, man."

"Shut up, Jason," came the voice. "Peter does what he wants."

An egg flattened against Jason's forehead. He turned and faced Benny. "Aw, man, can you believe he's wasting food like that?" Jason's eyes brightened, as if he suddenly remembered something. He spun back toward the house and pointed up at the window. "You're on restriction, man."

"Restrict this," Peter shouted.

An egg shattered on the ground next to Jason.

The house's front door creaked open. A heavy woman in a riotous red, yellow, green and blue tie-dyed tent dress stepped out onto the porch and smiled down at Benny, Sharkovsky and Jason. Frizzy brown hair escaped from the bun perched atop her head. Chunks of crystal and a large alarm clock swung from leather thongs around her neck. She opened her arms wide in a greeting. "Welcome, Benjamin, to the New Family Way Group Home," she said.

Benny straightened up.

An egg sailed past his ear. He ducked back down.

The woman on the porch looked surprised, then scowled when an egg broke against the side of Sharkovsky's car. "Jason, who's throwing those eggs?" she asked, coming down off the porch. She planted both fists on her hips and looked back up at the house.

"I don't know, man," Jason said.

"Nancy," Sharkovsky said. "It's Peter."

"It is not Peter," came the shrill voice from behind the curtains. "It's somebody else. Somebody who looks like Peter. Thinks like Peter. Sleeps like Peter. But it's not Peter. Not Peter."

"The other Peter gone now?" the woman shouted at the window.

"Yes, Nancy," the voice replied.

The woman nodded and turned toward Benny and Sharkovsky. "Again, Benjamin, welcome." Raising her arms in welcome. "My name is Nancy and this," she said, pointing at Jason, "is my husband, Jason. We're the New Family Way facilitators here. Feel free to call us Nancy and Jason, or mom and dad if you like."

Benny glanced over at Sharkovsky, but the counselor's face told him nothing. Was this some kind of joke? He looked to Jason, who lit another cigarette with the butt of one just finished. Egg yolk shiny as oil stiffened on his forehead. This must be a fucking joke, Benny thought.

Benny turned back to the woman. "Hi," he said.

She smiled at him. "Benjamin, come in and see your new home."

Benny and Sharkovsky followed the wide roll of Nancy's hips up onto the porch. They entered a small vestibule with a scattering of shoes and winter boots on both sides. Benny spotted the spindly legs of a Barbie doll poking up from the pile on his left.

"This is the entrance hall," Nancy said. "Where we store our winter boots." She gestured off to the right. "That's the office. You can drop your bag there."

He eased the duffel off his shoulder and put it just inside the office door. The room seemed, to Benny, a paper version of the front porch. Mounds of files, like mismatched playing cards, covered what he took to be the desk. A rainbow shaped calendar hung askew on the far wall. Beside it hung a messy watercolor that might have been a painting of Nancy or a car, Benny couldn't tell. Papers seeped from the edges of the file cabinets and dripped to the floor like water.

"This way is the living room," Nancy said, pointing.

Benny turned and followed her through a double-wide doorway. Couches and chairs, each draped with a kid, were stuffed into the space. The kids seemed to be moving, sliding, dancing in their chairs -- but there was no sound, no music in the room. A large-screen TV, off, stared blind-eyed at Benny from the room's far side. The fireplace was a litter of charred magazines and what looked to be a blue pair of girl's underwear. Holes punched in the walls, by fists or heads, Benny couldn't tell, were ragged with plaster and lathe around their edges. The glass in two windows was held in place by yellowed strips of masking tape.

In a far corner a black girl, in bright yellow bib overalls and a pink tank top, stood up and began shimmying her hips to no sound

Benny could hear. He looked again and saw two wires running from her ears to a Walkman she held in her hand. Soon all the kids -- about twenty -- were on their feet, shaking and dancing, eyes closed; there was no sound except for their movement on the floor, the snap of their fingers and sharp breathy *huhs* and *yesses.*

Benny's palms felt damp. He rubbed them against his jeans.

"Let me introduce you," Nancy said.

Benny glanced over at her. "Don't worry about it," he said. "I'm sure I'll get to meet everybody soon enough."

"You're family, now," she said. She held the crystals and clock to her breasts and began hopping in place. Her hair flounced an odd rhythm with jumping. The entire house shook when she hit the floor.

Slowly, one or two kids opened their eyes and looked at him.

Nancy pointed at her mouth, and those kids tapped other kids, and those kids more, until all of the kids had stopped and lifted off their headphones. A thin hip hop beat from all the Walkmans filled the room.

"New Family Way," Nancy said, "this is Benjamin Taggart."

Somebody shouted, "So this the new boy, Sharkovsky? He look like a punk."

The kids said, "Whoa" and "Whooee." They all began laughing and jiving, giggling, slapping hands, bumping butts.

Benny felt his face get hot. Assholes. He put on his 'you assholes don't know bad' face. He looked at the farthest person he could make eye contact with -- a goofy-looking white guy: tall, gangly. The guy's little slits for eyes made Benny think he might be dangerous. But that didn't matter. He laid his face on the kid like a hot iron. When the kid saw Benny's face he stopped laughing and glared, hard, at Benny for a moment, before turning his back to him. But the look on Benny's face spread through the room, and soon all the kids were quiet. Some watched Benny's face. Most stared down at the floor.

Nancy looked over at Benny. "Well," she said, sounding startled, "why don't we introduce ourselves? Margo, we'll start with you and go around the room."

A blonde girl with a blue star tattooed on her cheek said, "Hi, I'm Margo." And the kids went one after another. The tall goofy-looking guy's name was Ronald. The black girl in the yellow overalls said her name was Chereese.

"Hi," Benny said. "I'm Benny." He smiled.

Nancy said, "Thank you, family."

Earphones clamped over heads, the kids dropped back into the couches and chairs. There was a rustling sound. The room quieted.

"Come on," Nancy said, "I'll show you to your room. Introduce you to your roommate." She turned to the stairs, then looked back at Sharkovsky. "Roy," she said. "There's no need for you to stay. I think Benjamin is going to do just fine here."

"I suppose," Sharkovsky said, nodding. "But I'd like to talk to him for a few seconds on the porch."

"Sure. Sure," Nancy said. She looked down at the large-faced clock that hung around her neck. "Jason, honey," she said, "isn't it time to start dinner?"

"Huh? What?" he asked.

"Dinner," Nancy repeated, "isn't it time to start?"

"Oh, right, man. Dinner." Jason smiled. "Yeah, dinner." He walked down the hall trailing smoke.

Sharkovsky and Benny went out onto the porch. The counselor held up his hands. "Listen, Taggart, I know everything you're going to say. I know everything. But there's nothing I can do about it. This is your placement. The court decides where you go. I know it's pretty weird in there. Just try and deal with it. Just get through the time. It'll be okay once you get used to it. Just learn the rules -- do the time."

"Sharkovsky," Benny said, pointing toward the door, "this place is a fucking zoo."

The counselor tapped a cigarette from his pack and stuck the filter between his teeth. "You are right, kid. It's a zoo. Good luck." He grabbed Benny's hand and shook it. "Oh yeah. Nice face, Taggart."

Benny watched as Sharkovsky drove around the van; his car disappeared from view. As he re-entered the group home, a rumbling began somewhere in the house. The house shook and groaned; the floor vibrated as if the house was trying to belch. Benny thought it was about to explode. He ran out the front door and kept going down the lawn. When he thought he had enough distance, he turned and looked back at the house. The sound grew louder. Benny reached up to cover his ears, wincing, waiting for the blast. The sound stopped. No one else left the house. Maybe I'm hearing things, he thought.

He walked back into the house, looking left and right to see if anyone else would acknowledge what he thought he'd just heard. No one did. He waited outside the office while Nancy talked on the phone. "That's okay. That's okay," she said. "You keep him locked up down there. Our van isn't running. We'll try to get down there tomorrow or the next day." She hung up the phone.

Benny reached in for his duffel.

"Come on," she said to Benny. "Let's go meet your roommate."

Nancy spoke breathlessly as she hustled up the stairs. "The boys sleep on the second floor, the girls on the third. Jason and I have a room up in the old servant's quarters in the attic. It's nice and cozy. We run this place on the honor system. If you do something wrong, just come and tell us. We understand. The food is all natural. Jason and I have a theory that food and clothing and environment are so important to raising healthy happy children. We also believe that the world is too adult-centrically based. We think you kids should be running things here, not us. That's our philosophy."

At the second landing, she turned down a hallway that smelled of urine and sweat. Holes had been punched in the walls. Someone using a red crayon drew a face around one, so the hole became a snaggle toothed mouth. Light fixtures hung down on wires. Some doors were closed -- others, knocked off their hinges, leaned against the wall.

Nancy stopped at a closed door and rapped twice. "Peter," she said. "Your new roommate is here."

"Peter kills roommates and eats their hearts," came a shrill voice from the other side of the door.

Benny wanted to turn and run down the hall.

Nancy smiled at him and tapped the door again. "Peter, I understand. Your room is your space, and I, in a non-adult-centric world, will not violate your rights. But Benjamin here has a right to one half of that room. He is going to come in, now. You, Peter, you are denying him what is his." Nancy turned and smiled at Benny. "We'll be eating in about an hour." She patted him on the shoulder and started down the hall.

"Hey," Benny said.

Nancy turned back and gave him a thumbs up, nodding. "You'll do fine."

Benny stood staring at the door. He raised his hand to knock and held it there. "Peter, I'm Benny Taggart," he said. "That fat thing is gone, so open up and let me into this room."

No answer.

Benny slapped the door. "Come on. Open this fucking door, man. Peter?"

He slapped the door again and grabbed the knob. It turned in his hand and the door swung open. Benny, hoping to avoid any more eggs, stepped back into the hallway and leaned to his left and right peeking into the room. A kid scrambled out an open window. The boy had blonde hair, a red t-shirt. Beneath the window lay an empty egg carton. Blue curtains rose and fell on a breeze. "Peter?" Benny said, stepping across the threshold. "Peter?" He heard shoes scrape down the roof. Benny rushed to the window. The boy was gone.

Benny took in the view from the window. If it weren't for the broken-down van and the lawn mower, the place would have looked pretty good. The damp air smelled clean and an idea came to Benny: there was no longer anything between him and all the air in the world. No fences -- no walls, there was him and he was in the world. An emotion welled in him, more electric than happiness. He tensed his body to squeeze all he could from the feeling. A small green car passed on the street. Benny smiled and waved. I'm out, he thought, and turned back to the room.

On either side of the window, two low bunks were covered with twists of sheets and clothes. It looked like Peter had been sleeping in both beds. A microwave oven sat atop a thigh-high refrigerator in one corner. A small color tv, on top of the dresser, was turned on -- sound down, an afternoon soap opera cut to a commercial for Mr. Clean. Benny thought the room was the nicest thing he'd seen in the house.

He dragged his duffel in and tried to decide which bed would be Peter's, which his. He had learned any number of things in the JDC, but the most important was making space for yourself. If you created the space, and didn't fuck with anybody else's, you would do okay. Benny knew he had to create his space and collect whatever juice he had coming. He weighed the issues carefully before deciding which bed, small closet and dresser drawers would be his. If he saw more of Peter he would have known. Size played a role in every decision.

He chose the bed by deciding which one looked slept in last. There was no telling, really. He knew that. But to do nothing only invited trouble. He stripped all the stuff off one bed and stacked it neatly on the other. He moved to the closets. Bent and twisted hangers hung in both, nothing else. Benny's would be the one directly behind his bed. Finally, he turned to the dresser.

Peter was the first one into the room, he should have the choice of drawers. Benny reasoned the top two should be Peter's. He opened the lowest drawer and picked up a bundled Buffalo Bills t-shirt. Something wrapped in the shirt dropped back into the drawer with a thud. The object's solid dead smack of metal against wood told Benny what it was before he saw it. He lifted it from the bottom of the drawer and held it on the flat of his hand. So small, so tiny, the gun looked like a toy. Benny never held a real gun before, but he knew about them. He'd seen them on TV, and the kids in the JDC talked about them all the time. They called them gats and heaters, four fives and three eights. They'd have laughed if anyone talked about a gun like the one Benny held in his hand. A BB gun, they'd have said. Shoot squirrels not people.

Benny closed his hand over the grip and pointed at himself in the mirror. He put on his baddest 'die motherfucker' face, then smiled at *Bad* Benny Taggart. He spun toward the window, crouched and said, "pow, pow." He stuck the gun it in his back pocket to see how it felt to carry a gun. He lifted it to his nose. It smelled of oil and exploded firecrackers. He put the barrel against his temple and smiled at himself in the mirror. Bang, he said and closed his eyes. I'm dead, he thought and laughed out loud. Benny opened his eyes, carefully rewrapped the gun in the t-shirt and put it back in the bottom drawer. He would take the dresser's top half.

He closed the last of the drawers and sat on the edge of the bed admiring his red sneakers. They were too cool for words. He had to make sure they didn't disappear. Really cool things always disappeared if you weren't careful. He pushed the sneakers into the bottom of his empty duffel bag and stuck the balled-up duffel in his closet. He would save them, wear them to school, be the *Bad* man.

Benny snapped JDC issued sheets onto his bed, lay back, hands behind his head, and stared out at the world. The trees were just budding. He imagined them with leaves, during the summer. It would be warm. He would wear shorts. He closed his eyes and thought he might sleep. The rumbling began again. Louder this time. Benny bolted up out of bed and moved close to the window as the entire place shook. Walls hummed. The window frames popped and clattered. And stopped. Benny's heart raced on. No one responded to the sound. He wondered if he was the only one who heard it. And if he was? He didn't want to think what that meant.

When an hour had passed, Benny went back downstairs and fell in line behind kids heading into the dining room. No one spoke. Each followed the other, plugged into their Walkmans. Benny grabbed a seat between two black guys. One had a martini glass design shaved into his head. The other didn't. Benny did as good a job of ignoring them as they did of ignoring him. In a week Benny would be a known quantity. On the first day, he didn't exist.

In the dining room, everything above the wainscoting had been painted institutional green, including some beams that crisscrossed overhead. The color reminded Benny of the lockdown ward in the hospital, where he spent the three nights following the second fire. Spots of food, hard like scabs, marred the walls and ceiling.

Steam rose from the pans of lasagna set in three places along the table large enough to hold twenty people. Nancy stood up at the head of the table, arms outstretched, and shouted a prayer asking the Earth Mother to welcome Benjamin into her arms and help him in everything that he needed. Benny thought that he and she were the only ones who heard the prayer. Jason stood in the corner of the dining room smoking through the meal.

After eating Benny went out onto the porch. It had gotten cool. He shivered. Goose bumps rose on his arms, but he didn't care. He could be outside. He could be alone. Being on the outside was everything people said it would be, everything he remembered. A match flared behind him. Benny glanced over his shoulder. Jason stood in the porch's far corner and lit his cigarette.

Benny said, "Hi, Jason."

Jason didn't answer. He acted as if Benny wasn't there.

Weird, Benny thought. Very weird.

Benny went back into the house at nine. Bent over the desk in her office, Nancy was scribbling something in a folder. Kids packed the living room. The large screen television broadcast snow and static. Two girls danced in a corner, spinning and jiving against each other. The rest of the kids, head-phoned or ear plugged, had draped themselves over chairs and couches.

Benny tried to figure out what was really going on in the New Family Way. All he really knew for sure was that he had six months. That's what the Judge Williams said, "six months transitional housing." Benny wondered if the judge had ever visited the New Family Way. He didn't think so. He counted the months on his fingers. September. He'd get out in September. Good deal, he thought. But he wondered what that really meant. His mother hadn't been to see him since the penitentiary, and he hadn't written or called her while in the JDC. Benny climbed the stairs and walked down the hallway to his room frightened by his future. What was he going to do? So much of his time on the inside was waiting to get out, but now what?

Benny opened his bedroom door and stepped into the dark room. As he reached for the light switch, a hand slapped his away. The door slammed shut behind him; someone was on his back, wrestling him to the ground. Benny felt his arm twisted up behind him. A knee pressed into the back of his neck. He squirmed a moment and lay still.

"Nobody touches Peter's stuff." The voice hissed out of the dark. "Understand?"

"Yeah," Benny said. "Yeah." He felt something cold and hard being drawn from the corner of his lips along his cheek.

"Do you know what this is?"

"I know," he said, feeling the gun.

"Don't move," Peter said. "Don't do anything stupid. Don't make Peter do anything" -- the weight lifted from Benny's neck and the light came on -- "that he doesn't have to."

Benny lay flat on the ground and squeezed his eyes shut. He heard steps cross the floor, the squeak of bed springs and quiet.

"Okay, Peter says you can move now."

Benny rolled over slowly and looked up to the voice. He gasped when he saw the most beautiful boy, maybe the most beautiful person he'd ever seen, sitting on the bed with the little gun in his hand. Peter's blond hair, streaked with light shades of brown and red, hung about his shoulders. His eyebrows, a shade darker than his hair, highlighted the freckles on his cheeks and drew Benny's eyes up from Peter's mouth.

Benny swallowed his drool. "Holy shit," he said.

"Peter could kill you right now." The boy raised his arm and sighted down the gun's tiny barrel at Benny's face.

"Okay. Okay," Benny said, mouth dry. "Please don't."

"Peter has friends and Peter has enemies. What are you?"

"I am a friend."

"Good," Peter said. He scowled and glanced around the room. "What did they feed downstairs?"

Benny thought dinner tasted pretty good. "Lasagna. They said it was vegetarian, but I couldn't tell."

"You like Mexican food? Peter loves Mexican. You want a burrito?" Peter asked.

"Yeah, I'll have a burrito."

"Coke?"

"Yeah," Benny said. "I like Coke."

Peter slid off the bed and crossed the room. He placed the gun on top of the microwave, pulled a package of frozen burritos out of the refrigerator and slid them into the oven. He punched some buttons. The machine began to hum. He tossed Benny a can of Coke and returned to the bed, leaving his gun on the microwave. Benny glanced over at it.

"If you're not Peter's friend," Peter said, "even that gun won't help you."

Benny nodded and said, "I'm a friend."

Peter popped the top of his Coke. Benny did the same and watched Peter drink. The boy's skin looked so smooth, Benny wanted to reach over and touch him.

"Peter's fifteen," Peter said suddenly. "Only friends know that. Peter fucked his mother and her boyfriend." He tilted his head to the side and looked at a spot on the ceiling. Benny followed his eyes. "Peter cut off his mother's boyfriend's dick." He took a sip of Coke. "Do you think men should fuck boys?"

Benny shook his head. "No."

"You think mothers should fuck sons?"

"No."

"Peter doesn't think so either." He took a sip of Coke. The

microwave timer rang. "Peter loves Mexican food, and these are the best," he said, as he handed Benny a burrito.

Benny took a bite; it burned his tongue. "They're good," he said, blowing hot steam from his mouth.

Peter shook his head. "They're the best."

Benny kicked off his sneakers and lay back on his bed eating the burrito. Warmed by the television's glow and a full stomach; his eyelids drifted together and apart. He was tired. He was out. He smiled and closed his eyes.

"Hey," Peter shouted. "Wake up." The boy poked Benny in the arm. "Wake up," he repeated. "Peter will take you out."

"Huh," Benny said. He felt as far out as he wanted to get. "We can't go out."

"No one tells Peter what to do," Peter said.

Benny rubbed his eyes and looked from Peter's beautiful face to the open window. I bet no one tells you what to do, Benny thought. But he wasn't going out. He would show Sharkovsky. He could do it. His counselor would be proud. "No," he said, hoping somehow Sharkovsky could hear him. "I'm too beat to go out."

"Peter will be back," the boy said, as he stepped through the open window.

Benny listened to Peter's feet scrabble down the porch roof. He sat up on his bed, pulled the sweatshirt off over his head, peeled off his socks and dropped his jeans to the floor. He shut off the television, the overhead light, and walked gingerly through the room back to his bed. Under the covers he felt warm and full and out.

Out, he thought.

***

The clock on Peter's microwave oven, its electric blue-glow digits reading 3:24, provided the only light in the room when Benny opened his eyes and sat up shivering on the edge of his bed. The floor tiles felt cool and gritty beneath his feet. "Peter," Benny hissed, "where's the bathroom? I've got to take a leak." He repeated the question to no reply.

The microwave glowed 3:25 when Benny crossed the room and switched on the overhead light. He squinted at Peter's empty bed and hugged himself against chill. He shut off the light and stepped into the hall.

At either end of the corridor, red EXIT lights poked crimson shadows along the walls. Benny didn't remember passing a bathroom either time he had come up the stairs. He turned in the other direction. After passing three doorways, quick-toed and shivering, he smelled dampness, soap, urine. There was no mistaking it.

Benny stepped in and fumbled for a light switch. He squinted at the bathroom's high ceiling as the fluorescent bulbs chinked on. Splotches of mildew and fungus crept across the yellowing white paint. Brass-handled drawers and cupboards filled one wall from floor to ceiling. The toilet stood in a far corner. The sink sat on a pedestal and seemed old fashioned. The medicine chest lacked a mirror; someone had written UGLY, in red crayon, where the glass should have been. The bathtub sat on big cat's paws; a shower curtain drawn tight around it.

Benny took a step toward the toilet.

"Jesus, the light," someone said. The shower curtains jerked apart and a dark-skinned boy sat up, rubbing his face. "No lights in here after midnight," the kid whined. "Come on."

"I've got to piss," Benny said. He ignored the kid, crossed the room and began to empty his bladder. As his need lessened, Benny smiled to himself and then became embarrassed by how long he was pissing. He tried to force it out faster, but it seemed there was no end.

"You some kind of fucking camel, or what?" the kid asked.

Benny shrugged his shoulders, concentrating on his stream.

"You are a fucking camel, the kid said. "Look at this guy piss."

Benny giggled. Started laughing. He wondered what the world record was for pissing.

"When's the last time you pissed?" The kid was laughing too.

"About ten minutes ago," Benny said, heaving with laughter. The kid hooted.

Benny's stream ended as suddenly as it began. The kid in the tub was still laughing. Benny had tears in his eyes. He tried to remember all he had drunk that day -- it didn't seem like much. He leaned forward and pushed down the handle on the toilet.

"Don't flush," the kid shrieked.

As the toilet bowl emptied, pipes hidden behind walls rumbled, creaked and groaned. The entire house shook -- light fixtures jiggled, doors rattled, window frames popped.

That's it, Benny thought. He put his hand on the wall. It squirmed and vibrated like it was alive.

"Man, you really fucked up," the kid said.

"What?" Benny asked, over the noise.

The kid looked toward the door. "Listen, shut off the lights and get in here. Under my mattress. And, don't say a fucking word."

"What?" Benny repeated.

"Okay," the kid said. "Be stupid."

Benny heard voices -- angry voices -- coming down the hall. The kid in the tub looked toward the door and back to Benny.

"They're coming," he said.

Benny leaped at the light switch, then climbed into the tub, worming his way under the kid's mattress.

"Don't make a fucking sound," the kid whispered, drawing the shower curtain closed.

Benny could hear the voices in the hall getting louder. The kid pulled a blanket up over Benny's head. The blanket smelled moldy and felt damp against his cheek. He heard the light switch, and a crowd piled into the bathroom.

"Who flushed?" a girl shouted.

"Who fucking flushed?" said a boy.

"Who was it? Come on, admit it," someone else demanded.

Benny heard the shower curtain jerked open. He felt the kid in the tub move.

"Carlos," someone shouted, "did you see who did it?"

"Jesus, no man," the kid said, acting as if he had been asleep. "I was sleeping."

"Maybe was that new punk Sharkovsky brought in?" a boy said. "Yeah," someone agreed, "let's go kick his ass."

"Maybe it was Peter?" Carlos suggested.

The bathroom got quiet. Benny could hear the kids breathing.

After a moment, somebody said, "Fuck it, I'm going back to bed." Someone else said, "yeah." There were a couple of sighs. Carlos pulled the shower curtain closed. "Don't forget the light," he shouted.

The bathroom went black.

After a few moments, Carlos lifted the blanket. "It's okay, they're gone."

Benny sat up and wiped his hand across his face. "Thanks."

"They would have fucked you up," Carlos said.

"I can see that," Benny said, as he climbed over Carlos and stood outside the tub. "Why are you sleeping here?"

"I'm Peter's old roommate," Carlos said.

"He's mine, now," Benny said.

The shower curtains slid closed.

"Yeah, I know," the kid answered.

Benny waited to see if Carlos had anything else to say. He didn't. As he crept down the hall and through his bedroom door, a match flared next to him. The shock snatched his breath away.

Jason stood at the end of Peter's bed and took a deep draw on the cigarette. "Don't flush toilets after ten o'clock, man," he whispered.

Benny nodded his head.

Jason shook out the match. The cigarette's glowing tip disappeared through the bedroom door.

Tears seeped from the edges of Benny's eyes as he closed the door and crawled into his bunk. He blinked into the dark, tinged blue by the microwave's digital readout, and knew that Sharkovsky had it all wrong. How could you follow the rules if you didn't even know what they were? And what kind of rules did they have in this fucking place, anyway? Rules that said a kid could sleep in the fucking bathtub? Rules that said people would fuck you up because you flushed a fucking toilet? Rules that said your roommate would be crazy and carry a fucking gun? Rules, huh? Rules? Fuck you, Sharkovsky. Fuck...

V

A boy wept in the hallway outside Benny's bedroom door. Benny lay with his eyes closed, wishing the boy and the sound would go away. The kid screamed something. The words didn't make any sense. Another boy shouted, "I'm gonna come down there and fuck you up, you keep screaming like that." The kid moaned, quick and frightened, and Benny heard him run down the hall.

Angry and tired, believing he hadn't slept at all, Benny opened his eyes and puzzled at Peter in the bed across the room. A blanket wrapped Peter's body from his shoulders to his thighs. His lips worked his right thumb like a nipple. Benny wondered when the boy had come in. It must have been very late. Or very early.

Benny slipped out of bed and pulled on the jeans and sweatshirt he'd worn the previous day. He went, without thinking, down the hall to the bathroom. The sweet smells of soap and shampoo masked the rotting dampness that rose up from under tiles and behind walls. Carlos was gone; his bedding was stacked on the radiator beneath a tiny window. Benny flushed the toilet. The pipes groaned and creaked. He splashed some water on his face and wiped it dry with the front of his sweatshirt. He glanced up expecting a mirror: UGLY in bold red. "Yeah, fuck you too," he said.

Benny watched Peter sleep as he sat on the edge of his own bed and tied his sneakers. Hair mussed, face calm, thumb between lips, the boy reminded Benny of something from a greeting card. He finished tying his sneakers, crossed the room and ran his fingers down Peter's cheek to his chin. The skin felt the way butterscotch pudding tasted. He stared at Peter for a moment, wanting to touch every part of the boy, knowing he couldn't. He shook his head. He looked back at Peter from the hall and closed their door as quietly possible.

The blonde girl with the blue star tattooed on her cheek sat on the bottom step as Benny jogged, loose-limbed, down the stairs. "Hi," she said, lifting her headphones. "Remember me? I'm Margo. Remember?"

"Yeah," Benny said, barely slowing down. "Hi."

"I guess Nancy forgot to tell you," her voice rose after him. "I'm your sister."

Benny stopped and turned around. "What?" he asked, thinking he had not heard her correctly.

Margo smiled at him. Benny liked that. He didn't know any girls, and he liked the way this one looked. Her hair, around the sides of her head, was buzzed as short as Benny's. The top locks were longer and hung down, circling her head like a cap. The tattoo, a solid blue five- pointed star just below her left eye, looked like it had been done in prison. "I'm your sister," she repeated, "in the New Family Way."

Margo ran a hand up under the cut hair and twisted a knot around her finger. "Don't look at me so funny," she said. "I don't know either. It's one of Nancy's ideas. We're all a family here, right? And in families you have brothers and sisters, right? So, I'm your sister."

Benny had heard stranger things. "Okay," he said. "And, I'm your brother, right?"

She smiled, nodded her head. "Right."

Margo reached a hand up to Benny.

He wasn't sure what to do.

He shook it.

She laughed. "You're funny," she said. "Come on. Help me up." No girl ever told Benny he was funny.

His ears and cheeks felt warm.

Margo dusted off the back of her jeans as she led Benny down the hall. The denim curved over her ass in a way that the boytoys in the JDC couldn't copy. Until that moment, Benny had believed the boytoys were his only attainable objects of desire.

Margo talked nonstop as Benny followed her ass down the hallway, through the swinging door and into the dining room. "I wouldn't be here if my brother didn't turn me in," she said. "They gave him a 'Just Say No' award at his school for it. We were on television together. I told them it really sucked that he turned me in. They didn't put that part on TV."

Twelve kids were spread out in chairs around the dining room table, leaving room for at least ten more. Some spooned cold cereal out of battered plastic bowls. Others sat, chins resting on hands or arms, and stared blank-eyed at the walls. Empty bowls, plastic glasses, and dirty silverware littered the tabletop. Carlos looked up at Benny as he drained a cup of milk. A white milk mustache marked his lip. Benny nodded and grinned, following Margo into the kitchen.

"That Carlos kid," Benny said. "What's the story?" He shut up and nudged Margo when he saw Jason leaning against the sink, staring at the door of the industrial-sized refrigerator.

"What?" the girl asked.

"Later," he said.

"Oh, you're not worried about him, are you?" Margo giggled, waving a hand at Jason. "Hey, Jason. Do you know where I can score some smack or crack or blow?"

Benny laughed, nervously.

"He's gone," she said. "Not gone all the time, but most. Forget about him." Margo pointed at three plastic bins of cold cereal. "There's no Fruit Loops or anything good," she said.

As he turned to look at the cereal, Benny glimpsed Jason's left eyelid sliding closed. He turned his head back. Jason's eye opened; the mannequin showed his brown teeth in an awkward smile. Margo didn't notice any of it. Jason's face looked stone stupid. Benny half listened as she explained that the big silver milk dispenser was called the cow. She offered to show him how it worked. He looked at Jason out of the corner of his eyes and told her that he'd already used one in the JDC. He didn't tell her they called it the tit.

Benny scooped out a bowl of generic Cheerios and asked Margo where they kept the sugar.

"Don't you know white sugar is worse for you than heroin?"

"Huh?" Benny said.

"Nancy and Jason don't allow white sugar in the house. It's their only rule. Do you believe it?"

"Jesus," Benny said.

"Yeah," Margo agreed. "What a pair, man?" she said, mimicking Jason's inflections. "Nancy told me they found each other after one of those three-day rock concerts they had in the sixties."

Benny laughed.

He believed Jason was more aware than he acted.

"No. It's true."

"I believe you," Benny said.

"See you later, Jason," Margo said.

As he followed the girl out of the kitchen, Benny looked back at Jason as he stared at the refrigerator. Benny knew he wasn't gone.

Benny sat down at the dining room table and spooned the first of his cereal into his mouth before he realized that everybody in the room, except Margo, stopped talking. He glanced around. All the kids were staring at him. He thought Carlos looked worried. He dropped his spoon into the bowl and looked around the table at each kid.

"Yeah?" he said as he looked from face to face.

The tall, dangerous-looking kid named Ronald said, "We want to fuck up that roommate of yours."

Benny put on his nothing face.

"Hey," Ronald said, "Are you listening to me?"

Benny nodded, slowly.

"That boy flushed last night, and goddamn motherfucking shitass pussy, I'm going to fuck him up."

Benny turned to Carlos, but the boy wouldn't make eye contact. "Okay," Benny said, shrugging his shoulders.

"You get him to come out into the hall," Ronald said. "He never comes out into that hall. You get him to."

Benny shook his head as he lifted a spoonful of cereal. "Nope," he said. He spooned the cereal into his mouth.

"What do you mean, nope?" Ronald demanded.

Benny pushed the bowl to the middle of the table and stood up. "I mean, you want to kick Peter's ass, fine. But I ain't helping." He stood up, nodded at Carlos and Margo and walked as fast as he could from the room, never looking at Ronald but listening for him to get up from the table. When he heard nothing, his heart slowed, and he climbed back up the stairs to his bedroom.

The room was empty, but as he closed the door, he heard footsteps scuffing up the shingles on the porch roof. The curtains parted, and Peter stepped into the room, carrying a brown paper bag under his arm. A sweet-smelling cologne trailed after him.

"Hi," Benny said. He wondered if he should tell Peter the others were going to fuck him up.

Peter ignored him, crossed the room and began rummaging through dresser drawers.

Okay, Benny thought. You don't talk, I don't.

Peter turned from the dresser, smiled at Benny and dumped

the contents of the bag on his bed. Two cans of Coke and three cellophane wrapped fruit pies bounced on Peter's mattress. "Breakfast is Peter's most important meal," he said, popping the top on the soda and catching its effervescence in his mouth. He giggled as he slurped. "Cherry, strawberry or mixed fruit?" he asked, pointing at the pies.

Benny sat down on his bed, smiling. "I don't know."

"Mixed fruit is Peter's favorite," Peter said. "You try it." He grabbed the pie off the bed.

Benny heard muffled laughter through their bedroom door. A chant started, the voices high pitched and almost inaudible. As the volume rose, the chorus became clearer, "Peter's crazy, Peter's crazy, Peter's crazy." The kids on the other side of the door modulated the words -- extending vowels, clipping consonants. "Peeeter's craaaazeeee," they sang, building in volume. Benny thought it sounded kind of funny and a grin started across his mouth. He looked over at Peter. The smile stopped.

Peter's left eye squinted down; the right opened wide. He trembled, crimson-faced, and crushed the fruit pie and the can of Coke in his hands. Soda ran onto the floor. "Peter is not crazy," he spat. He cocked his arm, and the pie's cellophane bag popped when it hit the door. Mixed fruit splattered, and gobs of the purplish filling began oozing toward the floor. "Not crazy," he repeated -- louder, harder. His voice sounded different -- deeper, older. The soda can ricocheted off the door and rolled under Benny's bed.

The kids laughed and whooped.

Benny heard them run down the hall.

Peter stood in the center of room, trembling, shaking, repeating, "Not crazy, not crazy, not crazy."

Scared, Benny could only sit on his bed and watch. A different voice erupted from Peter's body, a different face. As Peter continued shaking and repeating, "Not crazy, not crazy," Benny thought the kid was going to really hurt himself. He stood up and put a hand on Peter's back. "You're not crazy, Peter," he said. "It's okay. You're okay."

It had no effect.

Benny put an arm around Peter's shoulders. "Come on, Peter," he said. "You're not crazy. Okay? You're not." Peter didn't hear him.

Jesus, he felt so bad for the guy. Benny wrapped Peter in a hug and held his face next to Peter's neck. "That's okay, kid," he said.

"Let it go, kid." Benny told him it was important to cry, kids needed to cry. He hugged him closer and repeated, "Let it go, kid. Let it go."

Peter's trembles broke down into sobs, and his words no longer made sense. He buried his face in Benny's neck. His tears felt hot as they ran down Benny's back. After what seemed a very long time, Peter lifted his head and looked Benny in the eyes. Even wet and puffy with tears and snot, Peter was still the most beautiful person Benny had ever seen. Benny thought he was about to say something, but the boy didn't speak. He brought his face forward and kissed Benny full-mouthed on the lips. When Peter's tongue pushed past his teeth, Benny gulped for air. Peter's lips felt hot, his cheeks were hot, his tongue and spit were hot. He moved his mouth slowly over Benny's cheek and chin, then down his neck. Benny tilted back his head and felt Peter's hand on his crotch.

The boy undid Benny's jeans and bent to his cock. He took it into his mouth. Benny stared down at the face, the beautiful face and felt his cock hot, hard -- worked back and forth by Peter's tongue. Peter looked up at him. The boy looked like a god. Peter's right hand drifted up over Benny's chest. He moved it back and forth across Benny's nipples, then stuck his fingers into Benny's mouth. Benny sucked the fingers the same way Peter sucked his cock. He wanted Peter's cock. He wanted anything he could get from this boy. He wanted everything he could get from this boy. He leaned toward Peter. The boy's fingers slipped from his mouth. Benny's lips drifted across the back of Peter's wrist -- something smooth and hard rose from the skin just below Peter's palm. Benny opened his eyes as he flicked his tongue along the scar, raised and puckered. The fear of what it meant, the excitement of what it meant -- Benny's cock exploded. He moaned, "Again, again," as he tumbled to the floor and worked Peter's cock into his own mouth.

Peter slept, curled tight against Benny's back. The boy's breath feathered across Benny's neck and shoulders. Peter mumbled something and rolled over. Benny sat up and stroked Peter's cheek with his fingers. He leaned close and peered at the boy's wrists. White scars rose from both. Benny felt them in the pit of his stomach, as if they were his own. He leaned forward to kiss the most beautiful face he'd ever seen. Peter swatted at him as if he were a fly. He hit Benny in the lip. Benny didn't care. He loved Peter.

Eyes closed, under the shower, Benny let the water surge against his scalp. He rubbed the bar of soap over his cock and imagined washing off the seven months he spent inside. The seven months that, after the first two, became as easy to do as breathe. On the inside, you knew the exact size of your world: if you stood in the center of the JDC you could see the boundaries of the universe. But standing in the shower, swallowing mouthfuls of water to wash Peter's sperm into his stomach, Benny could not imagine any boundaries. He thought maybe there were none.

He turned off the shower and, like all the other boys who had been in the JDC, he squeegeed the water down his biceps and forearms with his hands.

Benny had one foot in and one out of the tub when Margo's voice surprised him in the steam-fogged bathroom. "Hi, Benjamin Taggart," she said.

"Ah. Hi," Benny said, struggling to maintain his balance. He stepped out of the tub, snatched his towel from the floor and wrapped it around his waist. Benny still couldn't see her; he peered around the bathroom.

"Over here," she said. Margo sat on the toilet seat, her chin resting in her right hand, her right elbow atop crossed legs. "Listen," she said. "There's a place not too far from here called Syd's where you can buy Cokes, pizza and sub sandwiches. You want to go?"

Benny felt a chill and crossed his arms over his chest. "I don't think so," he said. "I'm broke."

"Hey, I'm your sister," Margo said, standing up. "I'll loan you some money."

Benny didn't know what to say. He stood in the damp bathroom as the steam dissipated, dressed only in a towel with his arms crossed against a chill, staring at Margo.

"Besides," she said. "You're pretty cute, Benjamin Taggart." She said it so matter-of-factly, Benny laughed.

"So, shoot me." She shrugged her shoulders. "I think you're pretty cute. I'll buy you a piece of pizza. And, if you're not a jerk, maybe we can be more than brother and sister."

He swallowed hard. "Okay," he croaked. "I'll get dressed."

Margo's hand brushed against Benny's ass as she passed him. She looked back over her shoulder and smiled. "I'll be downstairs."

Benny rushed into his room, dropped his towel, and began tugging on clothes. His jeans and socks snagged on still wet legs and feet. Green fuzzballs from the lining of the sweatshirt dotted his face.

Peter still slept in Benny's bed, a thumb in his mouth, the other hand tucked between his legs. Benny barely glanced at him. He rubbed the fuzz off his face with his towel.

Peter flinched and made little crying sounds when Benny sat down on the corner of the bed to tie his sneakers. Benny glanced over at him and thought, you're not crazy, man. No more crazy than me, that's for sure. He reached out and stroked Peter's thigh. Not crazy, he thought. Not crazy.

Margo and Nancy stood talking just outside the group home's office when Benny came down the stairs. Nancy's voice had risen to a shriek. "I knew it," she cried. "I did your charts. You and Benjamin are celestial siblings. You're so close to each other," she stammered with excitement, "I think you two were brother and sister in past lives."

Margo nodded her head, smiling. "Cool," she said.

Nancy turned from Margo to Benny when he approached. "Smother hug, smother hug," she cried. She wrapped Benny in her arms, impaling him on crystals that hung from leather thongs around her neck. "This is the New Family Way, Benjamin, and I feel it's working for you."

Nancy's crystals poked into his chest bone; his face was smothered between breasts. He felt himself growing short of breath and began to choke. A loud metallic ringing began in his ears. He knew he was passing out. Nancy released him from her hug and shut off the alarm clock hanging around her neck.

"Jason," she shouted. "Jason. Time to start lunch." She looked back to Benny. "Oh, before I forget -- Monday, you're scheduled to start school. The bus gets here at 7:30." She turned back down the hall. "Jason, lunch," she cried.

Benny rolled his eyes at Margo and followed her out the door and down the steps. Benny didn't know what to say. He wondered if this was a date. He wondered what her tits were like. He knew he had to say something. As they stepped into the driveway, he said, "She's got to be the weirdest thing in this place."

"Who?" Margo asked.

"Nancy, who else?"

Margo looked at him from the corner of her eyes. "I don't know, Benjamin Taggart," she said. "Nobody's as crazy as your roommate."

They neared the end of the driveway. In the noon sun, the breeze smelled of asphalt, car exhaust. Benny stopped and looked hard at Margo. He challenged her with his face and stood waiting for an answer.

She seemed surprised. "Well, maybe he's a friend of yours," she stammered. "But he's fucking crazy." Margo held her left hand out as if she were trying to catch something in the breeze. "Listen, I don't know what you're here for. But I know you would never have tried to hurt anyone. Not like Peter."

Benny flashed his 'I don't know what the fuck you're talking about' face.

Margo placed her hands on her hips and looked left then right. "Okay, when they first brought him into the New Family Way, he was fine, okay? They had him so drugged up that he was just skyed all the time. I mean skyed." Margo laughed. "I was kind of envious. But Nancy and Jason don't believe in meds, so they started bringing him down. The closer he got to who he really was, the more fucked up he started acting."

"Aw, you're nuts," Benny said.

Margo's eyes widened. Her lips curled into a snarl. "Are you calling Margo a liar?" she screamed and grabbed at Benny's throat.

He back-pedaled away. "Jesus," he cried.

Margo hooted with laughter. "Your face was perfect. Just perfect. Now, tell me, Benjamin Taggart. Tell me Peter's not crazy."

Benny let himself smile. "I admit he's pretty strange. But..."

"Pretty strange?" she said. "Pretty strange? Jason and Nancy are pretty strange. Peter is Jeffrey fucking Dahmer."

"He is not," Benny said, suddenly pissed.

"Maybe Peter likes you," she said. "I suppose it could have its benefits." She smiled at Benny and began walking toward the street.

Benny didn't move. "What the hell is that supposed to mean?"

"I guess that's up to you. What do you want it to mean?"

"Oh, fuck you," he said.

"You know, you could have," she shouted. "But I think you'd rather fuck Peter."

Benny smoked her with his 'fucking asshole' face. He turned and stomped back up the driveway.

Peter was still sleeping in Benny's bed when he got back to the room. He pushed the door closed as quietly as possible, turned on the television with the sound down low, and ripped open the cherry pie's cellophane wrapper with his teeth. Benny seethed over Margo. She had small tits. She needed braces. The star tattoo sucked. She was a doper and a fucking asshole. A real fucking asshole.

He sat on the corner of Peter's bed and spent the afternoon and evening watching one old movie roll into another, the local and national news, a string of game shows and old sit-coms.

Peter never stirred.

Hours later, in the room lit only by the television, Benny heard Peter roll over. He looked at Peter's figure and saw him rise slowly from the blankets. He yawned and shook himself. "Peter slept a long time," Peter said. "What time is it?"

"Almost eleven," Benny answered.

The microwave glowed 10:47.

"Good," Peter said. "Peter will take you out to meet his friend."

"Okay," Benny said, thinking: Fuck you, Sharkovsky. Fuck you, Margo.

Benny followed Peter through the bedroom window and down an aluminum ladder propped against the front porch. He lowered his foot from the ladder's bottom rung slowly, as if stepping into a cold lake. At any moment he expected lights to blaze, sirens to sound, the voices of his keepers to shout challenges, scream commands. It didn't happen.

As Peter and he came around to the front of the porch, he saw Jason and waited for his reaction. A lit cigarette rose to Jason's mouth; its end grew brighter and smoke curled into the dark. When he said nothing, the surge of freedom that washed over Benny was something he was not prepared for. The farther he and Peter got from the group home the greater the rush became. Benny felt high. He felt buzzed. As they passed the van, squatting down on its flattened tires, he lifted his arms like wings and ran in circles down the drive.

He paused at the driveway's end, where the slick blacktop met the street's smooth, unreflecting asphalt. For a moment, the world seemed too big, too open. Anything that could happen to him, everything that happened, was out there. He looked up the street toward the neighboring houses. Security lights lit the lawns as bright as they did the perimeter of the JDC. Benny felt something coming together in his mind. The thought took shape: something to do with light against the dark, but he couldn't get the idea formed into words.

Peter jostled his shoulder as he ran past him and kicked a flattened soda can that lay in the street. It scuffed down the asphalt. Benny giggled and raced into the street after him, chasing down the can and missing when he swung his foot. A dog barked in the distance, and two more answered. Peter ran up and kicked the can again. It slid down the crown of the street and slapped against the curb. He shouted, "Peter scores," and jumped up and down, waving his hands over his head. The pistol made a dull flat sound when it dropped from Peter's pocket to the street. He shook his head and bent down for the gun.

"Where are we going?" Benny asked, eyeing the pistol.

"To see Peter's friend," Peter said, snatching the gun up from the street. Benny turned toward the group home and thought about running back.

"Come on," Peter said. "Meet Peter's friend."

Benny looked at Peter's eyes and lips. He didn't want to meet Peter's friend. He wanted to go back to their room, eat burritos and suck Peter's dick. He wanted Peter to suck his.

Peter pushed the gun into his back pocket and started down the street. Benny jogged after him. "Where are we going?" he asked.

Peter didn't answer. He walked ahead of Benny, leading him down one block and over three to a busy intersection. Four lanes of traffic, two in each direction, moved slowly past the corner. Headlights, stop lights, neon signs and streetlamps lit the road like a carnival. Benny grinned when he saw the street. It seemed wild and full of fun. The sign at the intersection said it was Franklin Street. Benny had heard of Franklin Street before. His mother went to places along Franklin. She'd say to her friends on the phone, "We'll meet on Franklin. At Joey's." Benny never imagined it as a street kids went to.

Peter turned left on Franklin and moved out closer to the curb. Benny walked beside him. Facing traffic, Peter slowed his gait and began swinging his hips from side to side. He adjusted his crotch, leaned both hands against a lamp post and leered at the street.

Cars slowed -- horns honked.

Peter waggled his tongue and began walking.

Benny giggled, then laughed. Peter walked like a cartoon of a girl. He hadn't thought that Peter could be funny. That he would do jokes. But here they were on Franklin Street and Peter was hysterical. Benny raised his arms and minced along beside Peter, laughing.

"Hey, Peter," Benny said, "when are we seeing your friend?"

A blue station wagon pulled to the curb.

"Now," Peter said. A man in the car leaned across the seat and the passenger side window went down. Peter stuck his head in for a moment, then opened the door and slid into the front seat. "Come on," Peter said.

"Where are you going?" Benny asked.

"Just come on," he repeated.

The man driving said, "Forget about him."

"Come with Peter," Peter said. He turned his head to the driver. "Are you a friend?"

"Yes," the man said.

"See," Peter said. "Come meet Peter's friend."

Benny looked up and down the street. He knew that he didn't have the strength to stop himself, and he hoped to see something that would. A traffic signal changed from red to green. A neon sign lit, one letter at a time, L I Q U O R. A car honked and flashed its lights. Benny slid into the front seat and pulled the door shut.

"I don't want you both. And I'm not paying for both," the driver said, as he pulled from the curb.

The man wore dark rimmed glasses and a dark baseball cap pulled down to his ear.

"Which do you want?" Peter asked.

Benny didn't get a chance to say, "Hey, no way."

The man put his hand on Peter's leg. "Who do you think?"

"Good," Peter said. "Now Peter won't kill you."

Benny's stomach dropped.

The man laughed. "That's funny." He leaned closer to the steering wheel and turned his head to Benny. "Your name's Peter, and I bet you like to suck peter." He laughed again. "Well, boys, I've got a good eleven inches..." The man groaned.

Peter had poked the barrel of the gun in the man's ear. "Peter thinks you should be quiet," Peter said.

"Yes," the man said.

"Quiet," Peter said, pushing the gun deeper. "Do exactly what Peter tells you and he might not kill you."

"Please don't kill him," Benny said.

"Peter does what he wants."

The man moaned.

"Quiet," Peter said.

Peter directed the man off Franklin to a side street. "There," he said. "Peter wants you to park there."

The man stopped the car beneath a streetlight. He slid the gear shift up to park and turned off the engine. The car grew quiet. Benny heard all their breathing. Peter's slow and easy. The man's wheezing sobs. His own, fast and choppy.

"Show Peter your wallet," Peter said.

The man fumbled it out of his back pocket.

Benny saw the man's face wet with tears. Small bubbles of saliva slid from the corners of his mouth.

"Open your wallet. Show Peter everything."

The man spread the bill fold. Peter lifted out the man's money. "You've got my money. Now..."

"Quiet," Peter said. "Show Peter everything."

The man thumbed through the plastic sleeves holding his driver's license and credit cards.

"Stop," Peter said. "What is that?"

"A picture," the man blubbered.

"A picture of what?" Peter demanded.

"A picture of my family."

"Peter will take that, too."

The man fumbled the photograph out of the plastic sleeve. His entire body quaked; a high-pitched moan escaped his mouth.

Peter took the picture and held it up with his free hand. Benny saw it was a photo of the man with a woman and three children -- two boys and a younger girl.

"Do you think men should fuck boys?" Peter asked. "Noooo," the man sobbed.

"You think mothers should fuck their sons?" Peter asked. "No, no, no, " the man cried, sobbing -- his head rolling from side to side.

"Good," Peter said. "Then you are a friend."

He turned to Benny. "Peter thinks we're done here."

Benny pushed out of the car and prepared to run. Peter climbed out next to him and stooped looking back into the car. "Peter thanks you," he said, before closing the door.

The car's engine roared and its tires screeched. Peter watched after it until it rounded a corner. He turned to Benny and said, "Peter's very tired." He stretched, yawning. "Peter's going home."

Benny walked beside Peter, trying to get up the nerve to ask all the questions that rolled through his mind: Shouldn't we run? Will that guy call the cops? You do this every night? For how long? Are you afraid of the cops? Did any of your friends ever come back? Did any ever fight? Did you ever shoot anybody? Would you? What do you do with the pictures? Are you fucking crazy, or what?

They rounded a corner and Benny spied the New Family Way van parked halfway up the driveway. He imagined the lawn mower frozen in its place. He turned to Peter and said, "You wouldn't have really shot that guy, would you?"

Peter pulled the gun from his back pocket, crouched and pointed up at a streetlight. The muzzle flashed. The lamp shattered.

"Shit," Benny said.

"Peter's a great shot," Peter said.

The pistol shot echoed in Benny's ears. "You are fucking crazy," he hissed.

Peter placed the gun barrel against Benny's head.

"Peter's not crazy," he said.

Benny's mouth went dry.

"Not crazy," Peter repeated. "Not crazy."

Tears welled in Benny's eyes. His tongue felt thick and heavy. He knew Peter would shoot him. He didn't want to die.

"Peter is not crazy," Peter shouted. "Not crazy. Not crazy. Not crazy. Say it," he screamed.

Benny tried to say, "not crazy," but only blubbering noises and moans passed his lips.

" Say it," Peter cried. He stamped his feet, his beautiful face melted in tears. Peter cocked his arm, placing the gun against his head. He pleaded with Benny. "Tell Peter he's not crazy. Tell him, please."

Benny's jaw clamped shut. He wanted to reach up and pry his

teeth apart. But he was too scared to move.

The pistol fired. Peter's eyes widened. He stood -- eyes fixed on Benny -- then his body tumbled to the ground.

A filmy trickle of blood coursed from the side of Peter's head toward the gutter. "Not crazy," Benny tried to say, knowing but not believing he was too late. The first sob snatched away his breath and he choked on his words. He stepped closer to the body. His hands and feet felt numb. "Not crazy," he said, trying to convince himself that the words would be enough to make Peter rise from the street. He knew it was stupid. Peter's face had frozen in the bullet moment -- eyes opened wide, lips twisted into a snarl. Benny moved in a slow, side stepping circle around the boy, trying to figure it all out. It seemed too simple: Peter was dead. Benny was with him. They would think he did it. Maybe he did do it? Wait. Did he *fucking* do it?

His shadow drifted across Peter's body. He stepped past the boy's head. His right foot slipped in something greasy. He dropped to a knee, caught himself with his hand. Peter's blood was not as warm as his tears, or hot as his sperm. The smear on Benny's hand looked black.

Blood. Dead. The words crackled in Benny's head with the clarity of shattering glass. Afraid of their sounds, he swallowed back the words: blood, dead, and pushed himself to his feet. Run, he thought. Run.

Benny turned to his right and bolted down the street, stopping at the next corner. He saw nothing in front of him that made sense. He turned in the other direction and ran back past Peter's body. He stopped beneath the next light and turned back again. He couldn't run. He had nowhere to go.

Clothes soaked with sweat, teeth chattering, Benny stumbled up the driveway toward the New Family Way Group Home. He had a plan. He'd be home in bed when they found Peter and he'd lie. Peter went out alone. I went to sleep early. Benny grabbed the side rails of the ladder and put his left foot on the bottom rung. A gash of light poked between the curtains in the window overhead.

Benny raised his right foot. A noise -- rough and abrasive -- rasped from a dark corner of the front porch. Benny froze and squinted into the corner, hoping he imagined the sound.

Jason re-struck the match and held it to a cigarette. His face --

eyes drooped into slits, head tilted to the left -- loomed momentarily above the flame. Benny could have imagined nothing worse. A small weak cry erupted from his throat.

Jason shook out the match. The porch returned to darkness. A cloud of cigarette smoke drifted out over the front lawn.

Benny's fingers tightened around the ladder. Margo had said Jason was spaced; Benny knew it wasn't true. He hissed Jason's name through chattering teeth. "J-J-J-ason," he said. The glowing tip of the cigarette rose to the man's face and brightened. He didn't answer.

Benny climbed the ladder, scrambled up the asphalt shingles and stepped through the bedroom window.

Damp towels from his shower lay balled in the corner; Peter's color television set was on, sound turned down; the empty Coke cans and wrappers from the fruit pies sat atop Peter's microwave oven.

Benny dropped down on his bed, shivering, and pulled a blanket up around his shoulders. He toyed with the idea that maybe Peter hadn't killed himself: maybe he never left the room, maybe it was all a bad dream. The momentary calm crashed about him when he saw the first blood-smudged sneaker print beneath the window. He followed tracks across the floor. They ended at his foot. He looked at his right hand. Blood smeared his palm. He groaned, felt like puking.

They had him.

He tugged off the sneakers without bothering to untie the laces and heaved them across the room. The right one left a rust colored imprint on the wall above Peter's bed. He broke down into choking sobs. He knew he had to clean up if they were going to believe he hadn't been out with Peter. Just clean up. He retrieved his sneakers and the damp towel from the corner, turned off the overhead light, and eased open the door, peering up and down the hallway.

In the EXIT sign's red glow, Benny crept down the corridor toward the bathroom. Once inside, he listened to Carlos' rhythmic breathing coming from the tub. Benny worked in the dark, opening the hot water tap slowly, turning his sneaker over and over under the flow, scraping Peter's blood from the treads with his fingernails.

Something rustled behind him.

A beam of light shone on the word **UGLY**. "Jesus, what are you doing?" Carlos asked.

Benny glanced over his shoulder. A small flashlight poked out from between the closed shower curtains. The beam crossed Benny's eyes. He squeezed them shut.

"Shit," the kid said. "What the hell happened to you?"

"Peter killed himself," he cried.

He blurted it out before thinking. He blurted it out to make sure somebody knew the truth. He blurted it out because he couldn't hold it back anymore. "I was there," he wailed. "They'll say I did it. They'll say I killed him."

Carlos climbed out of the tub as Benny spoke. In the tiny light's fragile beam the boy appeared even younger than Benny had first thought. Dressed in only his underpants, he crossed the bathroom, closed the door, locked it and turned on the light.

"Are you sure he's dead?" Carlos asked.

"He shot himself in the head," Benny cried. "Right in the head." He pointed to his own temple.

Carlos smirked. "Jesus, I wish I saw it."

"No, you don't." Benny shook his head. "No way."

"I'm telling you," Carlos said. "Fuck Peter. Fuck him. I sleep in the fucking bathroom because he was my fucking roommate. The fucker tried to smother me with a pillow. He pissed on my face. Fuck Peter. I'm glad he's dead."

Benny shook his head. "But now, I'm going back inside."

What?" Carlos asked. "Why?"

"I was with him," Benny cried. "They'll say I did it and even if I didn't..." He couldn't speak. His mouth no longer worked.

"Fuck, you ain't going nowhere you don't want to, man." Carlos pointed toward the door. "Just run the fuck away."

Benny's life seemed worthless and he knew it would stay that way forever.

"Are you sure he's dead?" Carlos asked.

Benny nodded.

"Okay, then. Come on." Carlos turned off the bathroom light, unlocked the door and returned with Benny to the bedroom. "Get some stuff together," he said, rummaging through the dresser.

Carlos jerked all the dresser drawers out and dumped them on the floor. Benny reached into the closet and pulled out his duffel bag, the red sneakers weighted the bag. When he glanced back at Carlos, the boy knelt on the floor digging through Peter's clothing.

"What is this?" he said, thumbing through a stack of photographs.

Benny looked over the boy's shoulder and saw they were pictures of Peter's friends. He almost said, "Hey, quit fucking around," but he knew that without Carlos he was lost.

"Found it," Carlos said. He lifted a white plastic band-aid box from a pile of clothes. "I knew he had a stash."

Sirens began in the distance.

Benny looked toward the sound, then back. "Found what?"

Carlos shook the box; coins rattled. "Peter turned tricks like a fucking rabbit," he said. "We'll split it."

Benny didn't want to tell him what Peter really did.

Carlos dumped the box on Benny's mattress.

A wad of bills flopped open.

"Holy shit," Carlos said. "You could go anywhere on this."

Benny picked through the jumble of clothes, pushing shirts, underwear, socks and pants back into his duffel. Where could he go?

"Got any friends you could go see?"

Benny thought for a moment. He didn't know anyone. Not anyone he could visit. He shook his head, and the tears began again.

"Listen, everybody knows somebody," he said. "Think, Jesus."

The sound of another siren, faster, more fervent, drifted in through the window.

Benny was shaking his head when it came to him. "I could go to Florida," he said. "My dad's in Florida."

"Will he turn you in?" Carlos asked. "Is he cool?"

Benny thought of all the bad things his mother had said about his dad. He nodded his head, almost smiling. "He's cool."

Carlos counted out the money. It totaled $487.33. He handed Benny $244, telling him, "It's more than half, but I ain't arguing over chump change."

Benny stared at the bills laying flat across his palm.

"Put some in your pocket and hide some in the duffel bag," Carlos said, as he stuffed his portion back into the band-aid box.

A red flash repeated itself between the curtains as a police car, siren off, rolled up the driveway. "They're here," Carlos whispered.

Benny, hands quaking, divided the amount in half and folded the bills in half and stuffed them into his hip pocket. He pushed half deep into his duffel.

"Come on," Carlos said.

He pulled Benny down the hall by the arm.

In the bathroom, Carlos closed and locked the door before turning on the light. The sudden brightness of the room churned all that was in Benny's stomach and brought him scrambling on his knees to the toilet. He vomited fruit pies and Coke, then reached up to flush.

"Don't," Carlos shrieked.

Benny looked at Carlos and took strange comfort in the realization that Carlos was scared too. He spat into the toilet and wiped his mouth on his arm.

Carlos scaled the linen closet shelves. Benny handed him up the duffel bag and his bloody sneakers, wrapped in his towel. Carlos pushed them deep into the cupboard's top shelf.

The cops rapped on the front door and shouted, "Police. Police." The house shuddered as feet dropped to floors and doors were flung open. Carlos hid Benny beneath his mattress and was climbing in on top of him when the doorknob jiggled.

"Jesus," Carlos whispered, "I forgot to unlock it."

As Carlos climbed back out of the tub, the kid outside slapped the door and shouted, "Stroke it faster, Carlos, I got to take a leak."

Benny remembered his puke in the bowl and stuck his head up from under the mattress. "Carlos," he hissed, "flush the fucking toilet."

As the water rushing through the pipes began shaking the house, Benny slid back under cover. It sounded like Carlos was talking to the kid in the bathroom, but Benny couldn't understand what they were saying.

He kept his eyes shut in the dark beneath Carlos' mattress. Benny shivered and sweated. It was harder to breathe when Carlos returned to the tub, but Benny was glad not to be alone.

In the bottom of the tub, cramped beneath Carlos' mattress, Benny could sense movement in the house. He knew when the cops came through the door. He pictured the sullen faces the kids would wear to greet them. He imagined the search. The kids trooping upstairs, trailing Jason and Nancy, who followed the cops. They'd search his and Peter's room first. They'd find Peter's stuff trashed and his stuff gone.

He hoped they'd believed he'd already run.

Benny held his breath when he felt the cops tromp into the bathroom. His heart throbbed. He could hear nothing but his own fear. He lay completely still and thought, 'Go away. Go away. Go away.' Carlos shifted above him and Benny felt the boy's knees pressed into his chest. He knew Carlos was kneeling over the edge of the tub, talking with the cops. He could feel the words. The cops left more quickly than they arrived. It all seemed too easy. Benny choked and gagged on the smell of his own fear.

The house took a long time to quiet. Benny felt people moving about for what seemed like hours. When it seemed completely calm, Carlos pulled back the mattress. "Come on," he said. He scrambled up the front of the linen closet and tossed down Benny's duffel and the bundled towel holding his sneakers.

Carlos' feet slapped the tile floor when leaped down from the shelf. He opened the bathroom door and stuck his head into the hall.

"Where?" Benny whispered.

"Shut the fuck up," Carlos hissed.

Carlos led Benny down the hall to his and Peter's old room. "Hide in there. Lock the door," he said, quietly. "Leave tonight."

"Where do I go?" Benny whispered.

"The bus station. To Florida."

Benny nodded and closed the door. He dropped the duffel beside his bed and sat down on the now bare mattress. Both beds had been stripped of sheets and blankets. Peter's color television and microwave were gone. Benny figured the other kids had rifled the room. The pictures of Peter's friends lay heaped like playing cards in one corner. The bloody sneaker prints scarring the floor and wall, two crushed Coke cans, the cellophane wrappers from fruit pie and the pictures were all that remained. Benny gathered up the photographs of Peter's friends and huddled in the closet behind the duffel bag.

Squatting in the dark, Benny's stomach churned every time footsteps sounded in the hall. He imagined cops, bursting back into the room, firing wildly into the closet. Three hours. Five hours. Seven hours. Benny watched the crack of light along the bottom of the closet door grow bright. Using that light, he studied the pictures of Peter's friends. There were forty-two photographs. He didn't recognize anyone in the pictures, and no one looked like Peter. Most were pictures of families -- moms, dads, kids. Benny imagined the men in the pictures, grinning and joking as Peter slid into their cars, then weeping and pleading for their lives. Benny wondered if Peter had killed any. He didn't think so, but? Some of the pictures were browned and faded faces of boys and soldiers, they looked like old movies. There were two pictures of babies and one of a black dog wearing sunglasses. Benny tried to figure out what the pictures meant to Peter. He decided it didn't matter what they meant. Nothing mattered. As the light dimmed, he put the pictures down, and huddled against his duffel bag. He listened for sounds -- felt for vibrations. When there were none, and he was sure the house was asleep, he slid out from behind the duffel and opened the closet door.

A match flared on the far side of the room. It drifted up through the darkness to a cigarette angling from Jason's mouth.

Benny moaned.

Jason took a drag and held it. "What now, man?" he asked.

"Huh?" Benny said.

"What are you going to do, man? Where are you going? How are you getting there? Do you have a plan, man?" Jason giggled. "You know, a plan, man." The tip of the cigarette bobbed in the dark.

"I'm going to Florida." Benny paused. He remembered saying it before, but this time it was true. He repeated it. "I'm going to Florida," he said. "Miami. My dad lives in Miami."

The cigarette bobbed again. "That's cool. That's a plan, man." The glowing ash drifted closer. The duffel bag was lifted from Benny's hand. "Come on, man."

Benny followed him out the window, down the ladder and around to the rear of the house. A black VW beetle sat next to a fallen-in garage. Benny didn't know what to say. What to ask. He followed Jason and did whatever he said. They pushed the car to jump start with the clutch. Motoring down the driveway, Benny noticed one of the head lights shone straight up, lighting the tree limbs overhead.

Jason didn't speak. He lit one cigarette after another, snuffing them in the tiny ashtray. Cigarette butts overflowed onto the floor. He drove past the bus station and parked two blocks down the street. His foot tapped a rhythm on the gas pedal; the engine revved in time.

Benny sat watching him smoke, trying to figure out what-the-fuck was going on. A bus roared by them. Benny looked after its brake lights. He wondered where it was heading. "I need to catch a bus, you know? Should I walk back to the station?"

Jason didn't turn his head. His eyes, appearing both glazed and focused, pointed straight ahead. "Look at you, man. You are the runaway. They'd be on you, like," he snapped his fingers.

"Why are you helping me?" Benny asked. It didn't make sense.

"It's my job, man. I'm like a care giver, dig it? Say you're my kid. I mean, you are my kid, right, man?" He turned to Benny for the first time. "Say some fucking pigs want to like lock your ass up, man. The fuck am I supposed to do? I can't let them put my boy in jail. Can I?" He shook his head. "What the fuck kind of father would I be, man, if I let that happen?"

Benny didn't know what to say.

"Don't worry, man. If you need to be in jail, they'll put you there whether I help or not."

Another bus passed.

"What if I miss the bus?" Benny asked. "What happens then?"

"Hey, man," Jason said. "You think I never did this before?"

Benny didn't answer him, but he guessed Jason had.

They sat for hours. Jason's cigarettes gave Benny a headache. His empty stomach churned acid. Buses passed. Jason smoked. The sky behind them changed from black to gray to pink. Without warning Jason pushed the stick into gear. The car jerked away from the curb. Air brakes and the low bellow of an air horn shook Benny's lungs. He squinted over his shoulder into a bus' headlights.

"This is your bus, man," Jason said. "Just tell the driver where you're going and pay him. You got money, right, man?"

Benny nodded, said thanks and tugged the duffel bag out of the car. He glanced up at the bus as the door hissed open. A white-on-black back-lit sign in the rectangle above the windshield read MIAMI.

VI

Bad Benny Taggart slept, outstretched, on the three rear seats of a Miami bound Trailways bus. The liquid in the toilet, sloshing against the thin partition beside his head, infected his dreams. The stench issuing from the little closet evolved in Benny's dreams into a stinking fog: gray, brown in color, it clouded every scene. The splashing of the liquid transported him to a desolate seashore, where Peter trudged up from the surf shooting himself again and again in the head -- to a battered wooden row boat, outside of which nothing existed, filling so rapidly with water the futility of bailing caused Benny to leap overboard into the void -- and finally, as the bus idled for fifteen minutes outside a diner in Waycross, Georgia, to a quiet comfortable space of slow gurgles and bubbles -- providing Benny a few moments of elusive peace.

As the driver wrestled the bus through a tight arc in the diner's parking lot, the jerking motion bucked Benny from his seat. He landed greasy-faced and stupid on the floor. Neither awake nor asleep, the fall and the grit scratching his cheek seemed all part of the dream. The driver braked hard; Benny's head bashed against the struts supporting the seats above him. He was awake.

Benny crawled back into his seat and, pawing sleep from his eyes, tried to focus on the rest of the bus. Dark, except for the overhead reading light shining on the seats two rows up from his. The bus smelled of the toilet, unwashed clothes and the musty breath of sleeping passengers. He leaned over and glanced toward the driver's reflection in the windshield -- arms and legs, draped over seats, hung out into the aisle. People snored. A baby cried out. Somebody said, "shhh," and started humming. One of the men sitting in the seat under the light said something soft and slow. The man next to him made a clicking sound with his tongue.

After twenty-eight hours confined to the narrow space of the bus's last row, the shock of Peter's death and fear of the cops had become part of the background noise of who he was. Benny had gone from crazed panic to numb acceptance. He knew what the bus was: it was time, and he just had to do the time. Everything else evaporated as large cities, small towns and interstate highway signs drifted by his window. At three a.m., next to a reeking toilet on a Trailways Bus heading south on a secondary road just outside of Waycross, Georgia, it didn't matter to Benny that all you saw when you peered out the window was your own reflection: time was passing.

Benny stared at his reflection, floating against the Georgia night and decided he missed the JDC. He knew he wasn't supposed to. But he missed fooling around with the boytoy, Sheila. He missed Sharkovsky, who could convince you that you were okay, and things could be okay. He missed being told what to do -- because he never really knew.

The voices of the two men in the seats two rows up from Benny's grew louder and snapped around the bus like a whip. One of them shouted, "What did you say, motherfucker?"

A passenger near the front hollered back, "We're sleeping here." Others said, "be quiet" and "shush." Benny peered through the gap between the seats. He saw an index finger, angled sharply at the second knuckle, pointing at something Benny couldn't see.

"What did you say?" the man repeated. "You know, motherfucker, you know you won't say that shit twice."

"Who you calling motherfucker?" said the other.

Some passengers stood up and looked back to the men. "It's the middle of the damn night," an old woman shouted. "Shut the heck up," cried a little boy.

Benny heard the sound of fist against flesh. One of the men groaned. "I told you, don't never call me no motherfucker." Benny heard another punch and peeked over the top of the seats.

Cramped and cursing, the two black men wrestled in the tiny space between the seats. Benny crouched for a better view. One, dressed in a faded green work shirt, had the other's shaved head pinned against the seats. His eyes were set and intense as he pumped punches down at the bald man. The green shirt's eyes suddenly widened, and he seemed dazed by something Benny couldn't see. He crumpled forward. The bald man thrust a hand up and caught green shirt's jaw in his palm. Benny saw muscles in the man's forearm ripple. He turned away, imagining the man's jaw cracking like an egg.

When Benny looked back, both men were on their feet. Green shirt's eyes were open wide with fear. The other man, his shaved head looking as hard and shiny as a helmet, had his free hand pulled back, measuring the distance from his shoulder to green shirt's face

The driver jerked the bus onto the road's shoulder and shouted, "That's enough of that. That's enough."

The two men tumbled out into the aisle.

The driver pushed through the passengers, shouting, "Stop that, now. Right now! Hear what I said? That's enough." Some passengers chimed in, above the shrieks and cries: "Stop it," they shouted. "Break it up," they shouted. "Lord, Jesus, have mercy," they shouted.

Everybody stopped when the bald man drew a knife. Its gray, cold-metal blade cast no reflection, and scribed a high arc above green shirt's head. The bus motor idled, vibrating a loose rivet in a window frame. A woman shushed a bawling baby. The bald man pressed the blade against the other's throat. "Don't make me use this," he shouted.

Green shirt wept, "Oh, my god, this mad man is going to kill me. Oh, my god."

Benny slid onto the floor and under the seat in front of his.

The bald man shouted, "If you all don't listen and do exactly as I say -- EXACTLY -- I am going to kill this motherfucker."

Green shirt blubbered, "Oh my god, ohmigod." Benny turned his head. The men's shoes, both wore cracked, black leather work boots, had stopped just in front of the small toilet's door. The bald man hollered, "I want everybody off this bus -- starting with you, driver."

Benny squeezed his eyes tight and listened to the sound of the other passengers fleeing the bus. He thought, for a moment, about making a noise so the bald guy would know he was there. He'd stand up, say, "Excuse me," and slide past him down the aisle. The thoughts that followed kept him motionless on the floor: the cops? The cops for sure. Where you from, kid? Got any I.D.? Where'd you say you were headed? Give us an adult we can contact.

When Benny opened his eyes, the two pairs of boots moved lockstep toward the front of the bus. "Hurry up," the guy with the knife said, "get the fuck off this bus." Green shirt sobbed quietly. Benny could see no more of their feet. He heard them reach the front of the bus and the air muscle sound of the door closing.

"Get in that seat and drive," the bald man said.

"I don't know how to drive this damn thing."

"You better learn."

The engine revved and slowed. The gears ground a high-pitched whine. The bus jerked forward. Benny braced himself against the struts.

"You know how we're going?" the bald man asked.

"And if I don't?"

"I asked," he said, "you know how we're going?"

"Yes, yes, I know."

"Well, get us there. I'm going to sleep."

"Why do you get to sleep?"

"'Cause you driving."

Benny said fuck to himself eight times in a row. Maybe if he had gotten off the bus, he could have just walked away. Not talked to the cops. Not talked to anyone. Fuck, he thought.

No sound came from the two men for a long time. The bus slowed and sped up jerkily, as the guy driving forced it around curves and through turns. Benny couldn't think of any reason to steal a bus. In the JDC he'd met thieves who talked about stealing everything; none of them ever mentioned a bus. These guys were probably crazy. A near empty soda can rolled against his cheek. A drop splotched onto his nose; it smelled like Coke. Fuck it, he thought, crawling back into his seat. It was not a matter of if they caught him, only when and what they would do.

Benny stretched across the seats and thought about a plan, but after a few minutes he knew that was bullshit. Someone else's plan might have worked, but not one he thought of. He'd tell them the truth, fuck it.

After about two hours, the bus slowed to walking speed. The driver muttered and cursed as it jostled over humps in the road. Just as Benny was able to see the silhouettes of trees, the bus stopped. A wooden, bullet scarred sign hung sideways from a pole: *"Okefenokee Wilderness Area: Unsafe Bridge, No Vehicles."*

"Wake up," the driver said. "We at the bridge."

Benny heard the bald man's boots drop to the floor. He sighed and stretched. "Well, take it on across."

"Fast or slow?" green shirt asked.

"Shit if I know. Just don't stop. Don't stop."

"Don't stop," the driver agreed, mimicking the other's rhythm. The engine revved. Gears ground -- the bus lurched backwards.

"Wrong way. Wrong way," the bald man cried.

"I'm getting a running start," green shirt said.

Benny felt the rear tires slide sideways. The bus stopped. The blue liquid in the toilet sloshed.

The engine revved again and slowed. The gears bit hard. The bus lurched forward. "Don't fuck this up," the bald man said. "Don't fuck this up."

"Don't jinx me," green shirt said. "Don't you fucking jinx me."

The bus shuddered and trembled. Benny grabbed the back of the seat in front of him for support.

"Don't stop. Don't stop," the bald man chanted.

Benny glanced out the window. In the faint light the bus lurched from the firmness of the road onto something else -- something that roared and fought back as if it were alive. The bus rolled forward as the bridge heaved it from side to side and bucked it end to end. Suitcases in the overhead racks split open as easy as cellophane bags. Underwear and trousers, shirts and dresses, exploded throughout the bus like feathers jarred from a pillow. Cheap plastic toys, toothbrushes, hair combs and tubes of toothpaste rained like shrapnel into the aisle. The emergency exit windows swung out on their hinges. Benny raised his arms to cover his eyes and was jarred against the outside wall of the bus. The bus jerked back, catapulting Benny against the bulkhead that separated him from the small toilet.

"Don't stop, don't stop," the bald man shouted.

The high revs of the engine slowed, and he heard the two men laugh and clap their hands. One whooped a loud screech that sounded to Benny like a bird. The other repeated the call.

The bus stopped hard, heaving Benny to the floor.

"Shit," he cried.

"What was that?" the bald man shouted.

Benny squirmed under the seats, trying to hide. He knew it wouldn't work, but he had to try. He had to try something. The bald guy had a knife. He'd probably use it. Face down on the bus floor, Benny felt their footsteps as they approached.

Joints popped like knuckles as one of them crouched in the

aisle. The bald man's face appeared next to Benny's. He smelled of sour sweat and burnt wood.

"Aw, motherfuck, Jesus," he said. "It's a white boy."

The other moaned, loudly.

"They're going to be looking for him. You bet your ass they're going to be looking for him."

"Awwwww," the other groaned.

Benny squeezed his hands around the seat supports. The bald man grabbed the back of his neck and lifted. Benny thought the man was going to tear his head off. He felt like a puppet. The man jerked him to his feet and held him steady with a fistful of t-shirt twisted in his hand.

Benny tried his "nothing" face, raising his eyes slowly to the bald man. The man's eyes, burning with something more than hatred, melted Benny's face -- melted his entire being. Benny turned his head. Green shirt's face told him nothing. He shifted his eyes to the bald man again. The man's fist was already moving forward. Benny blinked, felt no pain and saw the brightest light he'd ever seen.

***

Benny listened hard to the voice as he stared up into the darkness. Thin and cracked as radio static, the voice circled above him like a bird in the unlit room. He squinted his eyes, tilted his head. Benny had no idea where he was. He knew it was dark, the air tasted of wood ash, there was a voice and nothing more. When he first opened his eyes, the voice and the darkness seemed to be one. "Um hmm," it said. Benny wondered if he had died and the sound came from an angel or a ghost. "Um hum," it continued. Listening and staring, it took Benny a few minutes to realize that the voice was making music: a slow mournful music that drifted somewhere between humming and singing.

Benny tried to sit up. His head ached somewhere behind his eyes, as if some deep bone was touched with a hot brand. "Ahhh," he said between clenched teeth.

"You ever see a hurt dog? Hurt dog don't move." The voice

sounded thin as string. "Hurt dog'll lay and lay and lay. Won't move. Why you moving?"

Benny tried to lay still, puffing out breaths, as if he could blow the pain out of his body. The voice said, "Hm hummm. Now, you know what hurt mean." Benny nodded his head and tried to swallow. His tongue felt covered with paste.

The voice picked up the tune again and swooped down next to Benny's ear. "You cry out in your sleep. Trying to wake the dead? Crazy man blood be on your shoes," it said. "What crazy man be he? You the one that killed that crazy man? You the one?" it rasped. "You kill him and slop in his blood like a hog. Crazy man like that need killing. Probably would'a killed you if he got the chance. But you ain't supposed to be wearing no crazy man's blood in Pa Old Ma's camp."

Benny's tried to work up some spit in his mouth, so he could speak. His tongue felt thick. "Piss," Benny tried to say. It came out "pith." "Piss," he repeated.

The voice began humming and moved away from Benny. He heard metal scrape against metal and a slow creaking sound. A door swung open and light flooded into the small room. Benny blinked shut his eyes and twisted his face away. Tears ran down his cheeks. He turned his head slowly toward the door and, through slitted eye lids, watched the owner of the voice. Against the bright light, he couldn't tell if it was man or a woman, black or white. It must have been old: stooped forward and thin as its voice. Its head was wrapped in a cloth. A dress, or robe, hung to the middle of its calves.

The voice leaned out into the day light and called, "Luther. Luther, help this boy make water. Um hmmm. Help this boy."

Green shirt appeared at the doorway and the figure stepped aside. The man ducked under the door frame and moved toward Benny. He stripped back the rough blankets and gripped Benny under his right arm. His hands felt rough and pebbled.

Benny stood naked waiting for the pain in his head and the dizziness to cease. He glanced around the room: almost square, no windows. A tiny wood stove angled out from one corner -- its stove pipe poked up through the roof. The walls were skinned logs, laid on end; cracked gray mud filled the spaces between them. Then green shirt hooked his hand under Benny's armpit and tugged him toward the door. Goose-bumped in the cool breeze, and squinting against the sun, Benny stepped out of the hut. In the world beyond the door, new leaves shimmered against deeper shades of brown and green. Beyond the leaves there seemed to be a forest. Beyond that Benny had no idea.

VII

Naked, except for a musty olive-colored blanket -- his only clothing since the bus -- *Bad* Benny Taggart shivered and hopped from foot to foot alongside the scorched flat stones coiled around a fire pit. The cold sand nipped Benny's toes; his empty stomach ached. The old one, Pa Old Ma, knelt beside him, humming and singing, as he snapped twigs onto the pit's ash dusted coals.

The sun had yet to burn off the morning's haze. A bone-white mist shadowed the cypress trees ringing the two small cabins and the lean-to that comprised the camp. The cabins appeared cozy in that light, but Benny knew they were anything but: hot when it was warm, freezing when it was cold. If not for the night sounds, he might've slept outside.

Benny spent his first two nights in one of the cabins in a darkness so rich it seemed he could see better with his eyes closed. During the day he lay naked alongside the fire pit, on the olive-colored blanket. From mid-morning to sundown, he pursued the thin warmth of the springtime sun as it arced across the sky. Lying on his back, he watched leaves flutter, clouds drift overhead and flocks of tiny black birds attack crows. Lying on his stomach, he watched Pa Old Ma. The old man's skin was the color of cinnamon and drawn tight as catgut over his face, calves and arms. He wore a woman's red flowered house dress, cinched at the waist with a yellow nylon rope. Pa Old Ma traversed the camp in a gait so stiff it made Benny wince. The old man went barefoot, the knuckles on his toes swollen to the size of pecans. He wore a Christmas print tablecloth in a turban around his head; a tarnished silver badge adorned the headdress above the spot between his eyes. When bending to the fire or the pot, he removed the turban with great care and placed it on the ground beside him. Wisps of white hair, thin and delicate as the moss hanging from the trees surrounding the camp, encircled his head. Benny didn't know when he learned the old man's name was Pa Old Ma, or that he was somewhere in the Okefenokee Swamp, but he knew Pa Old Ma had told him. The old man made sounds all the time. Sometimes just slow, mournful singing. Sometimes Benny would notice, as if coming out of a dream, that the old one, as he tended the fire, stirred the pot or crossed the camp, was speaking directly to him. The man reminded Benny of a radio left on all the time. His voice became the background sound of Benny's entire world.

***

During his first two days in the camp Benny got used to drinking water the color of strong tea, but the food tasted as strange as the old man looked. Pa Old Ma cooked all they ate in two blackened pots that hung from hooked rods out over the fire. A white mush called sofketee simmered in one pot throughout the day. Benny had seen the old man drop parts of a large turtle he had cracked open against a rock, the skinned carcass of a small animal and leaves he pulled from his pockets into the other pot. Benny could eat the mush: it tasted smokey, needed salt. The other stuff looked like a black soup. It tasted the way garbage smelled and made Benny gag. The drinking water was kept in a battered, sweating bucket under the eaves of the cabin where the two men who stole the bus slept. The bald man was called Chuntawba and the green-shirted one Luther.

Chuntawba and Luther were gone during the day -- which was fine with Benny. At the end of his first day in the camp, sitting beside the fire with the blanket drawn up around his shoulders, he had watched Chuntawba and Luther jog single file out of the woods. Dressed in the same clothes they had worn on the bus, they slowed as they approached Pa Old Ma and said something in a language Benny didn't understand -- a string of grunts and clicks, brought up from the back of their throats. The old man nodded and turned back to the fire.

Benny looked up to Chuntawba. "Hi," he said. "My name is..."

Chuntawba made a hissing sound and glared at Benny. "I don't need your name, whiteboy." He leaped across the fire pit and stomped the ground. Chuntawba squeezed his hands into fists. His entire body shook.

Pa Old Ma sang fast and loud. The grunts and clicks ran together like a rope stretched taut.

Chuntawba glanced toward the old man, kicked dirt in Benny's face and stalked off toward the cabin.

"Man, oh man," Luther said, "Chuntawba like to kill that boy."

"Um hmm," Pa Old Ma sang. "Um hmm."

"Why?" Benny asked, wiping sand from his face. "What did I ever do to him?"

"Chuntawba want to kill everybody," Luther said.

"Everybody? "Even you?" Benny demanded.

"I guess so," Luther said. He turned his head and spat over his shoulder. "Maybe, I better kill him first."

"Um hmm," Pa Old Ma sang. "Um hmm,"

***

A large bird, bigger than any Benny had ever seen before, descended out of the mist, squawked in panic and broke its tottering glide just above his head. The bird beat its wings for lift, throbbing Benny's chest and ear drums as it climbed back into the fog.

"Shit," he said, as startled as the bird.

He tugged the blanket tighter around his shoulders.

Pa Old Ma didn't acknowledge Benny or the bird. He bent to the fire pit. The words he sang became longer and between each he inhaled. Then, with long steady blasts, he blew the previous day's coals to life. A flame burst through the twigs; they cracked and popped as if startled.

Benny opened his blanket to the warmth. He felt thick headed. The dull ache in his stomach angered him. He snarled, "I need my clothes, you know."

Pa Old Ma lifted the turban back onto his head and, pushing both hands on his knee, began to stand, joints popping like the twigs in the fire. "Mans need a lot of things," Pa Old Ma sang. He pushed the hooked iron rod into the ground and hung a fire blackened pot on it. "Um hmm, mans need a lot of things," he repeated, as he twisted the pot out over the flame.

"No, old man," Benny snapped. "Not a lot of things, just my clothes."

Pa Old Ma moved slowly. His right hand rose up and tore the blanket away from Benny. The fingers on his left-hand gripped Benny's shoulder. The pain so great, Benny crumpled to the ground.

Pa Old Ma draped the blanket across his own shoulder. "Um hmm," he sang, turning toward the lean-to.

"Hey, give that back," Benny cried, laying naked in the dirt. The old man ignored him.

"That's not fair," Benny cried.

Pa Old Ma turned around, "Yes summ. Um hmm. What's fair?" he sang.

"You took my clothes," Benny said. "I want them back."

"Burned them. They was marked with a taint. Crazy man blood. Can't be bringing crazy man blood into Pa Old Ma's camp."

"You're crazy," Benny shouted after him. "You're crazy."

"Um hmm," he sang, "but I got clothes. I got clothes, me."

Shivering and naked before Pa Old Ma's feeble blaze, goose bumps rippling up and down his body, Benny took a deep breath and yelled, "Bullshit."

"Bullshit. Bullshit. Bullshit," echoed back from the swamp.

Benny stood up, turned slowly in a circle, peering out at the trees. An echo, he thought, and hollered, "Hey."

"Hey. Hey. Hey."

Benny shouted "Yes, yes, yes." The sound of his voice came back at him. It was thin and squeaky like Peter's. Benny wondered if that's what he really sounded like. He didn't think so. He shook his head, laughed and howled like a wolf.

The echo came back and died, but the howling continued out beyond the edge of the camp. Those howls raised others that echoed deeper into the swamp, until the sound became something immense. Benny's muscles tensed as he stared out at the fog and the sound.

"Um hmm, um hmm, fool with that swamp and that swamp will fool right back. Um hmm," Pa Old Ma sang, tossing a handful of twigs into the tiny fire.

"Are those wolves?" Benny asked, his eyes scanning the fog.

"Might of been once. Now, they just wild dogs." Pa Old Ma stirred the pot with a stick and began humming again. "I need more fire," he sang. "I need this kettle hot. If the naked man got me some wood, I might give him some food, find him some clothes. Um hmm."

Benny turned his head and tried to see Pa Old Ma's eyes. "You don't want me to go out there -- into those trees?"

"What scares you naked little man? You scared of dogs? You scared of dying? You scared of that swamp? You scared of Pa Old Ma? Was you scared of that crazy man whose blood you wear?"

Benny wanted to shout yes to every question.

"Be scared of nothing naked little man. Be scared of everything. But, if you ain't hungry and you ain't cold, I don't want you to do nothing. But if you is cold, um hmm. If you is hungry, um hmm. Tell me what you want to do. Tell Pa Old Ma what you want."

Benny's stomach ached. His teeth chattered.

"Dying be a long time coming, um hmm. You ain't freezing dead in this weather. You got some fat; if you starved dead, you'd outlive me. Um hmm. Naked little man, shrivel dick froze -- hunger so deep he can't fetch a few sticks to warm his ass -- meat his bone. Naked little man."

Fuck you, old man, Benny thought. He was supposed to be in Miami, and if those two maniacs didn't steal the damn bus, he wouldn't be freezing his ass off. He'd be on the beach with his dad, fishing. "I didn't ask to come here," he declared.

"Um hmm, asking got nothing to do with it. White man don't ask no Blackafrican man if he want to be the slave. Red man don't ask my mother's mother's mother if she want him. Um hmm, ask. Ask where you be tomorrow, where you was yesterday. Ask? Um hmm. You right. You didn't ask. Um hmm. Now, run your scrawny ass into those trees and bring me some wood." Pa Old Ma raised his left hand and jutted a crooked finger in Benny's face. "I ain't asking," he sang.

Benny put on his roughest 'fuck you' face and stared into Pa Old Ma's eyes. The old man's response was flat as stone.

"I ain't asking," he repeated.

Benny walked toward the camp's edge with his left hand cupped over his penis. The sun's rays, cutting through the fog, looked damp and sloppy. Fuck. I'm going to get eaten by a wild dog. To hell with you, old man. At the camp's edge Benny glanced back over his shoulder. Pa Old Ma hadn't moved from his spot alongside the cook pot. The lean-to closer now, but the cabins less visible in the distance.

Benny stepped gingerly through low-growing bracken. Something chattered and skittered through the brush. Crouching, both hands out, Benny scanned the fog. He listened hard, over his pounding heart, for the low growl of a German shepherd or the panting approach of a rottweiler. He held himself still, listening and looking, until all he heard was his own breathing and the sound of his heart. Still crouched, he moved one slow, naked step at a time deeper into the forest. He turned his head -- left, right and rear, guarding against surprises. Benny gathered finger-sized twigs. He felt first with his toes, then snatched them up hoping to get back to the camp quickly. But the deeper he went into the forest, the more insubstantial the fistful of sticks became. He kicked up a branch as- long-as his arm. Then another.

Something darted out of the fog and stung his right thigh.

Jump back, stick scattered, shocked beyond sound -- Benny held himself still. Nothing moved. Nothing rattled the brush. He checked his thigh -- scratched and bleeding. There was something. It had gotten him. He moved side-step to the left, trying to make as little noise as possible. Two steps left. Three steps forward, crouched low, hands out. He touched it. Brittle, hard, it poked the palm of his right hand. He drew his hand back and grabbed out fast -- snatching a branch from a dead and down cypress tree, hidden by the fog.

"Shit," Benny said, giggling at his fear of a dead tree. He scanned the length of the tree, then worked quickly snapping off branches. Benny stacked the wood into an awkward brushy pile. It poked his legs and stomach when he squatted to lift it. "Ouch," he said, stepping back and rubbing the scratches. He snapped the branches smaller and stacked them in the crook of his left arm. He held a heavier branch club-like in his right hand and moved in what he took to be the direction of the camp.

The fog lessened as he walked through the forest. Cypress trees, low-growing ferns and broad-leafed saplings emerged, but Benny saw nothing he took to be the camp. He had seen no landmarks when he left Pa Old Ma. Now, as shapes became individualized, they only served to confuse him. He stopped near a burned cypress stump and turned in a circle: each direction looked the same.

He was lost. Lost. Shit.

Benny felt himself near tears. Everybody messed with him.

His mom made him go to school, even when he begged her not to. Sharkovsky sent him to the New Family Way, knowing a bunch of screw-ups ran the place. He trusted Peter to be his friend; look what he did. And that old man sent him out into the woods. Nobody gives a shit about me, he thought. Benny pushed the tears. He wanted to feel bad for himself. He imagined the old man laughing when he didn't come back. He imagined him singing, "Naked little man... shrivel dick cold... Lost in the swamp... Ate up by dogs..."

Benny smiled when he realized that it <u>was</u> the old man. He strode quickly toward the sound. Five feet before he stepped into the camp, he wouldn't have guessed it was there. He dropped the sticks in a heap next to the fire pit and rubbed flecks of bark from his arm and chest. "I found a tree," Benny said. "Do you want more wood?"

Pa Old Ma ignored the question. "Naked little man find his way back. Naked little man." He hummed and sang words Benny didn't understand, then stirred the pot, slowly. "Naked little man needs to feed the fire that will feed him. Um hmm, Naked little man."

Benny looked from the pile of branches to the small flame under the cook pot. "Um hmm," Pa Old Ma sang. "Um hmm."

Benny broke the branches over his right knee. He placed them carefully in the small fire until the flames licked the bottom of the pot. He no longer noticed his cold or hunger. Benny stared into the flames. He broke more sticks and fed them to the fire. Wood popped and sparks snapped out at him. Benny narrowed his eyes to slits. He knew that if he decided to burn the three boys, now, they would die. He might get caught, but they would die. He tried to picture O'Ryan and his friends scrambling to get away from the flames. He couldn't bring their images to mind. When he imagined death, he saw Peter. His face angry at life -- angry at its end. He could end O'Ryan's life, but he couldn't save Peter's. He looked into the flames. He couldn't save Peter's.

"Naked little man come get clothes, um hmm," sang Pa Old Ma. "Um hmm."

Benny looked up at the old man; he felt like he had just drifted back into himself. "Who are you?" he asked, but Pa Old Ma had already begun walking toward the lean-to.

The musty blanket hung from a peg driven into a log that supported one of the lean-to's corners. Benny reached for it.

Pa Old Ma shook his head. "Blanket need burning," he sang. "Full of crazy man sweat, um hmmmm." The old man ducked under the slanting roof. He walked to the building's far side and jerked down a green tarp, uncovering a pile of suitcases stacked as neatly as bricks against the lean-to's rear wall.

Jesus," Benny said.

Pa Old Ma grabbed the handle of a sky-blue, vinyl suitcase in the middle of the stack and jerked it out as neatly as a magician pulling a tablecloth from beneath a pile of dishes. He dropped the bag to the ground, removed his turban and knelt down. The locks made a metallic popping sound. Pa Old Ma flipped the suitcase open and, head bent, began rummaging through it.

"Jesus," Benny repeated. He had started counting the suitcases but stopped after thirty. There had to be at least twice that. "Where the hell did you get these?" Benny started across the lean-to to touch the stack, to make sure it was real.

"Same place we got you, um hmm," Pa Old Ma sang. "Same place we got you, um hmm."

"You stole other buses?" Benny laughed. "You steal buses?"

"They call it steal, naked little man, um hmm. They call it steal, um hmm. You let them tell you what you do -- and they'll own who you be, um hmm. They steal my fathers from Africa. They steal my mothers from the land. They steal all the worlds from my People. Um hmm. We take some back, um hmm. A few buses -- a few cars, um hmm. Now we took a white boy, um hmm," Pa Old Ma sang. "I ain't real for them out there, um hmm. When I take back, um hmm, I got something of theirs. But they got everything of mine, um hmm. No wrongs are never put right, just forgotten. Pa Old Ma don't forget though, um hmm. Don't never forget. I'm just taking it back, Um hmm. Just taking it back."

Benny tried to figure out what the hell the old man was telling him. If he would just talk to him, instead of singing that crap all the time it might make sense.

"Um hmm," Pa Old Ma sang. "This be fine for the naked little man. Um hmm." He left the suitcase open and returned to the stack. He stretched up and pulled down a round hatbox decorated with red and white stripes like a barber pole. Pa Old Ma drew a knife from the cord around his waist and popped the string holding the lid.

Benny thought of hats he had seen in movies. They were always worn by cowboys or gangsters. He smiled.

Pa Old Ma motioned him over.

Benny stood grinning before the suitcase as Pa Old Ma lifted a young girl's summer robe. He laughed. "No fucking way," he said. Repeating designs of pink and gray poodles, clad in sunglasses, using the telephone, shopping for clothes, sunning on the beach, covered the robe. "No fucking way," Benny repeated, "it's a girl's."

Pa Old Ma shook his head; wisps of white hair jiggled from side to side. "This be your clothes, naked little man. This be yours. Um hmm." Pa Old Ma gestured out of the lean-to. "Dogs out there got a smell of your fear. You got to let them know that you ain't afraid of no dogs. Um hmm. You got no fear. Um hmm. You wear their likeness. You wear their soul."

Benny looked out of the lean-to. The sun had burned off the fog. The cabins and the trees surrounding the camp looked hard and fast in the light. He imagined the dogs in the swamp moving, packed up and silent. The possibility of the dogs seemed more vicious in the bright light, when you could see them stalk. Benny took the robe from Pa Old Ma and held it up. "These are poodles," he whined.

"Um hmm," Pa Old Ma sang in agreement. "And they's as much dog as the wolf. Maybe more, um hmm. Maybe so."

Benny pulled the robe over his shoulders; it smelled sweet like vanilla and musty like the inside of a suitcase. The sleeves ended mid-bicep in gathers of lace. Benny giggled nervously as he popped the robe's snaps together. He patted two square pockets. In the left he found a safety pin and a tattered ball of tissue. In the right, a varnished wooden hair clip about the size of his little finger. *Hi, from Florida* was written across it in green script. Benny held the objects out to Pa Old Ma.

The old man hummed and nodded his head slowly. "Be good luck those things bring you. Um hmm."

Benny pushed the tissue and the safety pin back into the pocket. He squeezed the hair clip in his fist and wondered if it was a message from his father. He laughed at himself. What bullshit.

Pa Old Ma lifted the lid off the hat box and handed Benny a woman's green felt hat. It was shaped like a birthday cake, round and flat on top.

"Why are you dressing me in girl's clothes?" Benny asked. His head ached.

The old man took a step toward him and pushed the hat down on his head. "Clothes is clothes, um hmm. Clothes is clothes."

"Not where I'm from," Benny said, reaching his left hand up to the hat. He wiggled it back and forth, surprised at how well it fit. He studied Pa Old Ma's face to see if he was smiling or laughing -- to see if the clothes were some kind of joke. It didn't seem so.

Pa Old Ma, still kneeling, snapped shut the suitcase, put the lid on the box and lifted his turban onto his head. He pointed at the bag and the hat box. "Put these up," he sang to Benny.

Benny's first steps felt clumsy, the girl's robe strange. He bent to the suitcase and grabbed the handle with his left hand. The girl's smell was as close as his own. He heaved the suitcase up onto the pile and pushed the hat box up as well. Benny stared for a moment at the stacked bags and wondered what the girl looked like. He smoothed his hands over the robe trying to imagine how she felt.

"Cinch that up, naked little man, um hmm," Pa Old Ma sang. He held a piece of rope at arm's length. "Cinch that up."

Benny wrapped the rope around his waist and fumbled trying to tie the knot. Pa Old Ma slapped Benny's hands away and fastened the knot so it rode on Benny's hip. "Naked little man find him some clothes, Um hmm," Pa Old Ma sang. "No shrivel dick froze." He lifted one end of the tarp and motioned for Benny to get the other. Together they covered the wall of suitcases.

***

Steam rose from the cook pot as the sofketee began to boil. Benny snapped the remaining sticks in half, feeding them to the fire.

Pa Old Ma leaned out over the pot and stirred the mixture. "Naked little man, um hmm," he sang, "need more wood, naked little man, need more wood."

Benny said, "okay," and walked toward the camp's edge. As long as he didn't look down and see the poodles, wearing the girls' stuff didn't seem like that big a deal. He liked the smell. He liked the thought of the girl's body. But he didn't want to run into anybody and have to explain what was going on, because he didn't know.

Benny stopped alongside the lean-to and stared out into the woods, trying to focus on landmarks that would help him find his way back. He realized he had no idea where the downed tree was and nearly laughed at himself for being so stupid. As he struck out into the forest, he was surprised how noisy it was. Something up in the trees buzzed all the time. The occasional breeze rattled branches and dried leaves. Benny stopped every few steps and turned in a circle, making a mental picture of where he was and what he saw. He shouted, "Shit," when a chipmunk ran in front of him. He flushed a group of birds and ducked behind a tree, crying, "Jesus, shit," as they rocketed into the air.

After the birds spooked him, Benny scanned the forest floor for something he could use as a club. The sticks were either too thin or they snapped when he picked them up. Finally, he twisted a sapling off its stump and stripped it of branches. He walked on, brandishing it before him, making its tip whistle through the air.

Benny wondered if he would ever find the downed tree. He stopped and turned slowly in a circle. Looking back from where he had come, he could see the lean-to's back wall and the brighter spot that was the camp. To his left, where he thought the tree was, he saw only forest.

On his right, about thirty feet off, the cypress trees grew thicker; in the gaps between their trunks, he saw sky reflected on water. The swamp, Benny thought. The swamp. As he moved toward the swamp a softer mud squeezed between his toes. Benny climbed through the cluster trunk of four trees. He stared from his perch at some kind of plants poking up through the water's surface. They looked like gnarly carrots that grew the wrong way. He turned his head toward some movement and saw two turtles slide off a sunlit branch into the water. He moved closer. A school of small fish roiled the pond's surface as they darted from the shallows. At the water's edge, Benny looked out at the moss draped trees, the gnarly carrots and the lilies scattered about the swamp's surface and half expected to see a dinosaur, because this place was like history -- only older.

Benny looked into the water directly beneath him and jumped back from the reflection; it took a moment to realize that it was him. He laughed and leaned over the water. The green hat cocked on his head, the poodle robe gathered at his waist, he thought if he had a feather, he'd look just like an Indian. "Indians," he said out loud. "Maybe they're some kind of Indians." Benny waved his stick in the air and hopped through his version of a war dance. A log drifted toward him across the water's surface. Benny leaned out over the pond and poked it with his stick. Jaws thrashed open and snapped shut on the sapling. The alligator rolled beneath the water, twisting the stick from Benny's hand.

Benny yipped and jumped back. Goddamn. Goddamn. He ran toward Pa Old Ma's camp, weaving left and right through the forest. Benny tripped over an exposed root and tumbled against the trunk of a tree. He lay still, hat tipped forward over his eyes, robe up around his waist, waiting for the pain in his toe to stop.

Before he could move a hand gripped his face, covering his mouth and nose. He remembered the man's smell from the bus: Chuntawba. He felt himself lifted. Benny jerked once. Chuntawba tightened his grip on Benny's face until he squealed and held still.

***

"I told him we should've just left it. The having part don't matter, only the taking," Luther said, not looking up from the fire. "But he just had to bring it on in. Just had to get it into the swamp."

Chuntawba pointed at Benny. "It ain't the bus. It's the damn white boy. I told you we should've killed him and dragged him out of the swamp. If they thought he was dead, nobody be looking for him. But we got him. And we can't give him back. I say we kill him and move deeper into the swamp till they forget all about it."

Benny sat sprattle-legged in the sand, too tired to move or run. His face and neck ached from where Chuntawba had snatched him and carried him back to the camp. Benny knew there was no point in fighting, running or even crying. He looked from the smoldering fire to the three men.

Luther, his hands hooked in the bibs of his overalls, stood with his eyes focused on the fire pit.

Chuntawba shook his finger at Benny. "There's the problem,"

he hissed. "Get rid of the white boy."

Pa Old Ma hummed and ladled sofketee into wooden bowls. He rounded the fire pit and gave Luther and Benny each a bowl. When he tried to hand one to Chuntawba, the bald man stared hard at Pa Old Ma for a moment, then took it and scooped at the mush with two fingers.

Chuntawba said nothing more while he ate. Pa Old Ma took a bowl for himself and dropped into the sand alongside Benny. The camp was quiet, except for Pa Old Ma's humming.

Benny stared at the mush in his bowl. When he was hungry the stuff tasted like shit. Now -- he shook his head and placed the bowl in the sand.

"Naked little man better eat up his food, um hmm. Eat up his food," Pa Old Ma sang.

"No fucking way," Benny said. He pointed across the fire. "If he's going to kill me, I ain't eating that shit. Fuck it."

"Nobody he can see will kill naked little man. Nobody he knows will make him dead, um hmm," the old man sang. "Nobody he knows."

Chuntawba snorted and threw his bowl into the fire. The fine ash, stirred into the air, drifted down around the pit like snow. "Why you protecting that boy?" he shouted at Pa Old Ma

"That boy, that boy," echoed back from the swamp. The fire hissed as globs of sofketee dripped down onto the coals.

Pa Old Ma hummed, looking down into his bowl, while scooping out the mush with two fingers. "It ain't the boy I am protecting," he sang. "It ain't the boy."

"Then who?" Chuntawba bellowed.

"Who? Who? Who?" returned from the swamp.

Pa Old Ma shook his head. He hummed a tune so sorrowful that it made Benny want to cry.

"Answer me," Chuntawba screamed.

"Me. Me. Me," said the swamp.

Chuntawba howled and dove across the fire at Benny. Wild-faced, he wrapped his hands around Benny's throat, foamed spit flecked his lips. Benny tried to crab backwards, but the man landed on his chest. He grabbed at one of Chuntawba's wrists and tried to bite him. He kicked his feet in the air and, though he struggled, he knew he was going to die. Chuntawba squeezed his windpipe; time slowed for Benny. A shadow began closing around Chuntawba's face. Benny fought back but his hands no longer worked. An idea, as subtle as the fog clouding Chuntawba's face, drifted into his consciousness: I am dying. He would have laughed if he could breathe. It seemed funny to him that dying took so long. The events of Benny's life, good or bad, took no time at all -- the fires, his rape, sex with Peter, the last time he saw his mom. But death, damn. It took years. Benny laughed in his head. Fucker started to kill me when I was fourteen and I didn't die until I was thirty.

Benny felt a movement, a shifting of weight and a loosening of the grip on his neck. He moved his head and felt Chuntawba's face, like Peter's, resting against his neck. As his eyes cleared he could see Luther, holding a large rock from the fire pit. Benny choked and coughed on his first gasp of air. He turned his head to the side. The man's weight on his chest made it difficult to breathe. He heard a moaning and crying that rose in volume and intensity. He lay beneath the body listening, trying to suck air deep into his lungs, wondering what was going on. He felt the weight of the body shift. It was gone.

Benny sat up choking and rubbing his neck. Luther squatted next to him, brushing sand from Chuntawba's face. Pa Old Ma rocked back and forth next to the body chanting and singing.

Luther shifted his eyes from Chuntawba to Benny. "I knew I was going to kill him," he cried. "I didn't like it but I knew." He moved his hand lightly across Chuntawba's face. "He'd gotten wild, like a dog gone bad, like a dog gone bad." Luther stood up and looked around the camp. Shook his head. "Come on," he said, reaching a hand down.

Benny followed Luther across the camp and down a trail into the forest. Pa Old Ma's chanting followed them to the water's edge. A dented and scratched aluminum canoe, the words Camp OkeFanoke stenciled on its side in blue paint, rested in soft mud, half in and out of the water. "You take the front," Luther said.

Benny walked awkwardly down the length of the canoe and squatted on the front seat. He turned back as Luther pushed them off into the water. "Where are we going?" he asked.

"No place you ever been," Luther replied.

VIII

Benny sat figurehead still as Luther paddled the canoe through a series of ever smaller creeks and sloughs. Rounding a bend, they spooked a large-winged bird from its perch. It cried once and flew ahead of them deeper into the swamp. Benny noticed the bird and the decreasing size of the waterway but didn't care. He focused instead on the tearing paper sound his throat made each time he took a breath. It wasn't the sound, really -- though hearing it made the act more real -- it was his ability to breathe. Breathe, he reminded himself, each time he exhaled. He never thought about breathing, until Chuntawba tried to stop him from doing it. Now, the muzzled tearing sound made him wonder if something was broken. Broken or not, he could breathe. His jaw and teeth ached from where he tried to bite Chuntawba, and his tongue, coated with an acrid dried sweat, tasted the way the dead man smelled. Dead, Benny thought, the air whistling down to his lungs. Dead.

When Chuntawba had his hands around his throat, Benny knew he was dead, or good as. He wondered what dead was like. Would you know you were? Would you know anything? Would he see Peter? He'd heard people talk about God and heaven and dying, but nobody told Benny anything he believed. How could you know? He blinked his eyes, shook his head: breathe.

The trees overhanging the waterway grew larger and blocked out the sun. Though just past noon, beneath the trees it appeared no brighter than dusk. The canoe's narrow keel hissed through the water. Luther's paddle made a gurgling sound with every stroke. A branch seemed to come from nowhere and slapped Benny in the face.

"Ow, shit," he cried.

"Keep an eye out, or you might lose one," Luther said.

Benny glanced back. "Huh?"

"Pay attention, whiteboy."

Luther nodded toward the front of the canoe. Benny turned just in time to duck beneath a cypress limb that swept the hat from his head. When he reached back for the hat, he found himself nose to nose with Luther, who had leaned forward as the canoe glided under the branch. "You didn't have to kill him," Benny said, before he realized he was going to speak.

Luther laughed quietly, his breath stinking in Benny's face. "Don't think killing Chuntawba had any more to do with you than the sun rising has something to do with a rooster crowing." Luther sat back up in the canoe and worked the paddle through the water.

Benny stared at him. What the fuck did that mean?

"Chuntawba wanted to kill everybody," Luther continued. "Me. Pa Old Ma. He wanted everybody on that bus dead." Luther worked the paddle sideways; the canoe swung through a curve. "Pa Old Ma says any man wants to kill that bad, wants killing himself. For some dying's easier than living." Luther lifted the paddle and shook it; drops spattered across the water's surface.

Benny thought of the scars on Peter's wrists, the way they felt against his lips. He wondered if dying was easier for Peter. Would he have pulled the trigger even if Benny had said 'not crazy?' Benny's nose smarted and he could feel himself beginning to cry. The memory of Peter's face, just after the tiny pistol sounded, told Benny that dying was not easy, no matter what Pa Old Ma or Luther claimed.

Luther grunted and leaned hard against his paddle. He forced the bow of the canoe up onto the stream's bank. "Jump out," he said.

Benny tried not to think of Peter as he stood awkwardly, rocking the canoe back and forth. He stepped from the craft; a soft, cold mud squeezed up between his toes.

Luther pushed again on the paddle. The canoe climbed higher up the bank. He leaped out onto dry land and strode into the forest.

Benny trotted after him, the poodle robe flapping around his thighs. They moved through a narrow breach in a wall of densely growing trees. Once through the gap, Benny stopped -- startled as if he had plunged into cold water. The trees formed a large circular enclosure; their branches arched overhead, canopying the entire grove. Small platforms made of sticks and branches, lashed together with vines and twine, rose from the ground like beds in a hospital ward and filled the grove off into the distance. Each held one or two bundles of sticks wrapped in cloth. "What the hell is this?" he shouted ahead to Luther.

"Shhh," Luther scowled over his shoulder. "It's the ancestors' camp," he whispered. "Don't talk too loud -- you might wake them. Pa Old Ma says there's some that don't like to be bothered with us."

The ancestors' camp? Benny looked more closely at one of the platforms. The bundle, wrapped in faded red cloth, lay like a sleeping person. Benny's eyes grew wide when he realized the sticks poking through the ragged cloth were bones -- a skull and teeth emerged. Jesus, shit, Jesus. He ran toward Luther, stirring dust and leaves into the air.

"Did Chuntawba kill all these people?" Benny gasped.

Luther snorted. "These are the ancestors," he said. "Only Pa Old Ma knowed these peoples. They moved on to this camp long before Chuntawba was even borned." Luther stopped and began gently brushing twigs and branches off one of the platforms. "These is Blackafricans, the Peoples, and half-breeds the Whitemans didn't want. They talking to Pa Old Ma all the time."

Benny laughed, though he was more scared than amused. "No, they're not," he said. "These people are dead."

"The dead talking all the time, whiteboy. Pa Old Ma say the dead make more noise than the living."

"Yeah, what are they saying right now?"

"I don't know. They don't talk to me." Luther leaned over and blew tiny bits of twigs and dust from the bundle. "This, here, is Sari." A moldy brown skull protruded through the frayed blue cloth.

Crooked teeth poked up at Benny from the jaw. The bones, thin as sticks, were etched with tiny teeth marks.

"She is old enough to know somebody who knew time in Africa." Luther nodded. "She talk with Pa Old Ma all the time."

"That's crazy," Benny said turning left and right, looking for ghosts -- listening hard for their language.

"Sure is," Luther said. "Ask her a question. She might answer." Luther grinned at him and walked on.

Benny stood alongside the scaffolding, with his hands pressed down into the poodle robe's pockets, thinking the dead don't talk. He turned to follow Luther, but the idea of getting an answer to a question made it difficult to move. Luther continued across the grove without turning back. Trying to think of the question, Benny looked at the sunlight penetrating the tightly woven branches overhead. He closed his eyes to try and focus and it was nearly a full minute before he realized that he was squeezing the Hi from Florida hair clip in his right fist. He saw the script like skywriting across his mind -- *Hi from Florida*. He turned back to Sari and reached out with his left hand, sliding his index finger up and down the cool smooth length of bone. My name's Benny Taggart. And I'm just a kid, though that don't really matter, does it? I'm not lost you know. I mean, I don't know where I am, but I know where I'm going. I'm going to find my dad. And we're going to live together, because him and me are alike.

Do you know where he is?

Benny tried to slow every thought in his brain, every action in his mind. He wondered what Sari would sound like if she spoke. What if she answered his question and he didn't hear her, because she was old and all she could do was whisper? Or what if she spoke a language he didn't understand? Benny's left hand rested on Sari's skull. He closed his eyes and listened hard. A crow cried out overhead. The wind whispered through the grove and Benny's breath hissed in his throat. The sound he thought to be the wind grew louder. It sighed, grunting and clicking the way Pa Old Ma spoke to Luther and Chuntawba. It was an old woman's voice. She may have been weeping. Benny squeezed his eyes tighter. Speak English, he pleaded. The sound stopped. Please, he thought. Please. The voice began again, so sad, so sorrowful, that tears leaked from Benny's eyes. "Old ways lived," the voice said. "Old ways died. Old ways dead." An image of Peter sucking his thumb as he slept, drifted through Benny's mind. He saw his mother kissed by a man. She smiled. Sharkovsky leaned back in his office chair and tossed a chewed cigarette into a garbage can. A boy sitting across from him shouted, "Fuck you, asshole." Mr. Singerman stood before an Environmental Studies class holding his nose. The students laughed. O'Ryan rose up out of flames; Blume and Lewis stood at his side. An old Black woman dressed in rags appeared. She carried a club, waved it at the three boys and they disappeared. She turned and faced Benny. Her right eye was sealed closed. Her left eye clear and wide.

"Old ways dead," she cried. "Old ways dead."

Benny opened his eyes. It wasn't bright in the grove, but he blinked against the light and wiped tears from his cheeks. He looked for Luther and found him sleeping, his back against Sari's platform.

Benny poked him with his hand.

Luther's eyes blinked open.

"Sari must have given you quite a ride, whiteboy."

What did she say? Benny thought. He looked at the skull, its empty eye sockets. "The old ways are dead, Luther. She said so."

"I know that. What else?"

"That's all," Benny said.

"Ain't much."

Benny shrugged.

"Maybe it means something to me. I don't know."

Luther nodded, stood up, brushed off the back of his overalls. He pointed to the far side of the grove. "We need to make a place for Chuntawba. Put him somewheres he won't be fighting all the time."

As they crossed the grove, Luther gestured to different bundles: "That's Cries in the Night. He was half white and fat. Pa Old Ma claimed he ate his sofketee by the pot." He pointed to the next bundle. "That's his mother, Big Susan. She pushed a knife into a soldier while he pushed Cries in the Night into her." Luther paused next to a scaffold where the cloth wrapping was still intact. "This is Pa Old Ma's woman. He never say her name. Chuntawba claimed it Reebie. But I don't know."

Benny stopped and stared at the bundle. He never thought of Pa Old Ma as being a boy, or a young man with a woman. "Luther," Benny said, as quietly as he could, "Are you Pa Old Ma's son?"

He shook his head. "Pa Old Ma is my mother's uncle."

"Where's your mom, now?"

Luther shrugged.

"Never met her. All I ever knowed is Pa Old Ma."

"Luther," Benny said, focusing carefully on the sound of each word, "who are you guys?"

Luther looked around the grove, then back at Benny. "The last of the People's Blackafricans," he said. "We holding the land and talking with the ancestors, so they don't forget where they are. But Pa Old Ma say that cause you made it into the camp, it's time for us to go, cause the People ain't never coming back."

"The people?" Benny asked.

"The People, who world the Whiteman stole -- like he stole the Blackafrican out of his land."

It didn't make a lot of sense to Benny, but it made some. "You don't have to leave," Benny said. "Just get me out of here, give me some real clothes. I won't tell anybody."

"That ain't it, whiteboy. It ain't you, but it is you. That's just the way Pa Old Ma say it. It ain't you, but it is you."

Benny looked up into Luther's eyes. His breath hissed in and out of his throat -- it ain't me, but it's me.

Luther said nothing else as they crossed the grove. On the other side, they began shifting bundles from one platform to another based on a plan Luther mapped out as they worked. "This man killed that man's uncle thirty years before his mother was born," he said. "They need to talk it out. This woman stole that woman's man. Don't even let their shadows touch, they'll start fighting and we'll never get out of here."

Benny followed Luther's instructions, because they made as much sense to him as anything he'd heard before. He wondered how long the bodies had been there. Patches of cloth that still covered the bones had dried into dust and flecked off the bundles in a fine powder that clouded Benny's eyes and tongue.

While moving the bundles around, Benny became afraid. Someday the person he knew as *Bad* Benny Taggart would only be so much bone and cloth. If the dead couldn't talk, at least to each other, when he died it was over. Moving the bones of the People around, he realized dead meant there would no longer be a Benny Taggart.

When they finished, Luther stood alongside an empty scaffold and surveyed their work. "Chuntawba gonna do good, right here," he said, nodding. "Yeah, he gonna like it."

Benny looked around at the scaffolds and, for Chuntawba's sake, as well as his own, he hoped Luther was right. As they recrossed the grove, Benny slid a finger along Sari's platform.

When Benny and Luther returned to Pa Old Ma's camp, they found him sitting on the ground, chanting, beside the bundle that was Chuntawba's body. Straight black lines, finger thick, ran down from Pa Old Ma's eyes to his jawbone. The old man's singing slowed. He repeated the same couple of lines over. Then he wrapped Chuntawba in a white sheet, drawn tight enough for Benny to recognize the bald man's features. The bundle rested on a stretcher-like frame of branches, lashed together with pieces of yellow nylon rope.

Luther began punctuating Pa Old Ma's chants with quick snapped cries of his own. "Yess'm. Um hmm," he sang.

Pa Old Ma stood and stepped next to Benny and Luther. He opened his left hand. It held a piece of charred wood. He dabbed it with the index finger of his right and drew lines, first down Luther's cheeks, then Benny's. He tossed the burned wood away and moved to the front of the stretcher. "Naked Little Man, stand by me," he sang. "Naked Little Man, do as I do."

Benny stepped up next to Pa Old Ma. Luther walked to the stretcher's opposite end. The old man's chant became more rhythmic.

Luther exhaled, hard. "Huh," he said. Pa Old Ma repeated the chant. "Huh," Luther cried.

Pa Old Ma bent at the knees, chanting. Benny bent too. The old man grasped the stretcher. Benny did the same. Pa Old Ma's chant ended. Luther shouted, "Huh." They all stood and moved Chuntawba toward the canoe.

Pa Old Ma chanted constantly as Luther paddled through the swamp. He and Benny sat in the canoe's bow. Chuntawba's body straddled the gunwales. Luther paddled in the stern. The tiny craft rode low in the water. Pa Old Ma reached beneath the surface from time to time and scooped up handfuls of water, letting them run back into the stream from between his fingers.

They reached the ancestors' camp at sundown. Benny stumbled in the dark as they carried the Chuntawba's body across the grove to the platform he and Luther had prepared.

Benny expected something to happen after they put Chuntawba on the platform. He wasn't sure what, but some kind of praying or something. But once they'd arranged the bundle, Luther and Pa Old Ma turned away from it and began back across the grove. Benny thought about saying a few words, but being left alone with Chuntawba, dead or alive, proved too frightening and he jogged after them.

Benny fell in behind Luther, who followed Pa Old Ma across the camp. The old man stopped alongside the platform that Luther claimed held his wife's body. He removed the tarnished silver badge from his headdress and placed it alongside the bundle. His singing didn't change at all, but Benny saw him reaching slowly for the cloth wrapped figure. His hand stopped just short of the bundle and wavered momentarily in the air. His fingers squeezed into a fist; the hand jerked back and he began walking again.

When they reached the breach in the trees, Pa Old Ma stopped, turned back to the grove and began chanting louder. Luther stood next to him. Benny just behind. The old man chanted each phrase twice. The words didn't make sense at first, but when Benny heard him sing the name *Sari*, he listened harder and caught *Cries in the Night* and *Big Susan*. Finally, Pa Old Ma chanted, *Reebie, Reebie* and *Chuntawba, Chuntawba*. He sang a few more words and was silent. As odd as it had been for Benny when he noticed that Pa Old Ma sang all the time, it became even stranger when he made no sound at all. Benny wanted to ask him what was wrong, but he suspected that he, Benny, was what was wrong.

They returned to the canoe and Luther paddled through the night. Benny knew Pa Old Ma was near him; he could smell the old man. But without his sounds there seemed to be less of him there.

***

Benny, lying in swamp water puddled in the canoe's bottom, drifted in and out of sleep. He noticed a rhythmic vibration but couldn't muster the energy to wonder about it. The poodle robe was soaked; the green hat crumpled beneath his head like a pillow. The canoe buzzed and stopped. Buzzed and stopped. Benny opened his eyes. He remembered the endless canoe ride from the previous night, but not falling asleep. He judged, by the light, it was early morning. The vibration buzzed and stopped. He stretched and sat up. Luther lay backwards across the canoe's stern, his arms hugging his chest. He snored a deep vibrato that buzzed the canoe's aluminum rivets.

Benny didn't recognize where he was, other than in the swamp: moss like Pa Old Ma's hair draped the trees, birds cried out, fish jumped and slapped back beneath the water's surface. He lifted the crumpled hat from the bilge, pulled it on and stood - turning toward the shore.

There, beneath a rough lean-to, loomed the Trailways Bus. Benny yipped and stumbled overboard into the shoreline's slimy mud.

He scrabbled to stand. His hands and feet slid through the ooze as smoothly as if it were water. He flailed and twisted -- clawed and struggled, making no headway. Benny thought about shouting to Luther, but not yet. Not until he knew he couldn't get out on his own. He closed his eyes and relaxed into the mud. It felt cool and smooth. He rubbed his cheek back and forth and dug his hands into it. Benny rolled onto his back and sat up, facing the water. He scooped handfuls of mud onto his head. He rubbed it on his face, chest and crotch. Benny heaped mounds of mud over his legs and sat looking, he imagined, like a mud statue. He could become one, he thought, if he sat long enough. When they found him, they would make up stories about him -- call him the Mud Boy.

Once upon a time, Benny began, a boy got lost in a swamp. He shook his head, then remembered, statues couldn't move.

He began again -- there once was a boy who lived with his mother and father on the edge of a huge swamp.

No, that wasn't it either.

A long time ago there was a boy, he started. A boy who got into trouble and had a very hard time getting back out. Benny stared into the swamp. That's it. What next? The Mud Boy had a pet bird named...

"Naked Little Man." The voice startled Benny. "Get up out of that mud."

Benny twisted his head around. There before the Trailways Bus stood Pa Old Ma, dressed in a luminescent orange suit. The collar of his white shirt flared out from his neck like the wings of a bird. In his right hand, pressed close to his thigh, he held a rectangular wooden box. He wore a white straw hat and oversized white shoes.

"Jesus," Benny said.

"Luther," the old man snapped. "Luther, boy."

Luther's snoring ended. He opened his eyes and dragged a hand over his face. "Yeah."

"It's time," Pa Old Ma said. "We leaving."

Benny crawled slowly up out of the ooze. The mud coating his body gave him purchase and it was easier to get out than he thought. Benny stood and looked down at the muck coating the poodle robe, felt it sliding off his thighs, easing down his chin.

He grinned at Pa Old Ma.

The old man shook his head. "This ain't no time for fooling around." He pointed past Benny's shoulder. "You get in that water and rinse off. Luther," he said louder. "It's time."

He turned and walked up under the lean-to.

Benny stood looking after him for a moment. His world kept getting stranger and stranger and he wondered when it would be normal. He shrieked, "Crazy!" to confirm it to himself. Then peeled off the poodle robe and slid standing, like a surfer, back down the mud into the pond. The shore dropped off and he fell in over his head. He ducked under and scrubbed the mud from his face. He surfaced, treading water, and rubbed his arms and belly. Luther, his head turned to the side, had begun to snore again.

Pa Old Ma shouted, "Luther, let's go."

Luther waved vaguely.

Benny laughed, and shouted, "Come on Luther, let's go." He swatted the water, splashing the sleeping man's face.

Luther bolted up out of his seat. He stood, while the canoe bobbed up and down and side to side. He pointed at Benny, who, floating on his back, kicked up more water with his feet. "Whiteboy," he shouted, pumping his fists open and closed. "You ever, again..." He stopped and his eyes rose above Benny's head. He leaned forward and hissed quick and hard, "Whiteboy, take my hand. Take it now."

Benny stopped laughing; Luther's face scared him. He glanced over his shoulder and saw three logs drifting toward him. Adrenalin stunned his muscles. He stroked his arms broadly and frantically pumped his legs, but he traveled no closer to Luther. Something cold and hard bumped against his thigh. Too scared to scream, Benny tried to lunge away from whatever lurked beneath the water. He stopped paddling and shook his hand back and forth. A cry strangled in his throat. Luther's hand grabbed his and jerked him up out of the water like a hooked fish. Before Benny could get his bearings, Luther dropped him and he crashed down into the bottom of the canoe.

Benny lay shivering.

"Jesus, shit, Jesus," he said. "They would have killed me."

Luther nodded his head. "Uh hunh, they would'a." He stepped over Benny, walked to the front of the canoe and leaped off the bow onto dry land.

Benny sat for a moment looking back out at the swamp. The

three logs had disappeared; the water had calmed. He sucked in a deep breath just as the canoe jerked wildly into the air.

"Watch it!" Luther shouted.

Benny grabbed the sides of the canoe and screamed, believing an alligator had the canoe in its jaws.

A laugh boomed from Luther and stretched out over Benny's head and deep into the swamp. Birds grew quiet. Fish shadows darted beneath the water's surface. Benny looked over his shoulder. Luther smiled at him and shook the canoe again.

Pa Old Ma came around the back of the bus. "This ain't no time for fooling around. This is time for leaving," Pa Old Ma rasped at Luther. He pointed a finger at Benny, then turned to look at him. "Naked Little Man, get up on that bus and find some clothes. We leaving." The old man stalked away.

Luther grinned at Benny, then followed Pa Old Ma.

Benny sat for a moment, waiting for his racing heart to slow. He imagined what it would be like to get killed by an alligator. Its teeth, its skin. The bump of its snout against his thigh. Benny hugged himself, turned in the canoe and began a slow, careful duck walk up its length.

He glanced back at the water -- still, calm - no drifting logs -- before climbing out and working his way to completely dry land. He stepped over the poodle robe, a muddy twist on the ground -- the green hat, crumpled and mud scabbed, sat closer to the water than Benny knew he would ever go again. He turned to the bus and eyed its tooth-like chrome and moon- eyed headlights -- the word **MIAMI**, written across its brow. Branches, ripped from trees on its way into the swamp, poked from the Trailway's roof like a mad man's hair. Benny approached it with sidelong steps and eased around to the door.

The door's hydraulics sighed as Benny pulled it open. The air escaping from the bus smelled of plastic diapers and baby vomit, days old clothes and sleepers' breath. Though he was sure the bus was empty, something seemed to be lurking inside: something he didn't want to face. Benny climbed the short steps, past the driver's seat. A chipmunk squeaked and ran down the aisle.

Burst suitcases gaped down at Benny from the overhead rack, their contents heaved chaotically about the bus. Food left behind by the hijacked passengers had drawn vermin and flies. The door to the toilet, at the bus' far end, stood open and its chemical smell hung in the air.

Benny walked down the aisle: fingering a green nylon dress that hung body shaped from the overhead rack, wrinkling his nose at the smell of milk gone sour, waving his hand at the riot of flies that buzzed up from the remains of... he couldn't tell what.

He slowed as he approached the rear of the bus. Though it was less than a week since the hijacking, it seemed as if he was returning to a distant past. He scanned the three rear seats; they seemed cramped and small. Benny felt as if the boy who had slept in those seats was someone he knew from another place. A boy he might have been sorry for, but unable to help. Unable to help. It was less painful to think of the kid as somebody other than himself. So he remembered him as a boy whose name wasn't Benny Taggart, as someone who didn't have a real name, as someone they just called The Mud Boy. The Mud Boy was a boy who hid in the bushes, before going to burn three others; who acted tough in prison but was scared out of his mind; who couldn't say "not crazy," to Peter, not just because he was scared, but because he wanted to see what would happen. That Mud Boy, Benny thought, was worse than crazy.

He looked up and stared for a moment at his reflection in the bus' tinted windows. The mud still silted his skin and his close-cropped hair with a fine grey talc. A line of dirt, scar-like in its precision, angled across his chest from his left nipple to his shoulder. He picked at it, worked his fingers back and forth through his hair, and rubbed his arms and legs. The dried mud fell around him in a fine dust, but the more he rubbed the more there seemed to be. He gave up, believing nothing he could do would ever get the stuff off. "I guess I'm the Mud Boy," he said. The sound of his own voice startled him, and he knew he had to get out of the bus.

Benny climbed atop the three rear seats and found his duffel bag in the overhead rack, still clipped as tight as the day he left the group home. He slung the bag across his shoulder and walked quickly down the aisle. The boy whose clothes rested on his shoulder -- the boy who was himself, sort of -- could not be helped now. You couldn't go back and change things, he thought. You couldn't. That idea pained Benny nearly to tears. Standing before the bus's staring headlights, he undid the duffel's clip and dumped his clothes on the ground. The boy whose clothes these are knew nothing, Benny thought. He squatted beside jeans and t-shirts, underwear and socks, and red Converse Allstars. The wad of money from Peter's stash lay crumpled beside the shoes. A car's ignition ground on the bus's far side; he glanced toward it then back to the clothes. He wondered how the normal became strange and the strange normal. He decided with a little work anything could be normal, or everything could be strange. He lifted one of the sneakers. These, he thought, are both strange and normal at the same time. But underwear was stupid. He dropped the sneaker and held up a pair of jeans. Pants were weird, poodle robes normal. Benny laughed at the idea, then remembered the robe. He hitched up his trousers, slid shut the zipper, and bent to the money, cramming it into his pocket. He walked to the mud's edge. Using a stick, Benny hooked the poodle robe and searched its pockets; first one and then the other. He found the hair clip, pushing the mud off with his thumb.

Hi from Florida.

Hello, he thought, pushing the clip into the jeans pocket.

Benny pulled on a green t-shirt and the red sneakers. He stuffed his clothes back into the duffel and dragged it after him, along the side of the bus. He found Luther leaning under a car's hood. It was an old car. Huge and shaped like a long wave breaking against a beach, the car's white paint was stained by leaf shapes and windblown dust. Dusty metal washed back from the car's grill and surged around the windshield. Whitecaps curled over the trunk and ended, as if frozen, above the rear bumper. The emblem said it was a Pontiac.

Benny had never seen anything like it.

Luther jiggled the air filter housing and lifted it out of its seat. He poured something from a Coke bottle into the engine. He glanced at Benny as the liquid ran from the bottle but said nothing.

Pa Old Ma sat half in and out of the car's rear seat. The small wooden box lay open on his lap. It was filled front to back with papers on end. He ran his thumb back and forth over the paper; it made a quiet shuffling sound. Benny watched him for a moment, then looked past him to the car's interior. The red leather seats were stained with mold. Springs and white batting burst through small tears. The red and white metal dashboard, pocked with knobs, dials and buttons, wrapped around the front seat. The steering wheel was the size of a bicycle tire -- the gear shift, a baseball bat.

Luther slid behind the wheel, eyes focused down on the dash. He pumped the gas pedal and turned the key. A blue flame shot up under the hood. Gray smoke plumed out the tail pipe. Luther revved the engine. The car made farting noises. He grinned at Benny and pressed down on the gas pedal until the entire car shook. Benny laughed nervously; he knew it was about to explode. Luther eased off the gas. The engine slowed and ran smooth.

Pa Old Ma looked at Benny, licked a thumb and strummed it over the box's contents. He plucked a strip of the paper from the box and held it between two fingers.

Money green, Benny knew the moment he saw it. All the paper in the box must be money. They were rich.

Pa Old Ma turned the paper against his palm. They were rich.

It was a twenty-dollar bill. Benny smiled: rich, rich, rich.

"If you want to hurt a man, take what he love best," Pa Old Ma said, looking at the bill in his hand. "Whiteman don't care nothing for ancestors. Nothing for the Blackafricans or the Peoples. Whitemans only care about this paper."

"It's money," Benny said. "It's worth something. You can get things with it."

"Paper," Pa Old Ma hissed. He crushed the bill and threw it to the ground.

"Here, it's paper," Benny said, looking from Pa Old Ma to the bill. "Where I'm from, it's money." He dropped the duffel and bent for the money, uncrumpling it and smoothing the paper against his thigh. He held it up. "This is twenty dollars. You can get twenty dollars worth of stuff with this."

Pa Old Ma shook his head, growling, "Whitemans' lie."

IX

Sticks cracked beneath its tires and limbs sprung the antenna as Luther piloted the sedan through a cypress forest. Low growing branches clawed the car's length, like fingernails on slate, and set Benny's teeth on edge. Through the broad windshield Benny could see there wasn't a road; he wondered if there was a direction. They were leaving the swamp, for sure, but where were they going? He twisted in his seat and looked at Pa Old Ma.

The old man sat in back, his legs straddling the hump that ran down the middle of the car. Still as wood, he gazed out over his left shoulder at the swamp. The box of money, gripped in one hand, rested on his lap.

"Pa Old Ma," Benny said. He stopped, realizing he had never said the name out loud. "Pa Old Ma," he repeated, feeling the words in his mouth, and hearing for the first-time father and mother in the name. "Where are we going?" he asked.

Pa Old Ma didn't answer him.

Benny started to repeat the question, but Pa Old Ma held up a hand. The old man spoke without taking his eyes off the swamp. "When my camp belonged to my uncles, when I was a boy and the sounds of the People not long from the land, come to the fire one night a Blackafrican, big as a tree. 'Uncles,' he say to the old men around the sofketee pot, 'down on an island called Andros, in a place named Red Bays, the People's Blackafricans got a new camp. Leave now. Come down,' he say. 'The Whiteman's got this land.'

"My uncles say, 'the ancestors talk about the Blackafricans' camp. Talk about a big man coming up. They say bad time coming to your camp. They say don't go.' My uncles say, 'We watch the ancestors. They watch us.'"

"The big man laugh. 'Thank you, uncle,' he say, 'for watching the dead in their camps, but bad time already here. A camp of old men and boys. Leave now, he say.'"

"Ancestors say, 'bad time coming to camp,' my uncles say.

'They say the water going to reach out -- grab the Blackafrican man -- carry him back across. Your woman will have no man -- the People's Blackafricans will join the ancestors.'"

"The Blackafrican smile. 'It is your people that will die out. Only the ancestors will dance here.' The big man stood up and laughed. He say, 'Good news for you uncles. When you decide only the dead can hold this land, come down Andros way. When you decide the Red Bays be your home. Go to the river they call Miami and find the Blackafrican boat captain. Only the Blackafrican can take you to Andros. Red Bays be the camp's name,' he say. And he be gone."

Benny's heart skipped when he heard Pa Old Ma say Miami. He rubbed his hand over the hair clip in his pocket. "Does that mean you're going to Miami?"

Pa Old Ma looked at him and nodded. "My whole life been spent going to Miami."

"What?" Benny asked.

Pa Old Ma didn't answer. He looked back toward the swamp.

Benny sat forward in his seat and worked the hair clip from his pocket. Hello, Benny thought. He'd say that when he found his father. "Hello, my name's Benjamin Taggart. I think you're my dad." Or maybe, "Hi, I'm Benny Taggart, your son," holding out his hand for a shake. He was getting closer. He could feel it. But what if he got to Miami and couldn't find his dad? What if he found him and the guy didn't want anything to do with him? He tried to remember how he knew his father lived in Miami. Did his mother tell him? Was there a card? A letter? He had believed all his life that his dad was in Miami, but how did he know? Who told him? He wondered if he made it up. If it was all a lie told so often he no longer remembered the truth.

Luther gunned the engine. The car listed and rocked as it climbed a steep bank and emerged from the forest onto a roadbed of powdered sand. Luther coughed, and said, "Bridge just ahead."

Benny looked at Luther, then back to Pa Old Ma. The old man nodded slowly. Benny remembered the bridge and the savage way it fought the bus. He gripped the arm rest next to him and braced his feet against the floorboards.

Luther eased the car forward. Before them lay the bridge; it ran straight for about three hundred feet, planks and posts -- some rotten some missing. It appeared so tiny compared to the swamp around it. The only way in and out? Benny wondered. Luther started across, much slower than Benny remembered from the bus. The car swayed back to the front, like a boat cutting white caps. Its tires thumped the planks with a steady rhythm. It sounded almost musical to Benny. The noise stopped. They dropped back onto the sand road.

Benny wanted to ask Pa Old Ma if he would find his father in Miami. The old man knew things. Benny knew it. As he thought about the question, he wondered if he wanted to know the answer. If Pa Old Ma said no, what would he do? If he said yes, would he be right?

Benny looked back over his shoulder. Their eyes met. Pa Old Ma knew something, he could tell. "Is my father in Miami?" he asked, quick and fast. The question hung in the air like a smell.

"Without the ancestors, Naked Little Man, I don't know what you know," Pa Old Ma said. "Without the ancestors..."

Benny stared at him for a moment, then looked away because the old man was about to cry.

***

A short time after dark, the tires spun fast and hard, tossing gravel into the air as the roadbed changed from sand to macadam. The acceleration shoved Benny back against his seat. Looking ahead, through squinted eyes, his view of the future extended only as far as the headlights' beam. Luther swung the car through curves, bottomed out in dips and roared across bridges: wooden, grated and paved. The air rushing in the open windows whistled and fluttered through the car. Benny cranked his shut.

They approached a car, heading in the opposite direction. When its headlights were full on, Benny squinted and raised a hand to his eyes. Behind the shield he glanced first to Luther, who looked tired and frightened, and then to Pa Old Ma, who shifted his eyes from side to side as the car rushed by. Luther and Pa Old Ma were like him, now. They were all outside their worlds, and they were all scared.

The lights from the first house they passed startled Benny. He hadn't forgotten electricity existed; he just hadn't thought about it for a while. He turned his head and listed the details of the scene, as if to remind himself where he had come from: a night-lamp, on a high pole, shined down on the yard, the mowed lawn appeared gray, the trimmed bushes like cowered beasts. A car and a pickup stood side by side in the driveway, a yellow porch light was on and, off to the side of the house, a satellite dish bloomed under the night sky. The house was brick and just one story. Benny could see a light in a window. He wondered if anyone was up, watching tv, listening to a radio, worried people like himself and Luther and Pa Old Ma were driving by. No, he decided, people never thought that guys like him existed, at least not where they lived.

Luther tapped the brakes as they crossed two sets of railroad tracks. The slight rise lifted Benny from his seat; his stomach seemed left behind. Ahead, more lights shone from houses and poles set beside the road. Luther glanced over at him but said nothing. Pa Old Ma snored in the back seat. Benny choked back his shock when he saw a red light flashing in the distance. "The cops," he whispered.

Luther shook his head. His eyes, as they passed under a streetlight, were rimmed red and looked like open sores. "The light blinks red in Hickory," he said.

Benny took a breath. Jesus, he thought. They passed a sign, white letters on green: Hickory Village Limits.

Dawn close, Luther slowed the car. In the streetlight dim, they crawled through the town. He watched a dog lope across a lawn, a light flash on in a tiny house, bugs whir through the fluorescent lights in a SORRY WE'RE CLOSED gas station. At one intersection, lit more than the others, stood three churches.

Luther braked as they approached the traffic light. Red winked toward them, yellow down the crossroad. Benny read the highway signs: JCT routes one, twenty-three and 301. To the left an arrow pointed: Waycross, Georgia. To the right, Jacksonville, Florida. Hello Florida, Benny thought. His stomach knotted.

Luther stopped just before the light.

Benny looked toward Florida.

The car began forward, turning to the left.

"Hey," Benny shouted, leaning forward in his seat. "Where are you going? I thought we were going to Miami."

"Yeah," Luther said, "Miami."

"You're going the wrong way."

"No, Miami's this way."

"Luther," Benny said. "The sign back there says Florida's the other way."

"What sign?" Luther asked. "I didn't see no signs."

"By the side of the road." Benny shook his head. In the distance, stood another: *Waycross 36 miles.*

"Like that," Benny said, pointing. "Says Waycross, thirty-six miles."

"We ain't going to Waycross," Luther said.

"We are if you going this way. That's what that sign said."

"That ain't a sign. Whitemans don't make signs."

"What are they, if they're not signs?"

Luther looked at him. "Chuntawba told me."

"Yeah," Benny said. "What did Chuntawba say they were?"

"He called them passbys. They were put there by the Whitemans to keep the ancestors from traveling. He say when we cross a passby, the ancestors can't help us no more."

Jesus, Benny thought. "That's probably true," he said. "To the ancestors they're passbys. To me and my people they're signs. And that one says, if we keep going, we're going to end up in Waycross."

"Yeah, whiteboy, what does that one say?"

Benny looked ahead on his right. "It says, Seat belts it's the law. Georgia Highway Patrol."

Luther grinned at him. "And that one."

A tiny green sign stood alongside the road. It was covered by a series of numbers. "That one doesn't say anything to me," Benny said. "It's just a bunch of numbers. But you got to believe me. I know what I'm talking about."

"Luther," Pa Old Ma said. "Do what the boy say."

Luther looked into the rearview mirror.

"Do it," Pa Old Ma repeated.

Luther shook his head, pulled onto the shoulder and swung the car through a u-turn. "You better be right, whiteboy."

"Jesus, Luther, why would I lie about that?"

"Cause you're white."

Benny laughed. "That's the dumbest thing I've ever heard."

"Whitemans lie," he said. "But if you lying to me, I'll kill you."

Benny knew he would.

"Luther," he said. "You need to get to Miami, and I need to get to Miami. I can get you there. I know how things are."

"Luther," Pa Old Ma said, "you listen to the Naked Little Man. You do as he say."

***

Luther poked Benny's shoulder and gestured toward a billboard. "What does that one say?"

Benny opened his eyes to the endless pine forest that bordered the road. At first reading the signs aloud to Luther had been fun. "Tourist Information Center, Discounted Disney Tickets." "Best rooms at Epcot, Stay at The Sonesta." "Welcome To Florida, Drive Carefully." But as the sun rose higher, and the sign count closed on ninety, Benny wanted Luther to just shut-up. It wasn't just the billboards, though there were plenty. It was billboards and speed limits, county regulations, For Sale, Wetherell for Sheriff, weight limits, entering here, leaving there.

Benny pretended he was asleep. It didn't work.

"That one, there," Luther said.

Benny glanced at Luther, then the sign. "It says, "Closest rooms to Disney. Kids stay free. Kissimee Great Western Motel."

"And there." Luther pointed across the highway.

Benny looked at the sign. His stomach rumbled. "Here it is kids," he read. "Make them stop. McDonald's two miles." Big Macs, he thought. Benny grinned. "Are you hungry?" he said to Luther. He turned around, kneeling on the seat. "Are you hungry?" he asked Pa Old Ma. "We can stop there and get some food. We can use some of the money." He pointed at the box on Pa Old Ma's lap.

"What food they have, Naked Little Man?" Pa Old Ma asked.

"You know. Burgers, fries, shakes."

"No," Pa Old Ma said. "I don't know."

Benny grinned. He smiled so hard his lips ached. "You mean you've never been to a McDonald's?"

Pa Old Ma shook his head. "Never been."

He turned toward Luther. "You been to McDonald's, right?"

"What's a McDonald's?" Luther asked.

Benny nodded his head smiling. "Come on," he said. "Everybody's had a Big Mac."

Both of them shook their heads.

"Jesus," Benny said. "You must be the only people in America who never heard of McDonald's." He forced himself not to laugh. Benny didn't think much about Luther not knowing how to read; plenty of kids in the JDC didn't know how. But this was something different. If these guys didn't know about McDonald's, there must be a ton of stuff they didn't know. Unbelievable. "Okay," Benny said. "I'll handle it. Open the box."

Pa Old Ma lifted the lid and Benny stretched over the seat, pulling two bills from the box: both twenties. "Okay, Luther. Now, just do what I tell you." Benny sat back in his seat. Ahead, he could see an overpass arcing above the road they were on. Signs dotted the shoulder, but Luther didn't ask what they meant. Benny read each one to himself. "Junction I-95, One Mile." "Florida Lotto $9 million, You could be a winner." "Jesus is Coming. Are You Ready?" A quarter mile ahead, on the right, next to a green BP gas station, sat the McDonald's. Benny couldn't wait to get inside; it would be like going home. He pointed at the building. "See, that's a McDonald's."

"See what?" Pa Old Ma asked.

"Right there," Benny said. He watched Pa Old Ma as he leaned forward in his seat and peered out the window. Yeah, see what? Benny thought. See him and Luther and Pa Old Ma step into a McDonald's. See everybody stop and turn to look. As they approached the driveway, Benny nearly told Luther to forget it -- they'd eat something else. But when he saw the sign, "Drive Thru," he slapped his hands together.

"Okay, Luther, just do as I say," he said. "Pull in; we'll get it to-go. I'll do the talking."

Luther nodded.

Benny directed him in behind a blue van, with Michigan plates, idling at the drive through speaker. A kid pressed his face against the van's back window. He stuck out his tongue and stretched back his ears. Benny figured the kid to be about eight or nine and laughed at the face. The kid raised the middle finger on his right hand and mouthed 'fuck you' at Benny. The van pulled forward.

"Move up," Benny said. "Next to that right there." He pointed at the speaker. Luther bucked the car forward, tires screeching. "Luther, relax," Benny said.

"May I help you?" A girl's voice squawked from the box.

"Ahh," Luther said.

Benny leaned across the steering wheel and said, "Yeah, give us six," he eyed Luther. "No, make that seven Big Macs, three large fries, three strawberry shakes and three apple pies."

"Anything else?" squawked the speaker.

Benny looked at Pa Old Ma, then Luther. "No, that's it."

"Your total is twenty-two twenty-five," the voice said. "Pick up your order at the next window."

Benny sat back in his seat. "Now, pull forward, Luther. Up to that window over there."

The car didn't move.

Benny turned his head. Beads of sweat had broken across Luther's brow. His lower lip quivered. "Luther, relax. This is okay. People do this all the time. Relax."

"Behind us," Luther said.

Benny looked over his shoulder. "Shit. Fuck," he said under his breath, when he saw the rack of blue lights. "Shit. Fuck. Shit." He paused. "Luther, if we don't do anything funny, he might not notice us. So just drive up ahead to that window. Come on," Benny pleaded.

The car jerked forward, tires squealing. Benny shook his head. It was all over. As they came abreast of the next window Benny cried, "Stop here."

Luther did.

The car's momentum heaved Benny from his seat. He bounced off the dashboard and landed on the floor. "Luther, can't you drive any better?"

Luther's eyes were on the rearview mirror.

"What's he doing?" Benny asked, scrambling up onto the seat.

"Talking to that box," Luther said.

"Shit, shit, shit," Benny whispered.

A young girl with a thick scar cutting down her upper lip leaned out the window and said, "Twenty-two twenty-five, please."

Benny leaned across Luther and handed her the twenties. He smiled at her. She might have been pretty without the scar.

She handed him back the change and said, "Thank you."

Benny sat back in the seat. The car bucked forward.

"Stop," Benny shouted. "Stop, we don't have the food yet. Luther. Stop."

Luther stomped down on the brakes. The car stopped hard, rocking back and forth. Benny looked at Luther and shook his head. "Are you trying to get us arrested?"

"No," Luther said.

"Well, don't..." Benny stopped speaking. The girl was leaning toward the car with a bag of food. She looked confused. The backseat window was next to her.

"Pa Old Ma," Benny said. "You need to get the bag from the girl. Would you do that so we can get out of here?"

Pa Old Ma said, "Um hmm," slid across the seat and wound down his window. As he reached up, he said, "That mark on your lip mean good things for you."

Benny's head spun on his neck.

Pa Old Ma was smiling at the girl.

She blushed. "I hope so," she said.

Pa Old Ma took the bag and nodded. "It do."

Benny couldn't fucking believe it. What did these guys think would happen if they got arrested? "Luther," Benny said, calmly, as the warm smell of the burgers and fries filled the car, "Nice and slowly, drive away from the window, circle around the building and get us back on the road."

Benny tensed as the car started forward, but Luther had smoothed it out. The tires didn't make a sound, the car didn't buck. He eased out onto the road and turned up into the gas station next door.

"Jesus Christ," Benny shouted. "I didn't tell you to stop. That cop is right there." He jerked his thumb back toward the McDonald's.

"That's right, whiteboy, you didn't. This did." Luther tapped a gauge on the dashboard. "We need gas."

"Well, at least pull over to the other side."

"Whiteboy, if he didn't get us there, he just ain't looking for us. Shit, he can't even see us."

Benny looked back at Pa Old Ma.

The old man nodded his head. "Could be so. We was right there. Now we is right here. Could be so."

Benny didn't know what to think. He felt sweaty and cold and no longer hungry. Luther stopped alongside a gas pump, climbed out and grabbed the nozzle.

"Pay first," said a voice from a loudspeaker. "Y'all pay first."

"I'll get it," Benny said. He turned in the seat and plucked two twenties from the box. As he climbed from the car, the rear door opened, and Pa Old Ma eased out. "Now, where are you going?" Benny whined.

"With you, Naked Little Man," he said, adjusting his straw hat. Benny tried to think of something he could say that would get Pa Old Ma back in the car, but he didn't know what. "Fine," he said. "Just don't say anything in there. Okay?"

Pa Old Ma grinned at him. "Okay."

An alarm, triggered by an electric eye, chirped twice as they walked through the door. Benny saw Pa Old Ma look up and he knew the old man was looking for the bird. He touched Pa Old Ma's elbow and shook his head. Then he reached back and waved his hand in front of the electric eye. It chirped again. Pa Old Ma smiled and fluttered both hands past the eye. A flock of birds filled the store.

Benny grabbed his hands. "Don't do that," he whispered. He looked quickly over his shoulder.

Two pair of eyes, from the counter at the other end of the store, scrutinized him and Pa Old Ma over the tops of the shelves.

Benny grinned and nodded at the eyes. He let go of Pa Old Ma's hands and started toward the counter. The place smelled of brewed coffee and pine cleaner. It seemed to be stocked with everything you could want. In a single aisle Benny passed shelves of chips, pretzels and nuts, canned soups and meats, disposable diapers and laundry detergent. An ice cooler shaped like an oversized Budweiser can, stood near the counter. It was packed with ice, cold sodas and beer.

Benny's eyes grew wide as he approached the cash register. The man and woman on the other side of the counter were the fattest people he'd ever seen. The woman, perched on a stool, had a head the size of a basketball; a gather of skin ran from her chin to her chest. The man was dressed in an enormous pair of bib overalls. Benny had never seen clothes that big. The guy's right cheek bulged as if he had a baseball in his mouth.

"We want to fill it," Benny said, holding out the two twenties.

The lump in the man's cheek shifted. He raised his left hand and spit into a tin cup he was holding. "Filler up," he said. He reached over and flipped a switch. A digital readout above the toggle blinked twice and numbers raced by.

Benny glanced over both his shoulders, looking for Pa Old Ma. The old man wasn't there. He thought for a second about going after him but decided to just get the gas and get out.

"Looks to be a nice day," the woman said.

Her chins trembled as she spoke.

Benny nodded. "Looks like." He glanced up and saw Pa Old Ma's reflection in a fisheye mirror. The old man lifted a coffee pot from its warmer and sniffed it. He put it back and tore open a packet of sugar. He smelled it and smiled, before dumping the contents on his tongue.

The fat man cleared his throat and cocked his head so he was looking at Benny out of the corner of one eye.

When Benny looked back up in the mirror, Pa Old Ma had moved to the beer coolers at the rear of the store. He flattened a hand on the glass, then he leaned close and pressed his face against it.

"Pa Old Ma," Benny hissed.

The old man turned, grinned and started toward him. In the white shoes, straw hat and the glow-in-the-dark suit, he looked like a hallucination. As he came up the aisle, he hefted cans of motor oil, rattled a jar of nuts and fondled bags of potato chips.

The man shifted his chew noisily. "Is there something wrong with that old boy?"

Benny nodded, happily, and touched a finger to the side of his head. "He's not dangerous, though."

"Just one of God's beloved children," the woman said. "Amen to that, mother," the man said. He spit into the cup.

"Amen to that."

Benny looked outside as Luther put the nozzle back into the pump. "Amen," he sighed.

"Praise God," the man and woman said in unison.

Benny turned back to the counter. "How much?"

"It's twenty-nine, forty-three, mother."

The woman hit some buttons on the cash register. "Praise the

Lord," she said when the bell chimed, and the drawer slid open.

"Amen," said the man.

"Right," said Benny.

She took the twenties and counted out the change. Benny closed his fist around the money. When he turned to get Pa Old Ma, the old man was standing right next to him.

"One of God's beloved children," said the woman.

"Amen," said the man. "Amen to that, mother."

"They're all God's children," she said. "Like a lollipop?"

"He can't talk," Benny said.

"Okay," said Pa Old Ma.

"Praise the Lord and all his glory," the woman cried. "The dumb shall be made to speak."

"Amen, mother. Praise God. Amen."

"We've got to go," Benny said.

The woman reached under the counter and came up with a green lollipop. She spun the sucker between her bloated fingers. "Can you speak again for us, brother? In Jesus' name."

The man cried, "Praise the lord, mother."

"Okay," Pa Old Ma said.

The woman swooned.

"Mother, mother," said the man.

Pa Old Ma lifted the sucker from her fingers and grinned at Benny. "Thank you," Benny said, as the man leaned over the woman and fanned the air with his hands.

The bird chirped twice when they went through the door.

Benny stalked across the parking lot. Pa Old Ma moved after him spinning the green lollipop between his fingers. These fuckers are going to goddamn jail, cause they can't act right. Maybe they belong in jail, goddammit. If they can't act normal, maybe they ought to be there. Benny jerked open the door and climbed into the car.

Pa Old Ma slid into the back seat. Before he could pull the door closed, Benny twisted up onto his knees and shouted, "Are you fucking crazy, or what?"

"Okay," Pa Old Ma said, grinning.

"You just don't get it, do you?" Goddamn. Benny glanced at Luther. "Can we just get the fuck out of here?"

"Okay," the old man said.

Luther started the car.

Benny turned back on Pa Old Ma. "You think it's fucking funny don't you. You think they won't put you in jail. Well, they will. So just keep fucking around and we'll all be there. Okay?"

Pa Old Ma's face grew serious. He looked angry as he brought up a hand and stuck a finger in Benny's face. He held it there, staring at Benny. This is it, Benny thought. Pushing his lips together, lowering his eyebrows, he set his face -- his *Bad* Benny Taggart face. This is it, where we get into it. Okay-old-man, let's go.

"Praise lord, mother," Pa Old Ma said.

He sounded like the fat man.

Benny blinked while his mind processed the information. The laugh burst through his lips. "Praise the Lord in all his glory," he cried.

"Okay," Pa Old Ma said. He snorted like a horse.

Benny hooted. "And the dumb shall be made to speak."

"What's so funny?" Luther asked.

***

"These are Big Macs," Benny said, placing two before Pa Old Ma and three in front of Luther. They sat at a picnic table in the far corner of a rest stop alongside Interstate 95. "They're made with two all beef patties, special sauce, lettuce, cheese, pickles, onions on a sesame seed bun." A truck's air brakes wheezed in the parking area. A car horn blew. Benny lifted the large fries from the bag. "These are French fries," he said. "Just call them fries. And these are," he said, smiling, "strawberry milkshakes." He pushed a straw into one. "You do like this." Benny sucked up a long drink of shake: cool and sweet, he felt the pleasure of it all the way down to his stomach. Though the flavor seemed as familiar as his own reflection, he couldn't remember the last time he'd been to McDonald's. Before the fire, for sure, but when? How long?

He looked up. Luther and Pa Old Ma were staring at him. "Look like you went with the ancestors," Luther said.

Pa Old Ma nodded.

"No," Benny said. "I was just trying to remember something."

He shook his head. "Here," he said, handing them each a straw, "You drink through this."

Luther poked his into the cup right away.

Pa Old Ma held the straw up to his eye and looked at Benny through the tiny tube.

"Go ahead," Benny said. "It's good. "

Pa Old Ma forced the straw through the slit in the top of the container.

"Good," Benny said, "now you just sort of suck. Know what I mean? Just sort of suck."

Luther pulled the straw from his mouth and smiled at Benny with a mouthful of shake. "That's good, whiteboy."

"Yeah," Benny said. "I love them."

Pa Old Ma held the cup up and stared at it.

"Go ahead," Benny said. "It's good."

Luther said, "Yeah, it is."

"It might be," Pa Old Ma said. "But I ain't using this thing." He pulled the straw out and set it on the table. "I ain't using that thing."

"That's okay," Benny said. He reached over and peeled the lid off Pa Old Ma's shake. "You can just drink it."

Pa Old Ma nodded and tipped the cup to his lips. The old man's Adam's apple moved slowly up and down. Luther's lips worked the straw; his eyes crossed over the cup.

Great, Benny thought.

Pa Old Ma lowered the cup, grinning. Strawberry shake dotted his nose and mustached his lip.

Luther looked over at him. Pink spit flew from his mouth as he laughed.

Pa Old Ma looked surprised, then angry. "Luther," he barked.

Benny laughed as well.

Pa Old Ma straightened up at the table and scowled from one to the other.

"Here," Benny said, "watch."

He lifted the lid off his shake and took a drink.

The old man scowled when Benny lowered the cup but reached a hand up to his own nose and lip. He wiped at it, nodded, said, "Okay."

"Okay," Benny said, "watch this. Just do what I do."

Pa Old Ma and Luther nodded.

Benny unwrapped a Big Mac and lifted it out of its container. When he looked up, Luther and Pa Old Ma were staring at him. "Go ahead," he said. He waited while they did it. "That's good," he said. "You guys do this just like everybody else."

Benny looked around the table. "Now, the fries." He picked up a carton of French fries and dumped them out on the Big Mac's wrapper. "You guys like ketchup?"

They shrugged.

"Well," Benny said, "most people do. You should try it. Watch." Benny reached for a packet of ketchup, tore it open with his teeth and squeezed it over the fries. He looked up. "Did you get that?"

Luther and Pa Old Ma nodded and repeated Benny's actions.

"Okay," Benny said, "try a fry." He grabbed a French fry between two fingers, tilted his head back and dropped it between his lips like a live fish. Pa Old Ma and Luther did the same.

"What do you think?" he asked.

Pa Old Ma nodded. "Okay," he said.

"Taste good," Luther said.

"Yeah, see what I mean? Everybody likes ketchup. Everybody." He nodded. "Okay, now the Big Mac. Pick it up like this." Benny thought he was going to tell them things about the burger. How to lift it. Bite it. Chew it. But once in his hands, he couldn't help himself. He shoved it into his mouth and took a big bite. "Just like that," he said around the mouthful of McDonald's. "Just like that."

"This taste good," Luther said. "This taste real good."

Pa Old Ma nodded at Luther and took another bite.

"Yeah," Benny said, "I love this stuff."

After they ate Pa Old Ma and Luther stood up from the table and started toward the car. Benny stared at the wrappers, cups and napkins they left behind. "Hey," he shouted. "You can't leave this stuff here. It's litter. I thought you Indian guys were like against litter."

They stopped, turned around, looked at each other and then Benny. "Aw forget it," he said. He turned back to the table. Pushing the trash into the empty bag, he came across an unopened packet of ketchup. "Hey," he shouted after them. "Come here. Watch this."

Pa Old Ma and Luther turned back toward Benny as he gathered up the rest of the garbage and forced it into a can near the table. He jogged over to them, and repeated, "Watch this." He laid the packet of ketchup on the ground. "Keep watching." Benny stepped back and slapped his foot down on the packet. The ketchup burst the container, flew through the air and hit Pa Old Ma in the legs, staining his trousers just above the knees.

"Oh shit," Benny said.

Luther and Pa Old Ma laughed. The old man wiped at the ketchup with his fingers. He licked them clean. "Praise the Lord, mother," he said.

***

Benny sat up panicked. It was dark. He had no idea where he was. Something whistled overhead. As his mind cleared, he realized he was on the floor of the car they had driven out of the swamp. They had gotten gas, eaten McDonald's. He must have fallen asleep just after they got back on the road. That's what he figured. He fell asleep. He rubbed both hands on his eyes and twisted around to the back seat. Pa Old Ma sat up kind of crooked, the straw hat covering his eyes, his mouth angled open. Boy, that food must have knocked the hell out of everybody, Benny thought. He looked around, didn't see Luther and thought that he must have gone to take a leak.

Benny needed to go himself. He pushed open the car door and stepped out. It was warm and humid, but he felt a chill. He rubbed his hands over the goose bumps crawling on his arms, and yawned, wide mouthed, looking up as he did so. The noise, the repeating sound came from directly overhead. It was a bridge and the traffic made a whistling sound as it crossed. Benny wondered what the fuck they were doing there. Why were they under the highway and not on it? There were no lights along the road they were on. Jesus, he had to be watching all the time. Okay, he thought, no more sleep until Miami. He faced the car, pulled out his dick and began pissing on a tire. A car's passing overhead cast the surrounding trees into eerie silhouettes. Benny looked back over his shoulder. Luther walked toward him across the road. His boots made a strange sound on the pavement, like they were wet. They scuffed gravel ahead of him.

Benny heard him approach but saw him only when a car passed on the bridge. He hitched up his zipper and pushed his t-shirt into his jeans. "Jesus, Luther," he said. "Let me know when you're getting off the highway. We could get lost or any fucking thing. Jesus, I don't know."

Luther spoke quietly. "Pa Old Ma's dead."

"What did you say?" Benny asked.

"He's dead. Pa Old Ma's dead."

"That's not funny, Luther. You think it's funny, but it's not."

Luther inhaled noisily. "Whiteboy, Pa Old Ma is dead. He's in the back of that car and he's dead."

A car crossed the bridge. In its lights, Luther became a shadow, his arm extended as he pointed at the sedan.

"Yeah, we'll just see..." Benny had started toward the car -- he stopped and turned back to Luther. "When?"

"I stopped to make water," Luther said. "When I got out of the car, he was making his sleep sound. When I got back in, he wasn't."

"Well," Benny said, trying to control the emotion in his voice. "That doesn't mean he's dead, you know." But he knew it did.

Dead, he thought. Pa Old Ma. Dead. Tears ran down his cheeks and he sobbed. Dead. Pa Old Ma was dead as dead was.

Luther walked by him, opened the car's rear door and jostled Pa Old Ma's body into his arms. In the dim light of a passing car, through tear blotted eyes, Benny watched Luther lift the body from the back seat and walk slowly across the road. Benny couldn't decide if Pa Old Ma was so small or Luther so large. Dead, he seemed so tiny.

"Follow me if you want to, whiteboy." Luther didn't look back.

Benny hustled across the road.

Luther walked straight, never diverging, down through the roadside ditch. The water climbed past Benny's waist. Near panic, he had to dig his fingers into the dirt to scrabble up the other side and trail Luther into a pine scented forest.

Night sounds scrabbled before them across the needles littering the ground. Benny walked after Luther through the closed air. He followed him by sound, sight proving useless unless a car passed on the highway. Twigs and branches slapped his face, scratched his cheeks. It made it easier to cry. Benny walked into the man's back.

"Watch it, whiteboy," Luther said.

Benny stepped back.

He heard a rustling and settling of weight.

"Okay," Luther said. "That's it."

"That's what?" Benny asked.

"Let's go."

"Aren't you going to pray or sing or something, like he did when we left the ancestor's camp?"

"I don't know that. Only Pa Old Ma know it."

"Yeah, but you must know something."

"The ancestors will find him. Or he'll find the ancestors," Luther said. "We're no use to him."

A car passed on the highway. Its lights penetrated the forest in tiny pinpoints. Benny could see, for the first time, Luther had placed Pa Old Ma's body on a crude platform. "You built that?" Benny asked.

"It's the only thing I could do."

The only thing I could do, Benny thought. The only thing. He stumbled past Luther with his hand out. In the dark, the leisure suit's polyester fabric felt chill and damp, like the skin of a frog. Benny ran his hands over the body until he found one of Pa Old Ma's hands. It felt rough as tree bark. He reached into his own pocket and closed his hand around the hair clip. He pushed the clip into Pa Old Ma's hand and tried to close it. The fingers were stiff as claws and wouldn't move. Benny placed the hand on the platform and laid the hair clip on Pa Old Ma's chest. "Let's go," he said.

X

Benny's red sneakers scuffed gravel as he trailed the soft squishing sound of Luther's boots back to the car. Water-soaked from cuffs to beltline, his blue jeans sheathed his legs and crotch in a warm, damp second skin. Once under the bridge he reached out his right hand and braced himself against the sedan's roof. He took a deep breath, blew it out slowly. A car whistled across the overpass; its lights flared the night. Benny glanced back at the forest and the trees' black shadows.

The car passed on. The trees disappeared. He tried to think Pa Old Ma alive. It didn't work. The old man was dead. Benny knew what that meant. Water dripped from his trousers and floated in tiny beads on the dry soil beneath him. Dead meant that some part of the living died too. He chuckled wearily. Dying probably worked better for the dead.

"What's funny, whiteboy?" Luther's voice surprised him.

Benny shook his head. "Everything." He swallowed back his tears and choked on a sob. "Everything."

The driver's side door opened, and the dome light flickered on. Benny blinked his eyes. In the feeble glow he looked into the back seat, empty of Pa Old Ma. The box of money had spilled on the floor; bills lay scattered like scrap paper. Benny opened the rear door and pushed the money into its box. He heard the old man say, "Whiteman's lies," and he thought, maybe, maybe not." Here," he said, passing the box with money over into the front seat. "You better hold this, Luther."

As Luther took the box from his hand, Benny noticed Pa Old Ma's straw hat. Brim crushed, orange floral print head-band askew, the hat lay flattened against the far door.

"Can I have his hat?" Benny asked.

"What do you want with a dead man's hat, whiteboy?"

"I just want it," Benny answered.

"Maybe you hope that dead man'll talk to you."

"He's talking to me all the time, Luther."

"Take the hat," Luther said.

The car's starter made a grinding noise.

Benny climbed into the front seat. The engine turned over. Luther swung the car from beneath the bridge and pressed hard on the gas pedal; they sped up the interstate's ramp.

Slouched in the front seat, Benny held Pa Old Ma's hat on his lap, gripping its brim with both hands. The air, rushing in the open window, pushed on his face and made a loud fluttering noise in his ears. It felt good. Benny paid close attention to the road signs. He wanted to remember exactly where they left Pa Old Ma. He knew once he found his father, together, they would come back. They would -- well, he wasn't sure what. But he would come back.

The first sign they passed read, *New Smyrna Beach, Exit 84.*

He turned toward Luther. Dawn close, a thin line cracked the horizon. "I figure you must have got off at Exit 83 or 85," he said. "I'm not sure how the numbers go."

"It don't matter where we got off or got on. Getting to Miami is all that matters."

"Maybe to you. But I want to do something for Pa Old Ma."

"There's only one thing you can do for him."

"How do you know?" Benny snapped, feeling like Luther was trying to steal something from him.

Luther sucked air between his teeth. "Ain't you just like a Whiteman. You know what you can do for Pa Old Ma cause a what it can do for you."

"Fuck you, Luther," Benny said. "I'm pretty sick of all your Whiteman bullshit. My name's Benny. Not whiteboy."

Luther spoke quietly. Benny had to turn his head to hear him. "Whiteboy, you know I could reach right across this car and..."

"Well why don't you just fucking do it," Benny yelled. "Why don't you just fucking do it. 'Cause right now, I don't care."

"Because you don't matter to me, whiteboy. I need you, but you don't matter."

"Well, shit, Luther, you don't matter to me either. Just stop the fucking car and I'll get out here. Just stop the fucking car."

"You don't matter." Luther spat his words at the windshield. "But I need you to get me to the river in Miami. I need you to get me on a boat, with a Blackafrican captain. I need to get to Red Bays. Except for me, all the People's Blackafrican men are dead. Pa Old Ma knew you was coming... knew Chuntawba was to die... knew he was to die."

Benny turned toward Luther.

The man's eyes were focused on the highway. The dawn-line, off his shoulder, had thickened; trees and poles beside the road took shape. Luther shrugged his shoulders. "None of that mattered. The only thing matters is getting to Red Bays," he said. "The only thing."

Benny looked at Luther for a moment, then turned forward and worked Pa Old Ma's hat around in his hands. Pa Old Ma knew I was coming, and he knew what mattered? What did matter? Benny thought. Did it matter if his father was in Miami? Did it matter if he was *Bad* Benny Taggart? Maybe nothing ever mattered. Things only mattered when you believed they did. Benny nodded. If his father was in Miami, Benny would find him. If he wasn't, it didn't even matter.

Until that moment, Benny had thought his father would explain the world to him. Explain why he was a bad guy. Why he didn't really fit in. His next idea combined everything he knew into a single thought: his father was the past. The discovery made him giddy. His father had always been the past. By running away, or getting kicked out, his father had helped to make Benny what he was. Benny realized he wouldn't ask his father what to do or be, just show him what he had become. Who he was. He looked back at Luther. "You're right," he said. "Getting to Miami the only thing that matters."

***

The early morning light looked cool to Benny as Florida appeared outside the car windows. "Holy shit, Luther," he said. "That must be a palm tree." He had seen pictures in books and slow swaying images in movies, but the trees were stranger in person than he could have imagined. Clumped together by the side of the interstate, they rose out of the ground like French poodles' tails.

"What did you call them?" Luther asked.

"Palm trees," Benny said. "Where coconuts come from."

"What kind of nuts?"

"Forget it," Benny said.

Benny dozed and woke on the trip south. Hot and sweaty, he wanted to ask Luther to stop, get a drink, something to eat. But he knew Luther wasn't going to stop. Luther knew exactly what he had to do. Benny admired that, and wished he knew as well.

Interstate 95 gathered lanes. As they passed the sign Entering West Palm Beach, more and more traffic blew by. Horns blared; brakes squealed. Benny pleaded with Luther, "Can you go any faster?"

"I never seen nothing like this," Luther said. "Nothing."

A greasy blue pickup eased alongside them. "Get the fuck off the road," a guy shouted, waving his fist at Benny.

Benny gave the guy the finger and his bad face, cranked shut the window and pulled on Pa Old Ma's hat. It was a little tight. "Luther, you got to go faster. If you don't, the cops will see us for sure. Step on the gas. Pretend one of these lanes is a road and just go."

The car surged forward.

"That's it," Benny said. "That's fine. Just like that."

"Ain't so bad," Luther said.

Benny nodded his head and smiled when they actually started passing other cars.

Traffic slowed to a crawl as they passed the Ft. Lauderdale exits. They crept up a high bridge and from its top Benny spied a river and boats tied at docks.

"There's some water with boats down there," he said.

"Is that it?" Luther asked.

"I don't know," Benny said. "The boats look too small."

As they came down the bridge's far side, a sign in the distance read, *Miami 30 miles.*

"That sign says another thirty miles to Miami," Benny said.

"Does it say anything about the river?" Luther asked.

"No," Benny replied. And it doesn't say anything about my father either, he thought.

Between Ft. Lauderdale and Miami traffic flowed as continuously as water. Whenever Benny was sure the highway couldn't get wider, it grew two lanes and four times as many cars. Though Luther drove better -- he stayed in the same lane and moved at traffic speed -- he seemed tight as a spring and Benny knew it was his job to stay calm.

They passed signs: *Dania, Hollywood, Hallandale, Miramar,*

North Miami, Opa Locka. Benny read them quietly, hoping to learn something about the river, something about his father. But there seemed to be nothing. Behind the sign, NW 81st Street NEXT EXIT, stood another, Miami City Limits. They topped a small rise, and from its crest Benny spied tall office buildings, saw-toothed against the horizon. The buildings shimmered in the late morning light.

"Damn, whiteboy," Luther said. "Look at it."

"I know," Benny said, "looks like diamonds."

"Like what?"

"Jewels," he said. "You know diamonds, rubies. Like that."

Luther shook his head.

"Just drive," Benny said. "I'll look for the river." Benny turned to his left and right. Miami rolled away from him in every direction -- where in that mess, he wondered, could they have hidden a river?

Traffic crowded the road as it coiled through the city. Their lane ended in construction. Clouds of dust, powered by diesel engines roaring beside the highway, drifted across their path.

Luther, blowing hard as if he lifted a heavy weight, moved one lane to the left.

"Good job," Benny said.

Luther nodded. Beads of sweat flecked his forehead.

Benny read signs that seemed somehow familiar. From television? Movies? *I-195 to Miami Beach; Miami International Airport LEFT LANE; Orange Bowl NEXT EXIT; Downtown Miami NEXT LEFT.*

The interstate began a slow ascent and curved on pilings alongside the buildings in downtown Miami. Close now, the skyscrapers no longer looked like jewels, but stood as solidly as rocks. Luther flowed with the heavy traffic up a steep rise and onto a bridge. From its top Benny scanned all he could see: a silver commuter train, like mercury out of a thermometer, raced across a bridge to his left. Farther out, past the train, a body of blue water filled the horizon. The ocean? he wondered. On his right, below the bridge, two small tugboats jockeyed either end of a freighter on a narrow thread of water. Boats, ships, water: the river. "I found the river," he cried.

Luther punched the brakes and craned his neck.

"Where at?" he asked.

The sedan slid sideways; the sudden stop heaved Benny from his seat. Horns cried and tires squealed. Benny heard metal crunching metal behind them. He huddled on the floor, tense, expecting a collision. "Don't stop, Luther," he shouted. "Don't stop."

The car surged forward.

Benny climbed back into the seat and looked out the car's rear window. A small green car slid across a lane and bashed into a spinning black Cadillac behind them. The driver, an old man in dark glasses looked angry then stupid as his car was smacked from the rear.

"Luther. Go! Go!"

The car picked up speed on the slope down off the bridge.

"Go there," Benny said, pointing toward an exit. "There," he repeated, jaw clenched. "Come on."

When sure Luther was getting off the highway, Benny twisted up on the seat and looked back at the bridge. No traffic followed.

Luther eased up to a stop sign at the bottom of the ramp.

Benny said, "I thought you guys didn't know about signs."

"Whitemans always stop at this passby," Luther said. "I watch them, and I seen it. You want to get by, you watch what the Whiteman do and do the same."

Benny nodded, but he wasn't sure. If it wasn't what you thought, but how you acted, could you act a way you didn't think? Maybe that's what adults do, he thought. Maybe that's how they get by. It seemed too complicated, and he shook the idea out of his head.

Windows open, Pa Old Ma's hat pulled firmly on his head, Benny directed Luther left and right down neighborhood streets. He tried to take them back in exactly the direction they had come, but one-way streets and barricaded roads wouldn't let him. A queasy feeling rose from his stomach to his brain: he could get them from Georgia to Miami, but now they were lost forever. He had commanded Luther to turn so many times, he was sure they had gone in a circle. And the brief tour added to his anxiety: Miami was stranger than Benny had imagined. It wasn't just a warm version of his home. It was something else. The air, soft and humid, smelled like flowers, fried food and rotting fruit. Tree limbs, densely leaved, canopied some streets as thickly as in the swamp. Palm trees fluttered in the breeze; their shapes of their leaves made Benny think of sex, but he didn't know why. Women on the sidewalks carried open umbrellas even though it wasn't raining. At the stop lights, men waded through traffic selling flowers, oranges, newspapers, bags of onions. They spoke what

Benny guessed was Spanish, fast and clipped it rolled through his ears on a downhill slope.

As they idled at a traffic light, a man holding a fistful of white paper cones passed the car. Benny stuck his head out the window. "Excuse me, sir, do you know where the river is? How we get there?"

The man stopped and brought his face down next to Benny's. Tiny red veins sliced the whites of his eyes, he belched beer and cracked a grin. Very slowly and carefully he said, "No speak English." He waved the cones in Benny's face.

"No thank you," Benny said. He looked at Luther and shrugged. "I guess we just keep driving till we find the river."

"We near it," Luther said. "I can feel the water."

At the next traffic light, a man in a bathrobe and a grimy baseball cap approached the car and squirted the windshield with something from a clear plastic bottle. He began wiping it off with a rag, smearing the glass with road dust and grease.

"Hey," Luther, shouted as he stuck his head out the window, "don't do that."

The man snarled at Luther and walked around to Benny's side of the car. He stuck his hand, palm up, through the open window. Cracked and dirty, the paw floated in front of Benny's face like something that had crawled from a hole. Benny shook his head. The man's mouth fractured into a grin, and he grabbed Pa Old Ma's hat.

"Shit, Jesus," Benny shouted. The man squeezed the brim in his fist and tried to jerk it out the window. "Go, Luther," Benny shouted. "Go." He pulled the hand to his mouth and bit down hard. The car lurched forward. The man screamed and his hand disappeared. Benny clutched the hat to his stomach and leaned forward, gagging and spitting. His mouth tasted bitter and he imagined rat shit, human shit, grease and vomit. The car climbed a small rise. The tires made a deep and ominous buzzing sound.

"Shit," Benny cried, his head out the window, as he spat and gagged. He looked down through metal grates; brown water rippled beneath them. A bridge. "The river," he shouted. "It's the river."

He retched and spat.

"I could feel it," Luther said. "I knew we were close."

Benny lifted his head and examined the stream. It seemed too small. The interstate had been wider. Freighters tied along its bank --

listing toward shore -- towered above the water. His eyes moved quickly to another bridge, about a quarter mile down river. Without warning, it split in the middle and each half rose into the air. A drawbridge, Benny thought. As they dropped back onto the street, a bell like the one from Ottem Elementary began ringing. Benny turned his head. Two traffic arms floated down and blocked access to the bridge they just crossed. The bell clanged. Machinery groaned. The bridge's two halves rose slowly. Benny shook his head.

How does it work?

He turned and sat facing forward, Pa Old Ma's hat clutched to his stomach. He spat again. The man's taste coated his tongue.

On his right an electrical transfer station hummed behind a high chain link fence: transformers and wires poked from the ground like the skeleton of a dead beast. A brown high-rise loomed on their left. The interstate arced above it like a strange cement halo. The street beside the building ran toward the river and disappeared in the shadow cast by the highway. "Turn there," Benny said pointing at the street. "That way."

Luther nodded and drove slowly under the interstate.

The air cooler and damp, smelled of diesel and wood smoke, fish and urine. Cement pilings, thick as trees, carried the highway above black asphalt parking lots. Abandoned by drivers, the lots closest to the river were platted with tiny hovels made of scrap lumber, plastic and cardboard. Some of the shacks were painted and had doors. One, daubed with a bright blue paint, had a sloping roof topped by a television antenna. Others seemed mere paper and dreams, held together with bright colored cloth torn into strips, old sneaker laces, fishing lines and yellow ropes. Clothes and rags fluttered from lengths of twine strung between the pilings. Wood smoke curled up from the small encampment. A charcoal haze lingered beneath the bridge.

"Up there," Benny said. He pointed into a parking lot on their left. Luther turned in and drove slowly until the car nosed against a shopping cart heaped full of empty beer cans. They both climbed out and walked to the river's edge.

The river wasn't much larger than the one Benny remembered from the swamp. The water, black in the bridge's shadow, lapped against wooden bumpers that protected the interstate's pilings from boat traffic. Fish line, tangled and abandoned, rose on a breeze and feathered the air around the bumpers. A horn blew three times, rattling Benny's chest like a cough. He clapped his hands over his ears. A tugboat, towing a ship that eclipsed everything about it, rounded the curve and passed beneath the interstate.

"Whiteboy, look at that," Luther said.

Benny and Luther stared, open mouthed, as the tugboat working the rear of the ship ponied it through the curve. They looked at each other, heads shaking. The sound of the tug's motors punched the air like a fist. Benny screamed at Luther, "They're loud."

Luther pointed at his ears and shook his head.

As the boats moved on, Benny heard shouting. He turned and scanned the parking lot. A squat woman, her hair matted and dusty and wearing a dirty sack-like dress, moved around the car yelling in Spanish, as she slapped its hood and kicked its doors.

"Hey, lady," Benny shouted.

She screamed and waved her arms at him.

"What's she want?" Luther asked.

She slapped both hands down on the hood of the car. Luther and Benny jumped.

"I think she wants us to move the car," Benny said.

She kicked it, denting the fender.

"Okay," Benny shouted. He moved his hands like he was turning a steering wheel.

The woman nodded, scowling, and walked away from the car.

"Hey, wait a second," Benny hollered. "Do you know. . ."

The woman looked back at him over her shoulder. She shook her head and spat. "Chucho, Chucho," she shouted. "Chucho."

Benny glanced at Luther, then the woman. What the fuck was she saying?

She yelled again. "Chucho. Chucho."

Something rustled in a plastic shrouded GE refrigerator box. A kid, younger than Benny, popped his head out. "Mama?" he said.

She jerked her head toward Benny and Luther.

The kid's eyes met Benny's. They held each other's stares. "Yeah," the kid said, finally. "What do you want?"

Benny had to think for a moment. What did he want? He glanced at Luther then back to the kid. "This the Miami River?"

"What do you think?" the kid asked.

Benny gave him his 'just don't fuck with me' face. The kid smirked. "Yeah, it's the Miami River."

Benny nodded his head. "You know any Black boat captains?"

"How do you mean, black?"

"You know," Benny said. "Like him. Black." He flipped a thumb at Luther.

"Is he Haitian?"

Benny shook his head. "I don't think so."

"Can't he talk?"

"I talk fine," Luther said.

Chucho's eyes grew wide for a second. "He talks fine," he said, as he scrambled out of the box. The kid wore bright orange shorts and a faded blue t-shirt that read, *My folks went to the Superbowl and all I got was this lousy t-shirt.* Silver duct tape wrapped his sneakers. It looked like he couldn't take them off without cutting the tape. He was a head shorter than Benny. His legs were grimy and scarred as if something gnawed on them as he slept.

"Do you know any Black boat captains?" Benny repeated. He wasn't sure if the kid was messing with him.

"Just the Haitians," the kid said. "You know they eat cats?"

"What?"

"They eat cats. Cats." The kid clawed the air and hissed. "They eat everything. Rats, cats, spiders, roaches. You. Me. Everything."

"That's crazy," Benny said.

"No," the kid said. "That's Haitian. I seen a crazy guy eat a raw chicken once."

The woman shouted, waving her hands and jumping around. Chucho yelled something to her in Spanish. He turned to Luther. "She said if you don't move your car, she's going to kill you."

"She wouldn't do that," Benny said.

"She's got a gun," Chucho said.

"I'll move it," Luther said.

"Just put it over there." The kid pointed at the street.

Meters, heads broken, and uprights mangled, twisted from the ground like new sprouts.

"Don't worry about the meters," he said. "They're all broken."

"I can see that," Benny said.

Luther started the car and backed out. Once on the street, he eased forward. The right front tire rode onto the curb, then dropped into the street; the car continued to bounce as Luther turned off the engine. The woman stood beside the refrigerator box, gesturing and shouting up at the interstate. She fell to her knees and blessed herself.

"Who is she?" Benny asked.

"My mother," Chucho said.

Benny nodded but didn't know what to say.

Chucho said, "I know she's crazy, but she's my mother. In Nicaragua, where I'm from," he tapped his chest, "in Nicaragua, she's not crazy. It is only here that she's crazy."

"You could go back," Benny said.

Chucho pursed his lips and shook his head. "In Nicaragua, I'd be crazy."

Benny nodded. "Yeah, I know what you mean."

"Whiteboy," Luther said, holding the box of money in his hands. "I need to find the Blackafrican boat captains, now."

Chucho shook his head. "Not Africans. Haitians," he said. "You're looking for the Haitians."

"Okay," Benny said. "Where are the Haitians?"

Chucho pointed up-river. "That way," he said. "Two blocks. Just past the next bridge, at First Street. You can't miss it. You'll smell them. Don't eat their food."

The moment Chucho pointed, Luther strode off. Benny turned his head toward the man, then back to the kid. "Thanks," he said.

"Don't eat the food," Chucho said.

Benny jogged to catch up with Luther and almost said, hey, what's the rush? But he knew what the rush was. Luther didn't look at him. As they came out from under the interstate's shadow, they passed a yard of wooden crates, stacked higher than Benny's head. They passed a yellow warehouse that smelled like fish and walked beneath the bridge at First Street. Just past the bridge, Luther stopped and peered through a chain link fence. "This is it, whiteboy," he said.

Benny stared through the fence at five boats huddled at the docks. They were smaller than the freighter they'd seen, but larger than the tugs. Some were wooden, others metal. Box shaped, like floating houses, the wooden boats were all painted white, and trimmed in red or blue or yellow. Black and rusted, the metal ones looked more like boats to Benny. Their bows and wheelhouses seemed designed to withstand breaking waves. They looked newer, safer. The decks of all the boats were covered with bicycles, plastic milk jugs, old mattresses and rusting refrigerators. It appeared as if the cargo had been washed into place by a large wave. The boats all bobbed in the wake of a passing tug. Benny glanced over at Luther and wondered what he thought of these boats. Probably nothing, he decided. Only one thing mattered to Luther.

Weeds poked out of the oil-stained scrabble inside the fence. Boat parts burst life jackets and rusting metal lay scattered about the yard. Beneath a blue plastic tarp stretched between poles, a group of black men and women sat in a circle, on green webbed lawn furniture and picked food from styrofoam plates with plastic forks. The men wore pressed shirts and trousers -- the women in billowy light-colored dresses and straw hats, their dark skin radiant against the material. They spoke quick and hard in a language Benny never heard. They stopped speaking and turned their heads when he and Luther passed through the gate.

Benny waved and shouted. "Hello, is the captain of any those boats around?"

The people turned back to their food.

Benny looked at Luther and shrugged.

"Stay here, whiteboy," Luther said. He walked toward the tarp, the people beneath it glanced up at him, then back to their food. Luther crouched down beside a chair and set the box of money on the ground. He didn't speak for a moment. Then his lips moved. Benny strained to hear what he said. The people in the circle turned their heads toward Luther. Luther gestured toward boats and continued speaking. He took up the box and shook it. An old woman smiled and pointed to the boats. Luther nodded, then looked over his shoulder at Benny. He grinned.

On his way to the gangplank, Luther stepped aside for a boy toting a load of empty plastic jugs. He followed the boy up the plank and disappeared on the boat.

Benny wandered to the gate and sat on the ground, his back against a metal fence post. He could take me on the boat with him, Benny thought. He could've done that. Shit, I got him here. He watched as the people ate and others carried plastic jugs and metal canisters onto boats. A v-shaped flock of birds passed low overhead. Benny grinned when he recognized them as pelicans. This is Miami, he thought. They have drawbridges. People speak Spanish. Black people are called Haitians. Pelicans fly together. And somewhere out there was his father.

After nearly twenty minutes, Luther came down the gangplank, empty handed, and crossed the yard to Benny. He pointed up at a white broad beamed wooden boat sitting low in the water. Eye lashes were drawn in red around the vessel's hawser holes where the ropes snaked out to the dock. Red wing-like fins were painted near its bow. White and red scallops, like scales, ran the vessel's length and from the ship's rail to beneath the water line. Taken together the elements resembled a flying fish. The boat listed in the river's current. Blue barrels, bicycles and mattresses were strapped in varying heights along its deck. A slim Black man, wearing a white captain's hat, dark sunglasses and a sleeveless blue shirt, leaned from the wheelhouse that towered over the deck and shouted to someone Benny couldn't see. Luther pointed with his thumb up to the captain, "He's taking me to Red Bays."

"Good," Benny replied. "How much is he charging you?"
"What?" Luther asked.
"How much money did he want?"
"I gave him the box."
Benny almost said, that was pretty stupid. But he stopped himself. "When is he leaving?"
"When they loaded."
Benny nodded.
Luther turned, walked back toward the boat. Benny watched him for a moment, then feeling sorry for himself, started out the gate.
"Whiteboy," Luther's voice barked at him. "Whiteboy."
Benny turned around, smiling.
"Here," Luther said, tossing him the car keys. "I don't need them."
Benny said, "Thanks," but Luther already turned and walked away. Benny watched him move up the gangplank and disappear on the boat. I guess I really didn't matter to him, Benny thought. Fine. Fuck you, Luther. He tried to convince himself that Luther didn't matter either, but he knew that was a lie. Maybe Luther didn't care,

but Pa Old Ma did. He'd gotten them to Miami. He didn't do it for Luther. He did it for the old man. And he knew Luther wouldn't have made it without him. Benny lifted Pa Old Ma's hat from his head and waved it at the boat. "Hey Luther, good luck," he shouted.

And then, under his breath, "Fuck you."

The people on the lawn furniture grew quiet and turned their heads. Benny grinned at them, pulled the hat on and started, quickly, back to the car. As he returned to the interstate's shadow, Benny tried to figure out what to do next. Miami was so big. He had no idea how to find his father. Where would he begin? He decided to start by getting his duffel bag and asking that kid, Chucho, what he thought.

Benny opened the trunk of the great white car and the slung duffel bag's strap across his shoulder. With the trunk mawing at him and no use for the car anymore, Benny tossed the keys into it and slammed it shut. He started across the parking lot toward Chucho's hovel. He would ask him what he knew about Miami. How he might find his father. Halfway across the encampment, the interstate looming overhead, Benny paused. The world was so big and he was a very unimportant part of it. His nose itched. He thought he was about to cry. Nothing matters, he remembered, except what I think matters.

He stopped outside Chucho's hut. He could hear movement inside. "Hello," he said. "Hello?"

He recognized the gun's black barrel the moment it poked through the opening in the box. Someone on the other side of the plastic sheet made hissing noises and began speaking quickly and quietly in Spanish. Benny took two steps sideways and backed away from the hut. He moved slowly, until he got to one of the pilings and ducked behind it. Jesus, he thought. What the fuck? He placed the duffel on the ground and eased down onto it, his back against the upright. He shook his head, pushed back Pa Old Ma's hat.

Someone whistled off to his left. Benny rolled quickly to his right and lay flat out on the ground. The sound came again.

He peeked in its direction.

The boy, Chucho, was waving him to another piling, further out from the shack. Benny grimaced at him and shook his head.

Chucho nodded and waved a hand.

"Fuck," Benny said, under his breath, as he crept to Chucho's piling, dragging the duffel after him. "What was that all about?"

"My mother thinks you're the devil."

"That's crazy," Benny said.

"I know," Chucho said.

"Tell her I'm not."

Chucho smiled at him. "No, you tell her. See how far you get."

Benny shook his head.

"It don't matter." He thought for a second. "Listen, I'm trying to find somebody in Miami. How would I do that?"

"Who you looking for?"

"My father," Benny said.

"Your father?"

Chucho tilted his head to the left and scratched his neck.

"Yeah," Benny said. "I'm looking for my father."

Chucho nodded. "I don't know how you'd do that, but I bet Dog Ass would."

"Who?" Benny asked.

"Dog Ass," Chucho said. "Dog Ass knows everything. He was rich once. He owned two cars until the county towed them away. Parked them right there." The kid pointed toward two parking spaces occupied by a hut made of pallet wood with a television antenna on its roof. A combination lock hung from a hasp on the door.

"Where is he now?"

"Who knows during the day, but at night he sleeps right there. I'll ask him tonight. And tell you what he says tomorrow."

"Okay," Benny said.

Chucho nodded, then looked around. "But you got to get out of here before dark."

"I'm not worried about your mother."

Chucho shook his head. "It's not her," he said, gesturing around at the shacks. "It's everybody else. Nobody messes with me because of Mama. She's crazy and they know it. You. If they get you, they're going to mess with you."

"Shit," Benny said.

"It's no thing," Chucho said, patting his arm. "Just cross the river. It's different on the other side."

"Where?" Benny asked.

"There," Chucho said, pointing across the river.

***

Benny crossed the drawbridge at First Street with Pa Old Ma's hat on his head and the duffel slung across his back. The metal grated roadbed hummed and shook each time a car passed. Benny could see the river through the metal mesh. It made him nervous. He walked with one hand on the bridge's railing and tried not to look down. A man in a tiny house built right onto the bridge raised one hand to Benny as he passed. Benny nodded and said, "Hello."

On the bridge's far side, four men, beneath a tattered maroon canvas awning, leaned against a window counter outside a tiny grocery store housed in a squat square building. They drank something, Benny supposed from the aroma in the air was coffee, from tiny cups and talked a fast Spanish. The language made no sense at all to Benny. One man shouted louder than the others. The rest laughed and snapped their fingers. A woman speaking on a tiny radio blared from the store's entrance; Benny stopped. Just inside the door, on a small metal table, a candle in a red glass burned before a statue of a man on crutches. Tiny plaster dogs gathered at the man's heels; pink tongues poked from their mouths and licked his legs. Benny stared at the statue trying to figure out what it meant. Deeper in the store, just past the small altar, a cream-colored wire rack displayed fruit pies: blueberry, apple, and cherry.

Benny grinned as he stepped in and hefted a cherry pie in his hand. "Breakfast is Peter's most important meal," he said.

The man behind the counter rattled his newspaper. Benny turned around; the man stared at him. Thick black rimmed glasses goggled the man's eyes. Black strands of hair lay in a paste across the top of his shiny head. He shifted a cigar between his teeth and expelled a plume of smoke toward the ceiling.

Benny dropped the fruit pie on the counter and eased the duffel bag to the floor. Money? he thought. He heard Pa Old Ma say, "Whiteman's lies," and knew it wasn't true.

The man behind the counter folded his newspaper and placed it on the cash register. Benny pushed a hand into his pocket. His fingers touched the crumpled paper from Peter's stash. He pulled out a wad of cash and placed a twenty-dollar bill on the counter.

A thread of drool ran from the man's lips to the ashtray as he removed the cigar from his mouth. He flexed and snapped the twenty between his fingers. He held it up to the light and looked from the bill to Benny and back again. He pursed his lips and nodded. The cash register jangled. He slapped the twenty into the drawer and snapped out change. He counted the bills twice, before dropping them onto Benny's open palm.

Benny noticed a stack of newspapers on the counter next to him. Out of the corner of his eye he saw something familiar and frightening -- a face he recognized -- his own. His school picture from Halpert Middle School. Goofy smile, chipped toothed and moussed hair, the face, black and white and grainy, was inset in a larger color image of Pa Old Ma's camp. Men in uniforms and suits filled the picture. A military green helicopter stood in the background. A cop in a Smokey the Bear hat squatted beside the fire pit; another poked his head into the cabin where Benny had slept. A man wearing a suit spoke to a group of people pushing microphones into his face. His mother. . . His mother. . . stood beside the man. Benny, hand trembling, picked up the paper. *HIDEOUT FOUND* read the headline. Beneath it in smaller type: *Search for Boy's Body Continues.* His knees turned to water.

The man behind the counter slapped his hand onto the newspaper. "You read. You buy," he said.

Benny nodded and held out the money. He didn't pay attention to how much the man took. Holding the newspaper in front of him, he turned and started away from the counter.

"*Oye,*" the man said.

Startled, Benny glanced back.

The clerk held the fruit pie in his hand.

Benny reached for it and walked out of the store. He sat down on his duffel bag, in the awning's narrow shade, dropped the fruit pie beside him and tried reading the paper. The bright sunlight made him squint and it took a while for the words to sort themselves out. There were two stories on the front page, one about Pa Old Ma's camp and another about Benny. They said he was probably dead; they were still searching for his body. Pa Old Ma's camp was a haven for terrorists or outlaws. It might have been a cult. They said Benny was a troubled youth. They quoted from his file: what the judge had said about him; what Sharkovsky had written about him; what they thought happened the night Peter died. His mother said, "I loved him, but one day to the next I never knew what he was going to get caught doing. He scared me." He wondered if she were happier believing him dead.

At the column's end it said, *more on page 8.* He flipped back and discovered a whole page with more pictures: aerials of the camp and the MIAMI bus in the swamp; a map showing where the camp was in the Okefenokee Swamp. Beneath the headline, *LOCAL BANKER, BOY'S FATHER,* a man stared up at him.

It was the man whose picture his mother had hidden in the underwear drawer. The one she'd claimed was Meryl's brother. He was older. His hair was shorter, but it was the same man. William Taggart, the article began, Chief Financial Officer of IntelBank Miami, is the father of Benjamin Taggart, the troubled youth who was kidnapped on the Miami bound bus on May 3, 1994 and is now missing and presumed dead. Taggart, an eleven- year resident of Miami, said in a recent interview that he never knew the boy and felt terrible that such a horrible thing could happen. When asked about his relationship with the boy, Taggart said, "I didn't know him. His mother and I were young. We made mistakes."

At each revelation in the article Benny paused: William Taggart, my father's William Taggart; he works in a bank. He wondered what a Chief Financial Officer did. My father and mother were young once, he thought. They made mistakes. They made me.

The sky quickly brightened out on the street, and just as quickly darkened as rain raced toward Benny from the west. He lifted the fruit pie on his lap and folded the paper over it. A steaming humidity preceded the rain, dampening his clothes and freeing Miami's aromas from the dry ground around him. Benny inhaled the smell of his own body - rotting fruit - blooming flowers and frying food. A small rivulet ahead of the rain started at the curb carrying candy wrappers and leaves, cigar butts and dog shit. The water and the trash raced away toward the river. Just beyond the awning, the rain fell fast and hard in a line racing down the street -- faster and harder -- becoming a screen of water before his eyes. Benny backed against the wall and pulled his legs further beneath the awning. The men to his left leaned back against the counter and watched the storm in silence. As quickly as it began, the downpour disappeared. The last of the drops ran after the storm like slower children in a race. Bright sunlight returned as if darkness could never exist. Wisps of steam rose from the sun baked asphalt.

Traffic eased by on the street. The men at the counter recommenced arguing and smoking, shouting and snapping their fingers. They ignored Benny.

He reread the article about his father three times. Each time he hoped the words would tell him something else, but they never did. We made mistakes, his father said. Benny knew what that meant -- he was the mistake. The sun pushed longer shadows down First Street toward the river. Benny closed his eyes and believed he no longer cared what happened. He found his father. His mother had been right. His father didn't care. He said Benny was mistake, and he was probably right. A pay phone hanging on the grocery store's wall rang three times before an old man separated himself from the others, stepped over Benny and picked up the receiver.

He said something Benny didn't understand, then something he did. "No," the man said. "NO," he shouted. He fumbled the receiver into its cradle. It fell, swinging near Benny's head. The old man shook his fist at the swaying mouthpiece and returned to the circle of men.

Benny stood and hung up the phone. Words written with a fat tipped black magic marker daubed the small booth. Benny read the words both familiar and strange -- *pendejo*, faggot, *punta*, fuck. Images of knives and penises had been etched into the aluminum enclosure. A phone book encased in heavy brown plastic, held by a thin metal cable, hung down beneath the phone booth.

Benny opened the book and flipped through until he found the name Taggart. There were six listings. Taggart, W., he read, lived at 4403 Ponce de Leon. Benny pushed a quarter into the phone and punched the numbers. His stomach fluttered when he heard the first ring. He kept trying to hang up but couldn't. On the fourth ring, a tape machine clicked on, "I'm sorry we're unable to answer your call right now. If you leave your name and number, we will get back to you as soon as we can." Benny listened to the voice. It was deep -- a man's, a stranger – his father's. "Please wait for the beep," his father said. After the high-pitched tone, Benny said, "If I was your mistake, you were mine." His voice grew louder. "I could tell you a lot, you know. I could tell you what it's like… Aww what the hell do you care? You've told the world that I was a mistake. Well, you know what? If I'm your mistake, you're mine. What do you think of that? Mistakes are easy." The answering machine beeped and the tape ended. But Benny couldn't stop. "All I ever did was make mistakes. One after another. But my biggest mistake was what I thought about you. Who I thought you were. But just like I'm nothing to you, you're nothing to me. Nothing." Benny shouted into the receiver, "So why don't you just go the fuck to hell." He listened, ear against the phone, waiting, hoping and dreading an answer. After a moment he hung up and sat down on his duffel bag.

The men gathered near him snapped their fingers, clapped and whistled.

Benny spent the early evening sitting on his bag on the sidewalk outside the tiny store. He watched traffic flow by and listened as the men argued. He went into the store twice. Once for a Coke and a little later for a Snickers bar. Around 8 o'clock he asked the man behind the counter if he could use a bathroom. The man nodded, pointing at a tiny wooden door near a glassed front Budweiser cooler.

A mop in a bucket jangled across the floor as he pushed into the cramped room. The sink stuck out from the wall almost directly above the toilet. A black hose fastened to the faucet hung out of the sink and dripped into a puddle that covered the floor. He rested the duffel on the sink. After peeing, he caught a glimpse of himself in the smudged mirror above the sink. He lifted Pa Old Ma's hat from his head and stared into the glass, comparing his face to the picture in the paper. His skin had tanned; there were creases at the edges of his eyes; buzz cut hair lay across the top of his head. Benny smiled. His reflection smiled back.

When he left the tiny room, the man behind the counter pointed with his thumb and said, "*Cerrado.* You go."

Benny nodded, "I'm gone," he said, folding the newspaper into his duffel bag. Outside the store, he looped the strap over his shoulder, looked left and right. The lift bridge had risen again and the freighter he left Luther at glided past. Benny saw men in its wheelhouse but could not see faces. He lifted Pa Old Ma's hat from his head and waved it with his right hand. "Good luck, Luther," Benny said just loud enough to hear it himself. Then he said, "And, good luck to me." The ship's horn sounded. Benny knew it wasn't for him. Pa Old Ma would have told him, "That's a good sign." But Pa Old Ma was dead. Benny wasn't in the swamp. He was in Miami. He'd made it. It didn't hold the message he'd hoped for, but he'd made it.

He looked left then right and wished he was as sure of his future as Luther was of his. Wherever it was, it was forward not back. Not back at Halpert or the JDC or the New Family Way. Not Pa Old Ma's camp. There was no way back; only forward. The bridge's roadbed slowly lowered, the flashing lights on the barricades rose into the air and a sharp shrill bell rang. Auto traffic appeared at the top of the bridge and Benny noticed for the first time that he was beside a one-way street. He turned away from the bridge and began walking with the traffic, toward a thinning lip of sunlight in the western sky. Traffic flowed in two lanes beside him. Graffiti tagged plywood shuttered the store fronts lining the sidewalk. A sign at the cross street read SW 1st Street and SW 6th Avenue. Benny stopped at the corner and prepared to cross. An older light blue Chevrolet Suburban turned the corner in front of him and stopped, blocking his path. Its motor chugged rhythmically as the driver pressed and released the gas pedal. A plume of white smoke drifted from its tailpipe.

The passenger side window rolled down. An old man, his white hair pulled back in a ponytail, a white bandage covering half his nose leaned toward Benny from behind the wheel. "New in town?" In the lowering sun -- the man's eyes -- liquid whites and glowing dark irises -- surprised Benny in a face so old.

"Hello? I asked if you're new in town?"

"Who wants to know?" Benny asked.

"Charles," the man said. "Some call me Charlie."

"Hello, Charlie," Benny said.

The man smiled and pointed at the bandage on his nose. "Skin cancer. Too much time in the Miama sun for my lily-white skin."

Benny shrugged. "Okay."

"I tell you that because nobody told me. They just keep slicing more of me away, like a kid whittling a piece of wood. Someday, I'll just be a pile of splinters. That hat," he gestured with his chin. "That'll help some if you keep it on. And you? What's your name?"

Benny touched the brim of Pa Old Ma's hat and let the question roll around his head for a moment.

He smiled at Charles, "I don't know," he said.

"A good-looking young man like you must have a name."

"Oh," Benny said. "I see."

"See what?"

Benny smiled, shifted his hips to the left, tilted his head to the right then circled his lips with his tongue. "I suck your cock. Or you suck mine? How much?"

"Ha," Charles said, and laughed again. "Ha. Thank you very much. Maybe thirty years ago or forty, now. I was never one for minnows. I like my fish a little bigger – a little scrappier. Ha. Let's just say my needs have lessened - significantly."

"The fuck does that mean?"

"My cock, as you so graphically put it, seems to work only to micturate and sometimes that's a struggle."

"What?"

"My cock works to pee and little else."

"What do you want with me?"

"I'm eighty-three years old. I like company. You give me company. I give you a chance."

"A chance?"

"Where are you sleeping tonight?"

Benny looked left and right. "I don't know yet."

Charles gestured with his thumb. "Throw your bag in the back seat and get up front with me. If we're here much longer, I'm afraid the local constabulary may interrupt our conversation."

"What?"

"The cops," Charles said.

"I don't get it," Benny said. "Why?"

"Why? Because that's what cops do."

"No. Why me?"

"Do you think you're the only young boy who's blown into Miami, needing a hand?" Charles smiled. "How did it happen? You tell them you were queer? Or did they catch you with another boy?"

"What?" Benny said, "I'm not queer."

"Okay," Charles said. "Then I'm not either. Throw your stuff in back and let's go."

Benny measured his options, there were few. In a strange town with strange people there weren't many. Charlie or walking.

Charlie was old. Benny could take him if needed.

Benny opened the Suburban's passenger side rear door and threw in the duffel. "I'm not queer," he repeated.

"Right," Charles said. "My apologies. Get in."

Benny climbed into the front seat.

"Seat belt," Charles said, as he dropped the gear shift into drive and the Suburban rumbled forward. The car radio played classical music at a low volume. The car smelled of oil and gas and a sweetish medicinal cologne. "You remind me of a friend I had at your age. A boy like you. He died of something that killed boys back then. Scarlet fever? Polio?" He shook his head. "We played together from when we were small." Charles swallowed. "One day he was there. The next." He snapped his fingers. "Sometimes I think I've been looking for him ever since. His name was Richard. Poor Richard."

"Am I Richard?" Benny asked.

"No." Charles said. "Of course not. You're you, whoever you say you are."

"My name's Benjamin Taggart," he said. He unsnapped the seatbelt, twisted in his seat opened the duffel and fished out the newspaper. He turned the paper over and pointed at his picture.

Charles glanced at Benny, then down to his picture in *The Miami Herald*.

"Ha," Charles said. "I read that. You're that boy?"

"Yes," Benny said.

"That's a complicating factor. Isn't it?"

"What?"

"It's a dilemma," Charles said. "There are decisions you'll have to make. Not right now, of course. You should think about it."

Charles drove with his left hand on the top of the wheel, index finger pointing forward. His right rested in the gear shift. He guided the car through a residential neighborhood. Small houses side by side. Television's blue gray glow lighting most windows. "I sailed here when I was sixteen -- solo from Groton, that's Connecticut. Nineteen twenty-seven. One year after the big storm. That gives me sixty-seven years in Miama." He shook his head, as if trying to remember or forget. "When did you get here?" He glanced at Benny.

"Today," Benny said.

Charles eased to a stop sign. Looked right, past Benny, then left and pulled out onto a three-lane street. The Suburban sped up. Wind blew in from the open windows. Benny removed Pa Old Ma's hat and leaned back against the seat.

Charles nodded. "I ran away."

"Yeah," Benny nodded. "I ran away, too."

"And based on what I recall of the article, they're not looking for you. You're dead."

Benny thought for a moment. Everyone believed he was dead. He let his right hand hang out the window, buffeted by the wind. He opened and closed his fist. He wasn't dead. But he was to his past. Who knew where he was? Who cared? His mother? She had to. Sharkovsky? Who knows? The police? Their job. His father? He doesn't care. "You're right. They're not looking for me. I'm dead."

"Unlike most dead people, you have choices."

"Choices?"

"You could remain dead. Or, like Lazarus, you could rise."

Benny grimaced at the thought.

"There's two jokes," Charles said. "Well not jokes, really. Just things you say when you're old. One," he held up the index finger on his right hand. "There's no problem so big money can't fix – it's not true, but almost. The one I like is -- there's no problem so big you can't run from it." He smiled at Benny. "You can run, but you can't escape."

"I came to Miami to find something. Something I thought I wanted, and now I found it and it's not what I thought. Okay?"

"You arrived today. Are you sure it's not what you thought?"

Benny nodded. "I know."

Charles pulled to stop at a red light and flipped on his left turn signal. "None of what I'm about to say matters but try and remember this as you get older. Things that you're absolutely sure about right now will not seem so in the future."

Benny heard the words; they made some sense, but he was tired. He hadn't known how tired he was until he slid into Charlie's truck. His eyes drowsed. His head lolled on his neck. There was much to say and so little, and he was out.

Benny woke once in the night. He knew he was in a car, where didn't matter. He climbed into the back seat, pushed his duffel onto the floor and fell back asleep.

It rained in the night and he woke the next morning, his

clothes damp in the humid air. Mosquitos buzzed in his ear and sunlight warmed his face. He climbed from the car, stretched, lifting his arms over his head and peed against the Suburban's back tire. Before him stood a white, shake-shingled, two-story two car garage. A four-foot purple and red hedge wrapped the ground floor. A lace work of double stacked paned glass crossed the double garage doors at eye level. Steps on the right side rose beside the building to a second story wrapped in windows. To Benny's left, across a lush green yard, rose a white three-story shingled house, replicating the garage's style. Its first-floor windows reflected the scene in the yard back at Benny. Palms grew beside leafy trees in a green thicker than any Benny had seen before. Green and red birds flocked overhead, chattering as they flit from tree to palm to sky. The soft humid air smelled sweet of flowers and a pungent rot. Past the house Benny spied sunlight on a body of water. He followed a stone walkway around to the water's edge. A rusty ship's cannon mounted on rocks pointed out to a dock, where at its far end, a small blue wooden boat bobbed in the water. Benny followed the dock to its end. Two wooden oars crossed the boat's lone seat. Water puddled in its bottom. Ahead and to the right rippling water ran to the horizon. To his left, far away, Miami's skyscrapers rose as if afloat. In the morning light, the buildings appeared as solid as the reflection of water against the sky.

THE END

ACKNOWLEDGMENTS

Special thanks to:

The folks along the Creek Road who sustained me during my time in the woods. Brigid O'Hagan, who read the earliest drafts of my earliest work and nonetheless supported my efforts. Betsy Willeford, without whose encouragement Benny's tale would not have seen the light of day. J. J. Colagrande, my publisher and spiritual adviser. And, of course, Janet Kyle Altman, my wily associate and so much more.

ABOUT THE AUTHOR

Timothy Schmand fled upstate New York's oppressive winters and settled in South Florida in 1982. He has spent the ensuing decades immersed in the human experiment known as "Miami." Schmand's award winning fiction has appeared in literary journals, popular magazines and anthologies, regionally and internationally. Schmand's novel Just Johnson: The London Delivery was published in 2016 by Jitney Books, a micro-publisher celebrating the best of Miami's literary talent. He holds an MFA from Vermont College.

Made in the USA
Columbia, SC
30 October 2021